A Banyard & Mingle Mystery

Volume II

# THE GREEN INK GHOST

B J Mears

instant
apostle

First published in Great Britain in 2020

Instant Apostle
The Barn
1 Watford House Lane
Watford
Herts
WD17 1BJ

British Library Cataloguing-in-Publication Data

A catalogue record for this book is available from the British Library.

This book and all other Instant Apostle books are available from Instant Apostle:

Website: www.instantapostle.com

Email: info@instantapostle.com

ISBN 978-1-912726-32-5

Printed in Great Britain.

# Thanks

Special thanks to my beta readers Keith Munro, Matt Cooper, Revd Dr Simon Woodman and Henna Mears.
My thanks to Edward Field, Alison Hull, Julian Roderick, Kate Coe, Dan Sefton, Simon Lupton, Dr Alistair Sims, Joy Mears, Nicki Copeland and the fantastic team at Instant Apostle.

Special thanks to Phil Girdlestone Photography for the image of Baker featured on the back cover.

# Contents

# Camdon City

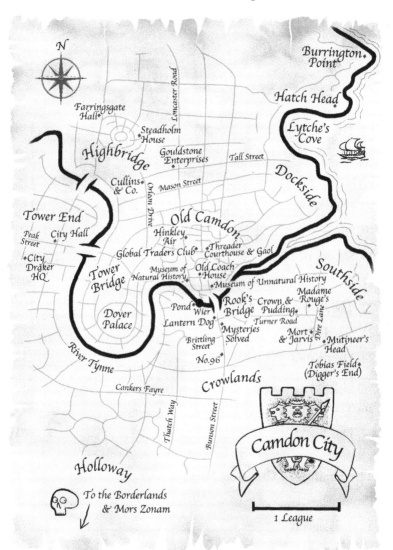

# The Eleven Months of the Earthorian Year

1st: Tithemoon

2nd: Doblemoon

3rd: Trimoon

4th: Quartersmoon

5th: Thripplemoon

6th: Sixthmoon

7th: Fipplemoon

8th: Hexmoon

9th: Honourmoon

10th: Twinemoon

11th: Elventide

**The year is 1795 AD (After Doon)**

*The threaders thread the silk.*

*The silkers wear the silk.*

# Prologue

Josiah's spade strikes wood around five feet down.

'That's it. Willard's coffin.' Standing at the edge, I peer into the pit.

'I think it *is*.' Josiah scoops soil from the lid, adding to the spoil heap. When he's cleared half of the lid, we swap places and I finish the job. The coffin is still intact and seems remarkably strong. Oak, presumably. Little else would survive as well, buried for so long. It even withstands Josiah's substantial weight. We clear the clinging earth from around the sides and gradually work the coffin up and out of the grave, laying it on the ground. It's awkward, slippery work.

Now for what is, perhaps, the grimmest part of the job.

We prise the lid off with the tips of our spades and look upon the withered remains of Willard Steeler. Josiah recoils at the sight. Steeler's skull leans, jaw yawning, hair fragmented and grey, falling to his pallid brow. He is little more than bones dressed in a gentleman's fine grey suit and black tie. All silk, of course. What flesh survives is dried out, the skin thin like parchment stretched tight.

There are superstitions surrounding the dead among the threader population, more so than with silkers. There are tales of witchcraft, of ghouls rising from the grave to haunt, drinking blood, preying on the living, but we silkers take a far more pragmatic view. The dead are dead. We observe a simple yet tempered respect for them.

Usually.

'It's all right, Josiah. There's nothing to fear.'

'But he looks so… alive!'

'Yes. He's half-mummified. But take it from me, he's thoroughly dead.'

Because the coffin is intact the interior is clean of dirt, except for the partial decay of the body, of course. This will make our job a little more bearable, for now we must search the corpse and the entire box. Unfortunately.

I take a half-crown from my pocket. 'Heads or tails?'

# 1

# The Unwanted Letter

*In which Banyard receives a letter and Mingle receives a clout*

My father's death was a mystery from the start. He was well one minute. Dead the next. It all happened in such a trice that, before I knew it, at the age of fourteen, I'd become the master of the house, proprietor of the private investigations agency Mysteries Solved, and sole comforter to my bereft and ageing mother.

A Draker, one of our city watchmen, found Father's body one night at the end of an alley in Old Camdon, not ten minutes' walk from our home at 96 Bunson Street. Nothing suspicious about that – each of us ventured across Rook's Bridge into the old town on a regular basis – and, with no visible damage to his body, the mystery was passed directly to our city's hard-drinking but capable coroner, Myrah Orkney, who quickly labelled it death by failure of the vital organs. I mean, could there be a vaguer cause?

And why?

*Why* had his body upped and failed like that without warning? Yes, he had suffered illness some six years before, but he had fully recovered. I'm no pathologist but it seemed most peculiar.

Among my inheritance came Father's old tricorn, now my favourite hat. I will not part with it for the world, though in a sea of toppers it is most unfashionable. It carries with it a sense of the man he was, as though all those years of use have imbued it with something of his nature.

Father's passing left his partner, Jeremiah Shrud, overwhelmed with work so we bought him out with some of Father's savings. He promptly wrapped up what cases he could before retiring from the business and moving away, leaving my mother and me to handle what remained.

In any case, that was five years ago, and I only mention it here to set the scene because, as I sit in the case room upon this sweltering summer's morning, my father's death becomes poignant once more, as you will see.

The office is humming today, a blur of activity. The air is stifling. We have many cases in progress and my operatives race around at a speed unusual for our dusty outfit. To be fair, it's become less dusty since we employed Elizabeth Fairweather as secretary – Lizzy for short. She sits primly at her desk, as shapely and smart as ever, dealing with a queue of clients. Mysteries Solved has never before been in such demand and we owe it all – well, most of it – to my esteemed partner, Josiah Mingle, and his inclination for *excellent ideas*.

Ridiculous ideas, more like.

Josiah, now rescued from his previous life as a threader, is gradually settling into the flow of silker ways and often lurches purposefully around the office, dictating, organising, reviewing, interviewing. With the sudden influx of cases, I saw fit to have him manage one – we'll see how that goes – and I fancy he carries his head all the higher because of it, which is a good thing because it might improve his muscle-bound stoop. He's still crowing over our successful recovery of Great King Doon's priceless remains and funerary urn.

Which he stole in the first place, by the way. Did I mention that?

But these new cases lose interest for me when I open the

letter delivered to my desk this hour. It's an unsettling, unwelcome message.

The paper is crisp and creamy. The same flowing script of green ink forms my name on the pristine envelope and the words inside. I unfold it and read as time pauses, my associates dashing in a haze around me. For me, all is quiet, all is frozen, at least on the outside. Within, my heart rises to my throat, pounding like the jibes of a dilapidated steam truck.

*Dearest Michael,*

*My story is long and involved and so I shall strive to remove myself from the episode about which I will here divulge certain facts. I have other reasons for wishing to remain anonymous, reasons that I am not at liberty to share. However, it is imperative that you believe I know the following details to be true and without question.*

*The first is this. Your father's death was unnatural. There are several other similar deaths you may also find of interest, each erroneously pronounced, those of Zacchaeus Mandon, Foster Keen and, lastly, Miss Martha Judd. Those responsible, a secret order of high social flyers, are long overdue their comeuppance.*

*I cannot name the culprits outright as yet, and I fear I may never do so due to circumstances beyond my control. Yet, suffice to say, I believe a little digging would reveal much. You should begin at the grave of Willard Steeler.*

*Yours truly,*

*Demitri Valerio*

The moment passes. The world continues to turn as questions flood my mind. I raise the page to my nose and sniff. Foreseeably, it smells of ink and paper. No help there, then.

In our reception room I grab Lizzy's arm as she passes.

'This morning's letter – did you see who delivered it?'

'No, Mr Banyard. It was on the mat when I opened up. I simply placed it upon your desk.'

There's an explosion of glass at my side as a large mass enters the room from the street, shoulders first, via the windows to land before me on the floor. Shards rain and settle and, after the briefest silence, a voice of fury follows Josiah's trajectory.

'And let that be a lesson to you, sir! I've never been so insulted!'

Josiah picks himself up and dusts himself down as, outside, the hulking figure in the top hat and cloak slouches away. Pedestrians on the street stop to watch. Steam trucks and clockwork cars continue to hurtle by. And that's pretty much how Josiah first entered my life, too; exploding into my world with shattering consequences and heralding a new atmosphere. He's an expense I can ill afford. Most of the time he's a kind of idiot. And just occasionally, a genius.

'Good morning, Josiah.' I brush a glistening fragment from my shoulder. 'Who've you been insulting now?'

'It wasn't an insult. It was a compliment,' he replies.

Lizzy interjects with a shrewd guess at the truth. 'You complimented Mr Farringsgate's wife?'

Josiah nods. 'A little too highly, I fear. You can take the window out of my wages.'

'Was it worth it?' I ask. I've noticed that Lizzy has been watching Josiah frequently and, on the odd occasion, has flirted with him. She flashes him a killer smile.

'You haven't seen Mrs Farringsgate,' he says. 'You'd have complimented her, too.'

Lizzy slaps him lightly on the shoulder. 'Oh, Josiah...'

I *have* seen Mrs Farringsgate but I choose not to correct him. 'Perhaps. Sweep this up and get on to the glazier at once. We have the security of the office to maintain.'

At least the airflow has improved.

'Right away,' he grunts.

We're all good. In fact, we're as thick as thieves.

'And work on your client relational skills. I suppose Mr Farringsgate will disengage our services now.'

'Naugh. He'll come around. I'll visit this afternoon and grovel. Farringsgate loves a good groveller.'

'I'm sure – and you'll gain another glimpse of the formidable Mrs Farringsgate, no doubt.'

'Why, Mr Banyard, whatever are you implying?' quips Josiah.

'You're bleeding,' says Lizzy, placing a hand on his shoulder. 'Sit down. I'll fetch a dressing.'

Josiah is one of those people who enjoys life to an irritating extent. He appears to relish Lizzy's attention as she brings dressings and scissors. She releases his tie, undoes several buttons and draws back his shirt to reveal the cut and several bulges of muscle before swiping the miniscule wound with iodine and taping a cotton wad in place.

'There. Good as new.'

He lunges to peck her cheek but she shoves him aside before he can strike. She slaps his arm again. 'Josiah Mingle, I'm not that sort of girl.'

Josiah closes his shirt and re-knots his tie, grinning. Lizzy smiles back at him. As he sweeps glass, my thoughts return to the letter and my father's mysterious death. Questions float to the surface.

Why has the writer waited until now to send a letter? Who is he? Can any of the information be trusted? If so, it is a report of four murders. Quite a claim, though it seems the author is for some reason unwilling to provide much assistance in naming the guilty.

Several phrases stand out upon a second reading.

*Episode:* A carefully selected term that conveys much. What this person experienced that led them to their conclusions must have happened over a reasonable period of time. It's safe to assume, then, that the conclusion was built upon a number of instances and is no mere whim. No reactionary cry, but a deliberated and calculated communication.

*High social flyers:* Perhaps this accounts for the lack of names as it implies people of influence and, therefore, great power. It follows that they might also be dangerous and fear has curtailed the writer's words.

*Unnatural:* The writer has gone to lengths to avoid the term *murder* and therefore to avoid an outright accusation. Perhaps again the threat of reprisal is the cause. They are not brave or able enough – for whatever reason – to name names.

Two further questions bother me.

Firstly, the author obviously knows more than he's saying. Is a second letter soon to follow?

Secondly, the message ends with a suggestion although, in keeping with the rest of the letter, an ambiguous one. More so, it's implied: exhume Willard Steeler's body from the grave. Is this truly what was meant?

For a while I'm too deeply entrenched to share this new development with anyone. I sit, attempting to digest it, recalling those last days of my father's life as I witnessed them. I remember him being insular at that time, constantly busy, always out in the field, following one lead or another. He went to work early each morning and came home late, exhausted and looking more haggard than ever before. Shrud, working an unconnected case, was unable to provide answers to the questions left behind. Even my father's case notes were of little help. It seemed nothing could be done and certainly nothing we could do would bring him back. To compound the general air of hopelessness, both Mother and the Drakers persuaded me to forget any thoughts of investigating. Our efforts soon waned in the overbearing shadow of Father's funeral and our grief.

This letter, however, has changed all that. One small page has quickly turned the whole thing on its head and now there's nothing left to do but investigate.

I make a cursory search for the casefile my father was working on when he died. Perhaps there is something in there that may help. From memory it is file number 2216 but the shelf by my desk only holds files as far back as 2300.

I lean through the doorway into reception. 'Lizzy, where are all the old files?'

Sitting at her desk, she looks up from a clipboard. 'They're boxed up, in the store room. Top shelf.'

'Right.' I enter the store and rummage until I have the file in hand. I pause, turning back to the boxes to root out a second file, this one fat and bearing no number but instead the word *Gawpers* written down the spine. It's an old file my father kept, holding records of every gawper encounter known to him.

Now, gawpers, in case you were unaware, are beings of legendary status. Many believe they exist. Probably more believe they don't. Gawpers come and go like the mist. No one knows how they do it or where they come from or where they go, but it is thought, by those who believe, that they come with ill intent. It is said that those who encounter a gawper are doomed; that if they do not perish immediately they will die soon after; that, if somehow, they manage not to die, some other tragedy will befall them. A loved one will collapse or become fatally ill with some terrible disease, for example.

Gawpers are tall beings with glowing white eyes of flame with which they probe your thoughts while you tremble, fixed to the spot like a statue. It is impossible to tell how the gawpers move. They appear to glide above the ground, or the water – wherever they happen to be.

You may be forgiven for thinking, 'My, my, Micky, you seem to know an awful lot about gawpers.' Well, there's a good reason for that.

I've seen them.

And each time it's happened, I have sweated blood.

I place the gawper file on the shelf over my desk before returning to my father's last casefile, wondering. Did he meet his end beneath the flaming white gaze of a gawper?

The file's rust-red cover is tatty, the edges worn. An elastic band holds it closed and a stamp in faded red ink on the front reads UNSOLVED. With my father's funeral and everything that followed, I can recall little more about the case other than the number and the general nature. It wasn't my case, after all. Father was investigating the death of a wealthy man of Highbridge. Even Shrud told me to let it go and, begrudgingly, I had done so.

Now my interest is piqued and I can't help myself. The name

on the spine reads Oliver Ingham. I open the cover and read. Oliver first came to Mysteries Solved with fears for the safety of his daughter, Tillie, who had received several threats in the form of badly written letters. Flipping through the file I soon find them. The writing is as terrible as my father's notes suggest, the letters poorly constructed, the words irregular, misspelled and speckled with misplaced capitals.

> Miss Tillie Ingham,
> ShoRt is yoUre time Now. DeAth comeS fore You.
> OOh, thE wurms wil Taist your Flesh and Go
> murMur.
> I wiL have JustiCe.
> DWeria PhilShaw

Was the hand that shaped these words crippled in some way or perhaps that of a child in early schooling? I take a new sheet of paper and attempt to copy the style. It's almost impossible, the written formations being so unnaturally peculiar. My closest attempts come when I swap to write with my left hand. All of a sudden a word leaps out at me from the letter.

RUN.

The first three capitals that are misplaced. Was that the true meaning behind the letter? A clear message in a simplistic code? One has to wonder.

Perhaps not, though. I jot down the rest of the unnecessary capitals.

ASYOETFGMLJCWS

Surely meaningless. Checking back for my father's remarks on the letters, I find he recorded no relating comment. It's frustrating because I'm desperate to know what he made of all this.

I move on to the second letter.

> Miss Tillie Ingham,
> Die whore. Die. I'm comminG for your hEarT. Black
> is the cOlor. YoU Traitor! DArkness awaitS You.

HOw yourE flesh wil fester wiTh ForGotten wurMs.
I wiL have JustiCe.
DWeria PhilShaw

There it is again! Am I mistaken? The first unconventional capitals! The message is unmistakable.

GET OUT.

Wondering who this *Dweria Philshaw* is, I read and reread my father's notes but there's no mention of the threatening letters other than a basic description of their unusual style. It's so peculiar because I'm sure this is where anyone else would have started. I certainly would have. It's almost as if some of the notes are missing.

And then it strikes me.

Mother…

# 2

# Dead Men Don't Write

*In which treasure is unearthed*

Ninety-six Bunson Street is a big old house that would have been grand in times gone by. Now it's a creaking shell, a little too worn in places. In the green room, I place the file heavily upon the table before Mother as an incriminating exhibit. Unable to conceal her discomfort, she gazes restlessly between the file and me.

I'm vexed and I look it. 'There are notes missing, aren't there?'

The accusation stings. She bluffs. 'I don't know what you mean. What is this?' She touches the file.

'Come now. You surely recognise it. It's Father's last case. His notes are incomplete. Would *you* know anything about that?'

She rises to step away, quietening for a few moments by the fireplace. 'It was for your own good, Michael. Everybody said so, even Lord Draker.' Lord Bretling Draker is the Minister for Criminal Investigations and chief of the Camdon watchmen.

'Bretling Draker? What has he to do with this?'

'I took the file to him after... after it happened. He said we should drop it. He held your father in high esteem, you know. Said if *he* couldn't solve the case then *nobody* could. I didn't want you running off and getting into trouble. Michael, you were young. You still are. You must understand – '

'I understand, all right. I received a letter today. One implying Father was murdered. If you still have the notes you removed from the file, please give them to me now.'

She considers this and leaves. For ten minutes I wait alone in the green room, brooding, while she clomps around upstairs, eventually reappearing with a fist full of papers.

'Here. For what good it'll do…' She's wounded.

'Thank you.' I take the pages, feeling I've been cruel in some way. I sit by the fire and reorganise the file, attempting to reconstruct its original order.

Mother pours me a port as if in apology and leaves me to it, though she's unsettled.

It's slow work but the task helps me to familiarise myself with the content and, an hour later, I have a good feel for what's in the file. The first section is Father's initial notes and the letters. I presume these are the originals as I see no reason to think otherwise. I find the missing notes about the Philshaw letters and see that Father's thoughts mirrored my own. I learn at least one new morsel: Dweria Philshaw is not a real name, at least, the *Philshaw* part isn't so, it follows, the writer must have invented the name to be sure they remained anonymous without landing an innocent party in trouble. I can't help feeling disappointed. Our most obvious line of enquiry, debunked.

I also find a faded imograph of Tillie Ingham. She was pretty with curling hair and a strong face, an attractive girl in her late teens, her unsmiling gaze fixed upon the camera lens.

The next pages are official documents – most likely copies – concerning the disappearance of Tillie: Draker reports, court statements and newspaper clippings following the story as it unfolded. Towards the back are further notes and some pages torn from my father's diary, detailing his movements during the later days of his investigation. The latter portion and most of what Mother removed concerns the murder of Tillie's father.

Gathering the pages together, I return them to the file and

head back to the office but, before I get far, Jinkers – our neurotic neighbour – steps out from his doorway.

'It's curious to see you here during working hours, Micky. Is something amiss?' His hair is riotous today, sticking up in tufts here and there. His eyes are as large and crazed as ever, roaming as though hungry for something new to devour.

'No, Jinkers. I needed to see Mother.'

'Oh, I see. And how is Mother?'

'She's fine.'

'Excellent!'

I'm not sure why he thinks this is excellent. He barely ever speaks to Mother.

There's an awkward pause while he continues to block my way on the narrow pavement before asking, 'Seen any gawpers lately?'

'Not for a while. You?'

'No. I wonder if they've all gone…' He mutters this as if talking to himself.

'Gone? Gone where? Gone from where?'

'I don't know. Just gone, I suppose.' As he speaks, a mottled-grey cat with black tiger stripes arrives to wind about his ankles. He reaches down and collects it in his arms. 'Do you think they've gone, Mr Kaylock?' Mr Kaylock stretches his neck and makes a noncommittal noise somewhere between a growl and a purr. He has menacing yellow-green eyes that flick to me as Jinkers continues. 'Mr Kaylock says he's not sure.'

'Right. Well, I'd best get on. Good day, Mr Jinkers.' I step into the road to pass him and walk on.

He calls after me. 'Micky, do you think there were gawpers before the cataclysm?'

'I don't know.' I give him a wave. He's an odd fellow but harmless.

It's not only a window that Josiah has cost me. He was a convicted threader when I first met him, a thief by the name of Silus Garroway, bound for the gallows. I intervened and brought him back to Camdon City, paid for his false papers and a wardrobe of silks, and set him up here, reinvented as my business partner. Our names are emblazoned in golden letters across the shopfront.

Banyard & Mingle: Mysteries Solved

He's one of a growing list of once-oppressed threaders I have secretly rescued, all unlawfully. I'll hang if my work is ever revealed to the silker authorities.

Out of habit I glance through a copy of the *Camdon Herald*. There's nothing much of interest other than a piece on a local threader court case. Mumford Foxer of Tower End has been convicted for the theft of a gold clock and for fleeing his master's domain. The Drakers caught him heading for Holloway with the clock in his possession, and a swift hearing followed.

Threaders are the low end of society, little more than slaves, who perform all the menial yet necessary tasks: washing clothes, cleaning, cooking, building, clearing the privies and cesspits, digging graves, mining, farm labouring, basically any hideous job that no one else wants to do. They are paid a pittance and generally treated like scum. There are harsher laws to govern the threaders, much harsher than the laws for us silkers. They are not permitted to wear silks, for one thing, although that is the least of their concerns. If found guilty of a crime they are generally dispatched by their silker masters or hanged publicly or, on occasion, banished to Mors Zonam, the zone of malignant desert stretching beyond the Borderlands. This is to be the fate of poor Mumford Foxer, who no doubt took his master's clock with hopes of selling it for enough money to make good his escape and survive for long enough to find an improved position elsewhere. In Mors Zonam, a place thought to be damaged by the cataclysm, it is understood he will suffer a slow and agonising death in the inhospitable terrain where undocumented beasts roam. The whole system is unjust and I would change it like a shot, if I could. And I would probably launch some hair-brained scheme to save Mumford Foxer if he hadn't already been transported. With a heavy heart I close the paper and set it on my desk, recalling my cousin's words in my mind: *You can't save them all.*

While the glazier thumbs putty around the new pane, we gather in the case room: Josiah; my debonair cousin Mardon; Penney, a recent but worthy addition to our team, with whom I'm utterly smitten; Lizzy and me. Joe takes the first of the Philshaw letters to read. 'Can worms actually murmur?'

Here we go. He'll probably spend the next hour deliberating the limitations of worm anatomy. 'I know it doesn't make sense. It's not the only thing about the letters that doesn't add up. Mardon?'

I've mulled over the case notes and the green ink letter alone for most of the day and now I want to know what the others think, even if it means pulling their heads from their respective cases.

My cousin Mardon can usually be counted on for enlightenment. His habit of late is increasingly to leave his Loncaster surgery in the capable hands of his business partner while he moonlights for me. I think he's bored with pox-ridden patients and the never-ending stream of battered threaders. I wait impatiently as he rereads the letters.

'I admit they're very odd. I imagine the illiteracy is deliberate. Too contrived to be anything else, which makes sense when you consider the hidden messages – though those are also strange.'

The others focus on Mardon.

Josiah asks, 'What messages?'

Mardon explains. 'Here. In the misplaced capitals. The first says RUN. The second, GET OUT. Hardly threatening talk. More of a warning, I'd say.'

'My thoughts precisely. And the following superfluous capitals?' I prompt.

Mardon grunts and sucks on his pipe. 'Nonsense, there to help disguise the main messages.'

'You did notice the same misplaced capitals follow these

warnings in both notes, and they appear in the very same order?'

He looks again. 'By thunder, you're right. Another code, then?'

'If so, it's beaten me. What else can you say?'

'Not much.' He shrugs. 'I'd need to know more about this girl's circumstances. Who is she?'

'*Was* she. My father believed her dead. She disappeared without a word shortly after receiving these letters.'

'Did your father notice the hidden messages?' asks Mardon.

'He did. Though I've only recently acquired the notes that include his comments. This is Tillie.' I give Mardon the imograph of the missing girl to pass around.

'She may still live. Perhaps she took the hint and escaped whatever perils were heading her way,' says Mardon.

'Perhaps. She was a bright girl by all accounts. In any case, Tillie was or is the daughter of Oliver Ingham, chief designer and engineer at Hinkley Air, based in Old Camdon. Oliver Ingham was the man who hired my father to investigate Tillie's disappearance. It seems he was murdered before my father was able to get very far with the case. My father died soon after.'

'How soon after?' asks Penney.

'Two weeks. Of course, the three events may or may not be connected. We should remain open-minded.'

'It all sounds very dubious to me,' says Mardon. 'First Tillie disappears, her father is murdered and then the investigating agent is found dead? I'd be very surprised if your father wasn't killed for getting too close to the truth. What did the authorities say?'

I fill them in on the details: the discovery of my father's body, the coroner's infuriatingly inconclusive report and the Drakers' insistence that the case be dropped.

'That's even worse!' says Mardon, billowing smoke. 'Clearly, your father was murdered by some clandestine means – poison or suffocation. It's a set-up, if I ever saw one. A conspiracy.'

'How awful,' Penney mutters. 'Would the coroner not have seen something to suggest that? I mean, if your father was poisoned.'

'Not necessarily. The signs may be easily missed.'

'How was Oliver Ingham killed?' asks Josiah.

I flip through the casefile and take out an imograph of the murder scene in which Oliver's broken body is sprawled unnaturally across a shattered barrel in a cobbled alley, blood pooling from his lacerated throat. Thankfully, imographs are only black and white. I pin the image to the corkboard on the wall. 'His throat was cut before he fell from the top of the Hinkley building.'

'So, he was killed by someone else at Hinkley,' says Lizzy.

'Apparently, but if my father's notes are correct, Oliver had good relations with his co-workers – was quite popular, by all accounts. My father spent the last two weeks of his life trying to get to the bottom of it all. He was confident that no one from Hinkley Air was involved.'

'That's a puzzle, then,' says Penney. 'He was killed by someone on the rooftop of the Hinkley building but not by an employee.'

'Supposedly. The entire case is peppered with riddles. No wonder my father didn't get very far.'

There's a pause during which an unspoken question hovers in the air around us. I think we all sense it.

*So why have you now gathered us to look at this old, unfathomable case?*

In answer, I produce the green ink letter from my waistcoat pocket.

'This morning I received a letter.' I read it to them, and when I'm finished, pass it to Mardon.

'Why now?' he says. 'If Demitri Valerio, whoever that may be, knew for certain your father was murdered, why wait until now to tell you?'

'Good question. Perhaps something has happened to prompt the gesture.'

'Surely that is why,' says Penney. 'Something has happened to change circumstances. And recently.'

'Like what?' asks Josiah.

'I don't know. New evidence?'

'"A secret order of high social flyers..."' says Mardon. 'Could account for the Drakers calling it off. One word from the right wig and they scurry beneath the nearest rock.'

I nod. 'Someone powerful is behind the killings, I believe. Someone with real money and influence. Do any of the other victims mean anything to you? Zacchaeus Mandon, Foster Keen or Martha Judd?'

The names draw a blank. Penney is perhaps the most highly connected among us because of her father's wealth. She shakes her head. 'I haven't heard of them.'

'Who says they're even real people?' asks Josiah. 'The entire letter could be twaddle. Someone's sick idea of a joke.'

I lean close to correct him with a whisper. 'You mean someone's idea of a sick joke...'

'That's what I said, isn't it?'

I continue. 'Either way, it will be easy enough to prove with a trip to the City Registry Office.'

Mardon holds the letter up to the light coming through the case room's frosted-glass windows. 'Demitri Valerio. Does that mean anything to you, Micky?'

'Well, it wasn't written by Demitri Valerio; not the original, at least. He was a renowned judge, his fight for justice for the poor made him famous back in the fourteenth century. I looked him up in one of Father's books.'

'You mean he's dead?' asks Josiah.

'Very.'

'Dead men don't write,' says Mardon.

'A ghost, then,' says Josiah.

'It made me wonder if it isn't a woman writing in an attempt to further disguise her identity. The whole thing has a distinctly feminine feel about it. I'd say the hand was female, wouldn't you?'

'Quite,' says Mardon.

'How can you possibly know that?' Josiah scoffs.

'Oh, it's a well-documented science. There's a doctor who's written a book on the subject. Fascinating stuff,' says Mardon.

'Is it?' says Josiah. 'I'll add it to my reading list right away.' I'm pretty sure Josiah doesn't have a reading list. His ability to read at all is questionable. 'Just because it's in a book it doesn't make it true,' he adds.

'There's an obvious element we seem to be avoiding,' Mardon points out.

I nod. '*I believe a little digging would reveal much. You should begin at the grave of Willard Steeler.*'

'Well?' says Josiah.

'Well what?' asks Penney.

Josiah looks at us all in turn. 'This Steeler fellow – are we going to dig him up or not?'

The City of Camdon Registry Office is a broad, stately building in the heart of the old town. As you'd expect, it's where all the official records of births, deaths and marriages are stored, mostly for use in court hearings and the like. The dusty corridors are tight and dark, its storerooms numerous, and the entire place smells of mouldering parchment and paper dust. I have to pester the moustached duty clerk several times before I find what I'm looking for, and his face alone conveys his growing irritation at my presence. He's a greasy-looking fellow with narrow shoulders and oiled whiskers and hair. His suit of dark-grey silks is faultless, probably because he never does an ounce of real work that might cause a wrinkle.

I've told him three times now that the individuals I'm researching are dead.

'You'll want the deceased section,' he announces curtly, with uncanny enlightenment.

'Isn't that what I've been saying?'

Finally!

'It's down the hall, second on the left.'

When I find the room I'm alone among the boxes of files, drawers and high shelves, each crammed with information on the dead. The following search is lengthy but this is what I learn.

Zacchaeus Mandon was a property developer who lived and worked in Tower End. His date of death is recorded as 5th of Quartersmoon, in the year 1783 AD (*After Doon* – Doon being the *Great King*). That was twelve years ago.

Foster Keen, a carriage driver from Tower Bridge, died the following year in Trimoon.

Miss Martha Judd was a dressmaker from Highbridge. She died just four years ago in 1791.

I write the details in my notebook for reference.

The fourth register I try reveals Willard Steeler to have been a city entrepreneur from Highbridge who passed, as rich as they come – yet no less dead – two years ago. An obituary kindly provides his current whereabouts: an overburdened cemetery, also in Highbridge.

The cemetery is overlooked by tall houses of golden stone, now a greenish hue in the moonlight as we creep, pulling a heavy machine behind us. It leaks a little steam and smoke as we move. The wheels were squeaking so we've oiled them and now they rotate almost silently.

Josiah, my accomplice in this foul act of illegal sacrilege, dumps the spades and the sack of coal he's carried onto the grass. I see no reason why the Drakers, or anyone else for that matter, might give their consent, and so we dig without any. A pale-blue watch lamp on the street illuminates the graveyard around Steeler's ostentatious tomb well enough for our purposes. I read the inscription.

> *Here lies the body of renowned industrialist*
> *Willard Steeler,*
> *much loved husband and father.*
> *Born 16th Trimoon 1711 AD*
> *Died 24th Hexmoon 1793 AD*

Before we can begin to dig, we must tackle the heavy capstone that covers the top and I'm grateful for Josiah's remarkable strength, without which we would not have a hope. With a huge effort we inch it sideways from the tomb. It grates against the stone edging beneath with a soft rasping noise and we lower it, dragging it perilously along one lip until it hits the ground with a dull thud. We let it rest against the side of the tomb as we prepare, although, if all goes according to Josiah's plan, we'll be doing very little of the digging ourselves.

My pocket watch displays a quarter past midnight. I tuck it away and look dubiously at the strange contraption we've brought through the streets. It has drivebelts, wheels and cogs, levers, a starter cable, a firebox, an iron rotation cylinder of spade blades and a funnel and, of course, the handlebar with which we pulled it. I help Josiah heft it over the edge and we lower it into the tomb where he stoops to check the pressure gauge before shovelling more coal into the firebox.

'It's good to go,' he whispers.

I nod. 'And you *are* sure it runs quietly?'

'Quiet as a mouse, according to Loegray.' Mr Loegray is Mrs Farringsgate's gardener, from whom Josiah has borrowed the steam-powered digging machine. 'Listen, don't worry about the digger. Just keep your eyes skinned.'

He's right. The Drakers make regular patrols of these streets at night and this corner of the graveyard is overlooked by two roads. Right now, there's no sign of anyone and, apart from the noises we're making, all is quiet. Deathly quiet. There's a faint breeze, but nothing strong enough to moan against the towers or rustle the leaves of the trees that are dotted here and there among the graves. Highbridge sleeps and every step we take is like thunder in my ears. Our breath, our whispers, the creak of our leather riding boots, each sound is amplified to me. It feels as though those in slumber around us are straining to listen in through their dreams.

'Well, what now?' I ask.

'Loegray said you just pull this cable to start it.' Josiah bends to take hold of a small brass handle on the end of a wire cable, most of which is wound within the machine, and heaves.

There's a flicker of life from the workings, a short-lived rattle and tick. A small belch of black smoke leaves the funnel and the machine stills.

'Is it broken?'

'Naugh. I expect I didn't pull hard enough.' He tries again, yanking the cable violently and this time the mechanism sparks into life with a thunderous clamour. Steam and smoke spew out and metal grinds and chugs.

'Turn it off!' I shout, closing on the machine in the vain hope I might find a way to silence the thing.

Josiah tweaks controls and pulls a lever. The engine accelerates and, if anything, the din increases.

'Turn it off! Now!'

'I'm trying!' He pulls another lever and closes a valve. The digger chugs on, blades rotating to chomp at the ground. In frustration he kicks it over. There's a clap and a rattle as it falls sideways, finally dying with a pop and a hiss of steam.

We stand shocked in an expectant silence.

'It seems Mr Loegray doesn't know the meaning of quiet.'

'Agreed.' Josiah watches the steam, fascinated by the mechanism, while I pace frantically around the grave, scanning the roads. Incredibly, it appears no one has come running to investigate. I can't quite believe we've escaped notice until several minutes have passed and still no one has arrived; not even a light has spawned from any of the surrounding windows. Calming, we each take hold of a spade. Despite the grand tomb, the body is likely to be buried deep – a measure that discourages grave robbers.

'Back to the old-fashioned way,' says Joe.

'Indeed.'

'Won't be the first time I've dug a grave,' he says, with a grim look.

We dig.

Several hours of back-breaking toil later, Josiah and I stand over the partially mummified remains of Willard Steeler.

I take a half-crown from my pocket. 'Heads or tails?'

'Heads.'

I toss the coin, catch it and slap it onto the back of my hand. 'Heads it is. Which end do you want?'

Dourly, he regards the corpse. 'I'll take the feet, I guess.' He makes the sacred sign with a finger, tracing a circle on his forehead and a line through it to the centre of his chest, before shuffling to the lower end of the coffin to begin.

I search the head for jewellery or anything else. Steeler has three gold teeth, which he can keep. We're not that kind of grave robber. There is nothing else on or around his head or neck. I work my way down the body, checking pockets, as Josiah edges up the shins. We meet in the middle, glancing with concern at the cadaverous crotch, neither willing to go there.

'His hands!' I move on and we both feel a considerable relief.

They are folded across his midriff, one covering the other. I have to poke the upper hand aside to reveal the one below, but it pays off. There, shining like new on the middle finger of the left hand, is a ring of gold set with onyx, a deep, glistening black. The ring is heavy and substantial, a statement of wealth and stature. I attempt to ease it from its emaciated finger, for it may hold meaning and it seems there is little else here to be found, but the digit snaps off in my hand as I straighten it.

'Oops.' I tuck the finger into the handkerchief pocket of Willard's silk jacket and we check the rest of the casket; the stained silk lining to the sides and, as best as we can, the areas beneath the corpse. Nothing. The ring is our only treasure. I slip it into my waistcoat pocket. 'Quickly, Joe, the lid.'

We replace the lid, tamp it down and hoist the coffin. We are preparing to lower it back into the grave when a watchman's shrill toot cuts the quiet of the night.

Josiah sees him first. 'Drakers!'

The watchman races towards us from an adjacent street, piping on his tin whistle. We drop the coffin.

'Run!'

# 3

# A Pocket of Frogs

*In which Banyard works alone*

The coffin hits the marble walls of the tomb and tips. The lid breaks loose and the body falls, disarticulating with a tearing of desiccated skin. The skull rolls away, the long bones slip from their silk coverings to topple in and around the tomb. Small bones rattle to the ground and, leaping graves, we dash for the closest exit, halfway down the graveyard. Behind us, Loegray's digging machine lies wounded, awaiting the Drakers.

A second whistle joins the first – shrieking, tuneless blasts – and the Drakers shout, the soles of their boots slapping the road as they approach.

'Halt! You there! Stop in the name of the king!'

We scarper, ditching our spades into a hedge to speed our escape, and weave through the southern streets of Highbridge. Two minutes into Old Camdon we lose the watchmen and pause in the moon shadows of the market hall to catch our breath.

'You and your brilliant ideas…' I wheeze.

'It's not my fault, Mr Banyard. The digging machine didn't get us caught.'

We watch for the Drakers, listening to their distant whistles.

'Not yet, it didn't.'

Our pace is more leisurely through Crowlands, crossing Rook's Bridge and nearing home but, as we skulk to our house on Bunson Street, an upper window of number 98 flies open and Jinkers pokes his head out. He's in a striped nightshirt and matching nightcap, his hair sticking out wildly at the sides. The whites of his rheumy eyes gleam large in the moonlight.

'I've caught you this time,' he hisses down to us through his flabby wet lips. 'Whatever are you up to, Micky? Sneaking in the dark. It's nearly three in the morning!'

'Shush!' I gesture for him to be quiet before whispering. 'Good morning, Jinkers. If it's all right with you, I'll tell you about it tomorrow.'

He throws down a suspicious look. 'You will? You promise?'

'I promise,' I lie. Well, it's not a complete lie. I'll tell him something. I have a few hours in which to invent a story.

'Very well.' He seems content. Excited, even. 'I look forward to hearing all about it.' He licks his lips and closes the window. He's a strange one, is Jinkers.


There is a phrase in these parts, its meaning much akin to *a different kettle of fish* or *opening a can of worms*, but these archaic sayings are only ever used these days with a melancholic respect for a distant and unreachable past. The cliché in question, however, is of a more recent origin. The words leap in my mind the minute Josiah and I study Steeler's gold ring in the lamplight of the green room. Sitting before the fireplace, we are the only souls awake in the house.

A proper pocket of frogs.

For some reason, it's all that is in my thoughts at this moment. Perhaps my mind has raced to forge a connection, and well it might, for the emblem engraved into the surface of the onyx stone set into the ring is that of a bullfrog, surrounded by a wreath.

'A secret order of high social flyers'… A golden signet ring bearing a frog motif…

… a proper pocket of frogs. Surely, the phrase has never been so apt!

Josiah and I quench our thirst with several glasses of port and sit, examining the thing, our heads growing slowly dizzy. I turn it in my fingers.

'What does it mean, the emblem?'

'I don't know but it's surely what we were meant to find. A sigil of the secret order, I'd wager. I'll research it tomorrow. Now get some sleep. You have a case to work come daylight.'

'Yes, Mr Banyard.'

'Listen, Joe, it's about time you started calling me Micky, or Michael at least. You only need refer to me as Mr Banyard in less-familiar company. When we're with a client, for example.'

For reasons I do not understand, this throws him. I can see it in his eyes.

'Yes, sir, Mr Banyard… Micky… Michael…' he hesitates but heads for his bed and we're no closer to fixing upon a title. I have to admit, both Michael and Micky sounded wrong. Perhaps we shall be forever stuck with Mr Banyard.

I'm left holding the ring. The more I scrutinise it, the more I'm convinced I've seen one like it somewhere before, but the recollection eludes me. It's more a sense than anything else – a feeling that someone else I have encountered wore just such a ring – yet I cannot make the connection, however hard I try.

More worrying is the thought of the Drakers tracing the digging machine to Mr Loegray, who would undoubtedly point them in our direction. The short remains of the night pass torturously as I attempt sleep.

The next morning, I visit Jinkers and spin him a most intriguing yarn about a drunken miller and a flirtatious barmaid of Tower Bridge. He soaks it up, eyes gaping at the highs, lips pursing at the lows. When I leave he's none the wiser, yet happier to know an adventure that never happened.

Josiah is already on his way to the Farringsgates' residence and my other operatives are absorbed by their cases. Even

Ebadiah, the street boy with a limp and a damaged eye, is busy assisting Penney on a robbery investigation that the Drakers could not solve. The Drakers don't like us much, mainly because people come to us when they have failed to get results. We then resolve the cases in good time and make them look bad. They pretty much hate us for it.

I find Ebadiah hanging around outside The Lantern Dog, a Rook's Bridge tavern known locally as The Dog. The tavern is so old that in several places its timber frame, warped by gravity and time, leans at odd angles as though built by a drunken carpenter. With a nod, Ebadiah limps over to join me at one side of the entrance.

I stoop to meet him at his level. 'A little job for you.'

'What's that, boss?' With his good eye he watches the street.

'I need you and your friends to keep an ear out for Draker movements. We had to leave Loegray's digging machine at a scene. There's a chance they'll trace it back to the Farringsgate residence. Then again, perhaps I'm giving the Drakers too much credit...'

'Right you are.' He removes his flat cap to hold it out.

With a sigh, I drop in a half-crown. 'You'll be the ruin of me, Shoe Shine.'

I walk to Mysteries Solved and sit in the case room to read more from my father's last casefile. The dates upon which Tillie Ingham received the strange letters are of interest. My father noted them down with a reference saying that soon after the letters were delivered, Tillie vanished. Instantly, I feel the need to revisit the City Registry Office as they keep copies of every newspaper ever printed in the city. The collection goes back decades and, somewhere, there's bound to be an edition carrying the story of Tillie's disappearance. There are several newspaper clippings in the casefile, but they are all from the *Camdon Herald*, my father's preferred read, and I wonder if the *Old Camdon Chronicle* might also have run the story.

I head out and spend several tedious hours searching old copies of the *Old Camdon Chronicle*. The oily fellow is still here, observing my every move with disdain. No matter. I care little when I find the article I've been hunting. I read the story set in tight columns halfway down page 8, keen to learn all there is to know about Tillie's last known circumstances.

> *Old Camdon Chronicle* – 13th Doblemoon 1790 AD
> Daughter of Esteemed Hinkley Air Designer Vanishes
>
> Following several letters of a threatening nature, Miss Tillie Ingham of Hill Street, Highbridge, daughter of Oliver Ingham of Hinkley Air fame, has been reported missing and concerns for her safety are rising. Oliver Ingham has offered a thousand guineas as reward for information leading to Tillie's recovery. Witnesses report that Tillie was last seen outside the Old Coach House late on the evening of 6th of Doblemoon, wearing a full gown of violet silk and matching bonnet. Anyone with information regarding her disappearance should contact the Highbridge Draker Headquarters post-haste.

Violet silk and matching bonnet – surely that should stick in someone's memory! She must have been hard to miss. I recall her face from the imograph. She had a striking look, so what with that and the silks... Closing my eyes, I picture her in her violet gown seated, waiting for a carriage as the world passed her by. The scene is sad and haunting.

There seems an obvious possibility here. Perhaps Tillie was last seen at the Old Coach House because she was there to catch a coach. If so, someone knew – and possibly still knows – of her last movements in Camdon.

The Old Coach House is an antiquated courtyard inn and stables on Witten Street that was converted into a working station some years ago. From here you can catch a horse-drawn coach directly to any district of Camdon or further afield. There is a daily service north to Loncaster and back, and carriages that go to Burrington, to Windstrome, Farringsgate, Lockingshire and Rochington – basically, anywhere in southern Londaland. All for the right price, of course. The company is old-fashioned in its outlook and keeps traditional values. There are no clockwork cars or steam trucks here. Nothing but good old horse power, and the evidence lies scattered around the cobbles, stinking in the sun.

I ask around and show everyone the imograph of Tillie, but soon have a feeling this is going nowhere. No one recalls her. The drivers waiting are a grim lot, dour, crude and unhelpful. Huddled in the depot, they all but ignore me while sipping their watered rum.

At the roadside a pair of horses stamp to a halt, shoes echoing against stone, their tack glinting, and a driver alights from a carriage.

I call to him. 'Sir, a moment of your time, if you please.'

He is tall, his broad forehead shadowed by the rim of his coachman's hat. The bold bones of his face are framed by brush-thick sideburns.

'I don't please.' He stomps past, heading for the depot waiting room.

'Sir, it won't take a minute.' I catch his sleeve, which he yanks from my grasp before turning with a glare.

'Get your 'ands off!'

Through the parting in his long coat I spy a blunderbuss swinging from his belt. The country roads are dangerous and some drivers carry a gun even though they have armed guards.

'Apologies, sir, but I'm investigating the disappearance of a vulnerable young woman, Tillie Ingham.' I wave the imograph. 'She was last seen at this station late evening on the 6th of Doblemoon, around five years ago, wearing a violet silk gown. Do you remember seeing her?'

His scowl morphs into a grin. 'Five years ago? You should 'ave said.' Back to the scowl. 'No, I don't remember nothin'.' He walks.

I ask others. No one can recall if they were on duty on the night she disappeared and, predictably, many of the coachmen and other staff are not even here right now, and then there are those who have moved on. I learn that a few have died, at least one in an unfortunate highway robbery. Half a dozen have new positions elsewhere. It's useless, but I leave my card with the station master anyway.

Pocketing the imograph, I turn for home but, across the road, stop. There before me is a cobbled alleyway I recognise. It's not until now that I make the connection, although there is no doubt: this is the alley where my father's body was discovered soon after Tillie disappeared, an alley that leads right to the gates of the Old Coach House. Had he traced the same clue to this place, only to find his murderer? Did he probe too closely at the killer's trail?

Back in the case room I clear an area of the corkboard by the grim imograph of Oliver Ingham and pin up a large map of Camdon City. The process engulfs me as I refer to my notes. Red pins mark each place where a murder or suspected murder has occurred. Blue pins show other associated locations, the Old Coach House, residences where the dead lived and their places of work. Every red pin holds a slip of paper in place bearing the deceased's name, including Willard Steeler and the three supposed victims mentioned in the green ink letter. The last pin I add bears my father's name. It overlaps the label of a blue pin marking the Old Coach House.

I quickly change Steeler's pin to a green one. He is not considered a victim but, rather, one of the frogs.

When reassured I've charted everything correctly, I lean back at my desk and consider the scatter of coloured dots that form a zone encompassing Highbridge, Tower End and Old Camdon, with Tower Bridge roughly at its centre. Notably, these are the high-business districts of Camdon City. There is only one pin in Crowlands (my father's house), and none in Dockside or Southside or any outskirts of the city where the grime of industry pollutes or where the threader workers dwell. Everything is centralised, precisely where the real money is.

Turning to a new page in my pocketbook, I draft a list of points for research.

> The gold ring
> Hinkley Air
> Oliver Ingham
> Zacchaeus Mandon
> Foster Keen
> Martha Judd
> Willard Steeler (frog?)

It doesn't look much on the page but the list represents an awful lot of work. The ring is problematic. I'm not sure where to start with that. Perhaps a jeweller's. There are several in the city, the most exclusive in Tower Bridge. No surprise there. Everything seems to point to the heart of Camdon so, deciding that is where I should begin, I grab my hat and waistcoat and head back out.

Chantrees is possibly the most prestigious of all the goldsmiths in Camdon. I enter, wearing a haze of road dust and my dog-eared tricorn, feeling like a poor excuse for a silker, knowing they'll want me off the premises as soon as they realise I'm not buying. The shop reeks of opulence. I glance around at the numerous displays of thick gold necklaces, chains, rings, brooches, armlets and earrings. Gemstones sparkle from every shelf: diamonds, rubies and emeralds, and many semiprecious stones. I take my time perusing the crimson velvet boards of rings set with onyx but find there are none bearing a frog motif.

A slight, pinch-faced assistant behind one of the two counters clears his throat, so I ask, 'Are all your designs on display?'

'They are, sir.'

'Do you, perchance, craft gold rings to order?'

'Why, yes, sir. Of course.'

'And could you make a ring to my specification in gold and

onyx?'

'Certainly, sir. We can design and fashion a bespoke gold ring set with onyx to meet your every desire.'

'Oh, good. I was hoping you'd say that.' I pluck Steeler's ring from my waistcoat pocket. 'Have you ever been charged to make a ring like this? Here, take a good look.'

He takes the ring, turning it in his fingers. 'It's a fine piece,' he says, but sure enough, four questions in, it's in the skinny assistant's eyes. They glaze over and his voice takes on a monotone drone. 'I'm afraid our clientele expect an exacting standard of privacy, Mr...?'

There is something else in his eyes as the onyx catches the light: recognition. Not of me but of the ring.

'Banyard. Michael Banyard.'

'Well, Mr Banyard, as I was saying, we have a strict policy at Chantrees, one that protects client information. I could not possibly tell you if we've made such a ring or for whom.' He hands the ring back and makes a point of closing the register between us on the counter. 'Now, will you be placing a legitimate order, or not?'

'Not today, thank you.' I turn to leave, but not before noting the spy holes in the luxurious panelling at his back. There, beyond the wall, is a flicker of movement.

It's mid-afternoon by the time the others start arriving at the office. There's an atmosphere of jubilation as Josiah enters with Penney on his arm. There is familiarity. Affection.

I leave my desk and stand in reception feeling coldly removed. 'What's going on?' Everyone seems happy but me. At her desk, Lizzy grins. Penney releases Josiah's arm. Mardon tucks his whisky flask away in his pocket like a child caught by the teacher. Even Ebadiah looks at me as though I'm the biggest party-killer who ever lived and lowers his handful of cake.

'It's Josiah,' says Lizzy, beaming. 'He's solved his first case. Congratulations, Joe.'

The Farringsgates had a break-in a while ago and the thieves took some jewellery and a little money that was lying around the house. It would have been a trifling affair if they had not also stolen some letters of a rather personal nature that were dear to the couple. Josiah has been close on the heels of the thieves for several weeks and has managed to name them and have them arrested. He also recovered and returned the letters to the Farringsgates. I must say, he's done well.

'Congratulations, Josiah,' says Penney.

'Well done, old chap,' says Mardon, deciding it's safe to break out the whisky again.

The tension eases although I'm left discontented, disconnected.

Adding my congratulations, I withdraw to the case room as the celebrations continue, leaving the door ajar. Lizzy passes around the cake. Mardon is trying his best to choke us all on his second-hand smoke. The noise of their chatter alone is enough to impede my focus but, to add to the din, they carry in a fiddler from the street and pay him a penny to play a merry tune. Lame Garrett sits in the visitor's chair, enthralled at this new-found appreciation of his art, grinning a toothless smile while drawing his bow enthusiastically. Alienated, I sit at my desk, brooding and staring at the map on the wall.

Ebadiah hobbles into the room. 'Mr Banyard! Dobson just reported in. He overheard a Draker down The Dog. They're on their way to the Farringsgate place!'

'Loegray's digging machine!'

# 4

# The Order

*In which Banyard and Mingle visit the Farringsgate residence*

I nearly fall off my chair hurrying to rise.

In reception, Josiah is still making merry but his face drops when I draw him aside and thrust his waistcoat into his arms.

'Sober up. We're going out.'

On Bunson Street I hail a carriage. The driver draws the horses to a halt and leans towards us. 'Where to?'

'Farringsgate Hall, Highbridge.' I check my pocket watch. 'There's an extra guinea in it if you get us there before four.' We might have ridden but circumstances demand caution. Our horses can easily give away our movements. When they are tethered outside the office it is obvious to any watchers we are there. Their absence can also tell others we're out in the field. When recognised elsewhere, it is a sure sign of our presence. A hired carriage is subtler if we can afford it. And right now, we can't afford to use anything else.

The driver steers us away and, minutes later, halts the horses in the driveway between the Farringsgate house and a huge fountain where leaping stone fish spout water into an ornate circular pool.

The mansion is a splendid turn-of-the century building with

well-kept grounds, long lawns, numerous water features and formal gardens, set on the northern edge of Highbridge. Farringsgate himself is an overweight politician for whom I have little love. His wife, as you'll have realised by now, is rather exquisite and he doesn't deserve her – my opinion, for what it's worth. Right now, there's no sign of either of them as Josiah and I snoop along the grand entrance to the side gate. Our problem is that we don't want to be seen here, not by anyone other than the gardener Loegray. We must get in quietly and convince him to keep us out of any investigation our little midnight dig has spawned, or we'll end up in gaol and the green ink case will be crushed beneath a barrage of Draker boots.

The house is tall and stark against the open sky and purveys a sense of power and authority. Josiah lifts the latch on the iron gate and it squeals open. Voices reach us from inside the house and I follow him into the rear gardens. Loegray is likely working back here somewhere because there was no sign of him out front.

'Yoo-hoo, is that you, Mr Banyard?' Mrs Farringsgate has spotted me sneaking in. It sounds as though she's somewhere near the front door. There's no hiding now. I nod towards the gardens ahead, gesturing for Josiah to go on without me, and turn back for the steps where she stands, halfway up, smoking a cigarette through a long black mouthpiece held delicately in her slender, white-gloved fingers. Her gown, pristine white, laced and frilled with azure, is drawn tight at her narrow waist and hugs every curve. Overshadowing this, her bosom is barely constrained. Her sensuous face is pale with powder, her lips a deep red, and a beauty spot resides above one corner of her mouth to the side of her nose. Her eyes are bright. Her teeth are white. A blonde wig of high luxurious curls completes her sumptuous guise.

'Ah! Mrs Farringsgate, there you are! I was just seeking the tradesman's door.'

She laughs. 'Oh, really, you are a cad.' Her eyes are unwavering, so much so that I'm forced to glance away or risk losing myself in their depths.

She seems oblivious to my creeping into her back garden with no real reason and I wonder why the rich always seem detached, distanced from the impact of reality.

'I'm calling to…' Why am I calling? I have no idea. Think! 'I'm calling to check that my associate Mr Mingle has provided a satisfactory service, now that the case is closed and you have recovered your letters. Is it so?'

'Oh, Mr Banyard, he's been simply marvellous.' There's something about the way she watches my reaction that leads me to suspect an undercurrent of some sort, as though she's enjoyed his attentions a little too much. It's worrying. We have enough powerful enemies already.

'That is good to hear. And would you consider using the services of Mysteries Solved again, should the need arise?'

'Of course. Without hesitation.' Her smile is utterly beguiling. 'And I shall tell all my friends.'

A horse-drawn carriage approaches on the road at the end of the lengthy driveway. Probably the Drakers Ebadiah warned us about.

'And the case has been concluded to your satisfaction?'

'Indeed, it has.'

'Very well. That is comforting to know, which leaves me no further reason to take up your precious time. I bid you farewell, Mrs Farringsgate.' I descend a step, one eye on the carriage as it turns in towards the house.

'Are you leaving so soon?'

'I'm afraid I must. These mysteries won't solve themselves, you see?'

She laughs again – a delightful sound like a soft peal of bells – and squints towards the coach and horses, sucking on the mouthpiece of her cigarette.

Now I'm stuck. Under her gaze, I can't join Josiah in the back garden and I can't saunter past the Drakers without being recognised. Nowhere to hide.

A voice from the house saves me. It's too faint for me to tell what is said but it's enough to call her away. She throws me a cursory smile and waves before going in and closing the door. For a few precious seconds I'm free to hurry back to the garden gate where I almost run headlong into Josiah.

'Hide. Quickly.' I point towards a neatly manicured privet hedge and we dash behind it. 'Did you find Loegray?' I whisper.

'Aye. He's all set. He'll swear the digging machine was stolen. No connection to us.'

'Thank Lychling.'

We hush then, because Bretling Draker enters the garden, looking surprised to find no one there. He must have seen me duck through the gate as he approached in the carriage with his officer. Let's hope I was too far away to be recognised. He returns to the front of the house and we hear him knocking on the door. We wait, wondering if we might overhear something that may keep us informed. In any case, we don't wish to risk leaving now and being spotted on the drive. Shortly, Mrs Farringsgate opens a rear door and calls into the back garden.

'Yoo-hoo, Gerald, are you there?'

'I'm here, Mistress.' Loegray appears, spade in hand, between two vast lavender bushes growing either side of a path further down the garden, and walks up to join them at the house. There follows a conversation of which we grasp but a few meaningless words. Mrs Farringsgate introduces Loegray to Bretling and the officer and, a few minutes later, they say their farewells and part. Mrs Farringsgate and the lawmen re-enter the house and we wait until the rattling sound of the Draker carriage has distanced before creeping away, disaster averted.

By five o'clock I'm in the case room again, pondering the green ink ghost when a small voice at my side takes my attention.

'You all right, Master Banyard, sir?' Ebadiah clenches his cap in both hands and his good eye pinpoints the imograph on the wall.

'Ebadiah. Oh, yes. I'm fine, thank you. Please don't call me master. You may return to the *fun* side of the wall.' Josiah, Lizzy,

Mardon and Penney are next door, enjoying a kind of post-party haze, doing little if any actual work.

But Ebadiah remains, gripped by the shocking image of Oliver Ingham. 'Cor! This your new case?'

'Hmmm. Although in a way it's an old one.'

'Can I 'elp with it?'

'Aren't you needed by Penney and the others?'

'Not really. Least, not right now. I 'elped Penney yesterday, Mardon before that. Joe's free, too. Well, he will be once he's filed his paperwork. We could both 'elp. Ain't fair me 'elpin' everyone but you, is it, sir?'

'No, I suppose not.' I show him Steeler's ring. 'Ever seen anything like this before?'

His eyes widen. 'Is that gold? Where d'you get it?'

'It's solid gold. We took it from the grave of a man named Willard Steeler.'

'You took it from a grave?'

'Yes.'

He pales and steps back. 'Bad luck, is that. What'd ya do that for?'

'I'm afraid it had to be done.'

'Well, keep it away from me.'

'Very well.' I tuck it back into my waistcoat pocket.

'What's it got to do with the case?'

'I'm not sure. I think whoever wrote the green ink letter meant us to find it.'

'Who's Willard...' He frowns, trying to recall the name.

'Steeler? A rich man. Well, he was. Now he's just a dead man.'

'And that were his ring?'

'It *was* his ring. I think the symbol could be important. Can you do a little poking around? See what you can find?'

The next morning, while Ebadiah wings the investigation to the Dockside streets – his old stomping ground – I take it to Old Camdon where resides the largest library of the city. There has to be a reference to the frog motif in a book somewhere, surely. I'm there for most of the day, perusing dusty volumes, and see nothing of interest until I check the index of history publications. Halfway through the filing cards is a book title that sounds promising: *Symbols of Londaland Throughout the Ages*, index number 413. Returning to the shelves I track the number but find no book where 413 should be. I find a bulging librarian at the front desk. She views me disparagingly as I approach.

'Excuse me, I'm looking for book number 413, *Symbols of Londaland Throughout the Ages*. It doesn't appear to be on the shelf.'

'One moment.' With a mighty effort and a glance that says *I hate you for this*, she rises to her feet and rifles though a shallow drawer of cards, eventually pulling one out with a shrug. 'It's not here because it was taken out and never returned. It's been stolen.'

'Oh? That's interesting – '

'Is it?' Clearly, she doesn't think so.

'Yes. Who stole it? As I understand it, each book that is borrowed must be signed for.'

She doesn't care about any of this. She only wants to sit back down and resume her role of doing absolutely nothing. 'Mr Black. False name. Fake papers, obviously. Fake address. Is that all?'

'Yes. Thank you.'

She rolls her eyes, turns and shuffles back to her resting place.

The second library I try is smaller and tucked away in a quiet corner of Tower Bridge, though it's a tall, ornate building with a reasonable collection. One book, however, is missing from its history section. You guessed it. *Symbols of Londaland Throughout the Ages*.

This is irritating.

There are several other folk perusing the shelves and one in particular bothers me. He's a tall man who looked shady from the second he entered, which was soon after me. He has yet to remove his hat despite the heat of the day and being indoors. Even in a public building it's considered improper not to remove one's hat, so this in itself is odd. His is a bowler, black, with a fine powdering of dust from the road. Not only did he enter soon after me but he has also consistently positioned himself at bookshelves where he has a good view of me.

I quickly leave.

Glancing back at the library doorway from the street, I catch him watching and hold his gaze for enough time to let him know I'm on to him.

There are ways to prevent a tail from following. You can turn corners and hide, double back through shops, hitch a ride on the back of a carriage or, if you're lucky enough to find two pausing on the street, you can enter one and pay the driver to go in one direction while you slip through the other door straight into the second carriage and head off the opposite way. I employ all of these methods before finally arriving, tail free, at the only remaining library in Camdon City.

This one is in Highbridge and I arrive close to closing time. No matter. It shouldn't take long to establish if they have the book or not. Five minutes later I have it in my hands. It's old and leather-bound, a great tome of a book, as dry and dreary as they come.

I open it and race through the list of contents, flip through its weighty pages and read anything that looks remotely connected to secret orders and societies. Ten minutes into my search, the willowy librarian, who's wearing spectacles and has a second pair hanging around her neck, rings the bell for closing time. In that instant I find the line I've been seeking all this time.

> *Between 1635 and 1639 the order used the noble crest with decreasing frequency, preferring instead the less obvious motif of a bullfrog within a wreath.*

The librarian leans her beaky nose over my desk. 'Sir, I'm afraid we're closing.' She fixes upon me, her eyes voluminous behind thick lenses. 'You'll have to come back tomorrow, unless you wish to sign the book out.'

'I'll take it, thank you.'

With one finger wedged between the pages, I sign for the book and leave, knowing it holds the information I've been seeking. It wasn't a complete waste of a day. On the steps outside I turn the corner of the page to mark the place before striding for home. It's then I notice the bowler-hatted man turning a corner and climbing the library steps. I tip my hat as I pass and wave the book at him with a grin.

'Good afternoon, sir. I'm afraid the library has just closed for the day.'

He stops mid-step and, without a word, watches me go.

Jinkers is sweeping his doorway when 96 Bunson Street enters my view. I sidestep into the long shadows and slow, waiting for the opportune moment as he finishes up and goes back into his house. He hasn't seen me. Good. I hurry to my door and slip inside.

A voice calls from another room. 'Is that you, Michael?'

'Yes, Mother.'

'Good. I'm just serving dinner.'

She's still speaking to me, then.

'I'll be right in.' I hang my waistcoat and hat next to Josiah's and walk into the dining room where the widow Koslyne Blewett, Mardon, Ebadiah and Josiah await.

Mother ladles aurochs stew into bowls and Josiah passes the bread. I sit at the table.

'I bumped into Miss Danton today,' says Mother. 'She's coming to dinner tomorrow night.'

'Oh?'

'I invited her.'

'Very well.' I'm not sure if this is a guilt offering or something else, but I won't complain. Penney and I have been so embroiled in our respective cases of late that we've barely exchanged a word, and now this green ink business has me consumed. Perhaps she might help me with it.

After we've eaten and retired to the green room, I finally get my hands back on the library book while Mardon lights his pipe and reclines in a grand Wexford across from me, near the cold fireplace. The evening has cooled to an enjoyable temperature. Josiah has already drunk too much wine, no doubt in celebration of his first solved case, and he folds himself into a chair to doze. Ebadiah brings port and crystal glasses.

'Any luck with your enquiries?' I ask.

'I put the word out. Should hear back tomorrow.'

'Thank you.' The port is rich and full-bodied, and it's an easy-enough job to find the page with the folded corner and backtrack to the paragraph before the mention of the frog motif.

> *The Order of Lithobates was founded around 1543 under sinister circumstances and has since been, to a large degree, a clandestine society enigmatic in nature. While rumours abound of its members' precise identities and purpose, it seems most scholars are agreed upon two of the more eminent aspects. Firstly, it is said to be a group of high-ranking noblemen, sworn to protect the king. This fits with the generally accepted view that King Osbert was highly unpopular and in certain need of protection. Secondly and perhaps more interestingly, the order has generally been associated with the study of gawper mythology. This is, perchance, owing to the well-known gawper obsession of King Osbert.*

I take a moment. The Order has an historic interest in gawpers. That intrigues me and I wonder what they might have discovered over the years. Another thought settles over me: For this reason, Father would also have taken a keen interest in the order.

I read on.

> *Today we view the Order of Lithobates through the haze of centuries and yet several of their symbols have survived in*

*startling clarity. In its infancy, the Order used a shield crest comprising four quarters, each taken from the heraldry of the noble houses in fealty to King Osbert: a boar from the House of Arthric, the three feathers from the House of Dover, the arrow from the House of August and the serpent from the House of DeCullis. Between 1635 and 1639 the order used the noble crest with decreasing frequency, preferring instead the less obvious yet simpler motif of a bullfrog within a wreath. The change marks a point in time at which the order became increasingly secretive.*

It's rather more information than I need but seems to confirm what the green ink letter says: 'a secret order of high social flyers'. But why use a bullfrog as a motif?

In the study are shelves and shelves of Father's old books. He loved them and spent many a contented hour in this room, seated in his favourite old chair, reading. I search for a title that might tell me more about bullfrogs and find just the thing: *Amphibians of Londaland and Amorphia.*

The common bullfrog; genus *Lithobates catesbeianus.*

Perhaps Lithobates has always been a name for the Order and it was kept secret until the seventeenth century. Who knows? It seems the reason for this choice may have been lost to time.

My ponderings are interrupted by Josiah. Bleary-eyed and subdued, he enters and waits for me to look up from the book.

'Yes?'

'How's the investigation going, Mr Banyard?' He yawns and sways slightly on his feet.

'Slowly. Have you signed off the Farringsgate case?'

'All paperwork submitted and filed. The final settlement is due tomorrow.'

'And the Right Honourable Mr Farringsgate has forgiven your… compliments to his wife?'

'Yes. All forgiven. He seemed rather pleased with my work, in fact.'

'Yes, so does Mrs Farringsgate.'

'Which leads me to ask, do you require help with the green ink letters?'

'Has Lizzy not already burdened you with another case?'

'No. She wanted to talk to you first but you've been out.'

'Very well. I'll fill you in.' I tell him about the newspaper report, the Old Coach House and the Order of Lithobates.

'You think your father was on to something.'

'Without doubt. It's the only thing that makes sense.'

'Then his killer walks free.'

'Not for long. Not if I have anything to do with it.'

'So, what's next?'

'I don't know. Ebadiah is using his connections to gather names of people who wear the frog rings, though I doubt he'll find much. They're hiding in palaces and royal houses, not in dockyards and backstreets.'

'Perhaps we should be looking there, then.'

He's right. 'But how?'

He replies with a wolfish grin. 'I can get us on the inside, Mr Banyard. You leave that to me.'

Oh, dear. This can't be good.


It's morning, just gone nine o'clock, and Father's case notes lie spread across my desk. I scan each page, hoping for some revelation. Father's old tricorn observes me from the end of the desk where it sits atop a yellowed skull, a memento from a past case that doubles as a good paperweight. Several times, Lizzy has begged me to remove the skull, saying it's a foul object to keep in an office, but I like it. And, anyway, it's not her office.

'Come on, old man. Give me something,' I ask the hat.

I hear my father's voice in my head like a memory. 'Use your eyes, lad. It's all there before you.'

'What have I missed?'

'It's in the details, son. It's always in the details.'

The hat's right. The hat's always right.

My gaze settles on a paragraph where Father has described the scene of Oliver Ingham's murder. I reread the notes. Oliver was found by a Draker on his nightly patrol at just after four in the morning. The body was stone cold to the touch, indicating that Oliver had been dead for some time before being discovered. Blood had run from his lacerated throat and from the other injuries inflicted by his fall, to pool and coagulate between the cobbles of the alley. There were no footprints in the blood, not even from the Draker, who trod carefully and saw no one in the vicinity during his watch except for the baker's boy on his way to work. Oliver's effects – his wallet, handkerchief, gold pocket watch, cufflinks, pen and wedding ring – were all present and in place, suggesting he was not robbed. His body showed wounds consistent with an impact upon the barrel and the cobbles from a great height, flesh and skin bruised and broken, bones shattered. There seems no reason to dispute the conclusion: Oliver had his throat cut before being pushed from the top of the Hinkley building.

The imograph on the wall is so grisly that it is disturbing to look at, but I force myself to study every detail before snatching it from the wall to stare at a small part of it. There, in the foreground, is an enigmatic curving shadow on the ground. I wonder, what was the cause of that shadow? Pocketing the imograph, I fetch Blink, my sleek black gelding, and ride for Old Camdon. Sometimes there's nothing else for it; you have to revisit the crime scene.

# 5

# The Unexpected Arrival

*In which a crime scene is re-examined*

The blazing sun bakes the cobbles as I tether Blink to an iron ring set into the wall. The Hinkley Air building is abuzz with workers, its many windows wide open to make the most of the disappointingly ineffectual easterly. A heat haze trembles the air over the crossroads nearby and I'm sweating by the time I arrive at the place where Oliver's body met with the ground. Hinkley Air is to my left as I stand at the entrance to the alley, which runs along two of the skyraker's edges. To my right climbs an office block less than half as high as Hinkley Air. It's owned by the Millers Society. The coroner's statement mentions the building's height as 'not in keeping with the extensive trauma to the deceased's body'. In other words, it wasn't the Millers building he fell from but one much higher.

There are around fifty skyrakers in Camdon City, most of them scattered around the northern edge of Old Camdon, the newer side, stretching as far west as Tower Bridge and Highbridge. There are none south of the river. In fact, to my knowledge there are none anywhere but here. Camdon City is the capital of Londaland and the skyrakers give it a unique cityscape.

Although the city at my back is bustling, this alley is not. Right now, it's forgotten. Much like Oliver and Tillie Ingham. There is no barrel standing where he landed. No trace of the one his body splintered. No blood between the stones. It is as if he never died here.

I take out the imograph and compare it to the scene. Apart from Oliver's wreckage, little has changed. I walk the length of the alley seeking clues about this man's horrific death but find none.

The alley is edged by a strip of shade that is ebbing fast as the sun climbs higher. The strip covers around four feet of the cobbled surface and has an odd shape to it, much like the one in the imograph although, because the picture was captured at a different time of day, the curve is in a different place. It's a shape that strikes me as wrong. Why is there a curve, a long low bulge along the shadow's shrinking edge? The Hinkley tower is square sided, its rooftop flat. I trace the building from ground to sky and find the cause floating from ropes high overhead, shifting faintly on the breeze, which, no doubt is stronger up above the city. There, a Hinkley Air ship floats, tethered to the rooftop.

Of course there's an airship. I recall the same branded ship floating over various parts of the city. Good advertising, I suppose. Its creamy white canvas stretches over a long oval form like an enormous fat cigar with Hinkley's red brand plastered across its sides in bold text. I backtrack to stand on the opposite side of the road, across from Hinkley. From here I can see more of the dirigible, though it's still mostly hidden by the building top.

This changes everything. Perhaps the ship had been moved on the morning of the grim discovery after this imograph was taken, and was never considered pertinent. Or perhaps the Draker who found the body simply never noticed it that morning.

That's when it happens again – that thing that occurs whenever a gawper is near. An overwhelming sense of nausea rushes over me and an inner pressure builds as blood seeps from the pores of my skin. I dab it from my forehead and temples with a kerchief.

Blink stamps and whinnies. It's unlike him, a clear sign something has unsettled him. I scan the streets, the banks, the offices, the barber's shop, the nearby milliners and other stores. There is nothing that could have spooked him, not even a steam truck on the road nearby.

I cross back into the alley, peer down it and walk to the elbow where it hooks around the back of the Hinkley building. Again, nothing. I untether Blink and ride back to Mysteries Solved, most of the way glancing over my shoulder.

The feeling that I'm being watched remains with me, even when I reach the office. I pin the ghastly imograph back up next to the map in the case room and consider calling another meeting. I've rather lost track of what everyone else is up to, except for Josiah, that is. He drank enough last night to sink a sloop. The doorbell jingles as he enters reception. I check my pocket watch. Five minutes past ten in the morning. Let's hope the extra sleep has cleared his mind because I could use some help.

I open the adjoining door to poke my head through. 'You're late, Josiah.'

He winces and gives a downward wave. *Quieter, please.*

He hangs his hat on the stand and sloughs off his waistcoat, draping it over the back of the old visitor's chair. The grand Wexford is bound in brown leather with patches of wear on its arms and a seat deeply sunken by years of compression. The upholstery is fixed in place by lines of brass studs that have a dull patina. He slouches, unshaven, looking pasty and sunken-eyed.

'Did you enjoy your celebrations, Josiah?' I ask.

Unrepentant, he grins back at me. 'I certainly did, Mr Banyard.'

'Lizzy, can you spare Mr Mingle for a time?'

Lizzy glances up from the ledger on her desk and fixes upon Josiah. 'We can manage without him for a while. He's not going to be much use today, anyway. You're welcome to him.'

I open the door wider and nod for Josiah to join me. He does so as Ebadiah limps in from the street.

'I got names,' announces Ebadiah. 'Some people wearing frog rings.'

'Who are they?' I grab a quill and dip the tip in ink.

'Thomas Hiddlesworth, Jacob Mansville and Fletcher Gouldstone.'

I scratch the names down onto a page of my pocketbook. 'Good work, Ebadiah. Are these names from trusted contacts?'

'As trusted as they can be. Cost me a pretty penny...'

'How much?'

'Three crown should cover it.'

I dig out three coins from my purse and drop them into his outstretched palm.

'Here. Anything else you know about these three?'

'Naugh. Just got the names.'

'Very well. Now run along. Let me know if your friends learn anything else of significance.'

'Right you are, boss.' Ebadiah tips his cap and leaves.

'It appears we have something to investigate, Mr Mingle.'

Josiah rides at my shoulder, sluggish in the saddle on his white dappled mare. He's named her Willow after a girlfriend from his previous life as a threader. Since I visited the alleyway, thin clouds have blown in from the sea to screen the city fleetingly from the glaring sun. Blink is frisky today, wanting to veer off track and tugging irritably at the reigns with his bit. Perhaps it's the weather.

'At least it's a little cooler today,' I say.

'It's still as hot as Mors Zonam,' Josiah mumbles.

We head for the Camdon City Office of Trade to search the registers for the names. It's a long and tedious job and, I decide, a suitable punishment for Josiah's excessive carousing. I check myself. Am I too hard on him?

'My head hurts,' he moans after a half-hour of silent

searching through files and registers.

'I thought it probably did,' I say, with little sympathy. 'We'll stop for black soup soon. Perhaps that will help.'

He grunts in reply and delves glumly into another drawer of files.

We find one of the names: Fletcher Gouldstone. A dusty file tells us he is an entrepreneur working in the Highbridge region. His main line of business is property development, although he appears to have a trading company and a toe in the cotton industry, mostly abroad on the east coast of Amorphia. I jot down his property development office address in my pocketbook with a pencil and we search on, hoping for other finds. An hour later we're weary of searching in the stifling rooms and have found nothing more. It's as if the other two men on Ebadiah's list are phantoms. Like they never existed. Not in Camdon City, anyway.

Revived by black bean soup we leave the offices with a clear plan of action. We must find this Fletcher Gouldstone fellow and watch him. Crossing town, we home in on his business address and find it without too much trouble. It's an office on the ground floor of a cream-stoned building on Tall Street. No skyraker, but a grand old place. His name is emblazoned in a black ironwork arch over the doorway and I guess he owns it all, even though other businesses have brass plates fixed on the wall to one side of the door. Among them we find Gouldstone Enterprises. We watch from across the street because, through the line of lower windows, we can see people working. It makes sense that one of them is likely Gouldstone himself, but time will tell. For now, we simply observe. Again, it's slow, uncomfortable work. We're hot and bored. And Gouldstone, if he's in there, remains inside. The waiting game again.

By five o'clock we've had enough for one day and return to Mysteries Solved. Josiah immediately collapses into the visitor's chair and, soon enough, Lizzy is pawing over him, fussing about the cut on his shoulder from his trip through our window and pestering to redress it. Josiah is not interested. Not in the dressing, anyway. He seizes the chance to topple Lizzy onto his lap as she leans across him and for a moment none of us is sure how this is going to end. With Lizzy it could go either way. She might laugh and clap him on the arm or she might punch him hard in the eye. You never quite know with Lizzy.

Luckily for Joe, she laughs and clips his shoulder. She likes him. This is clear as she's pretty slow to climb from his lap. In fact, she's still there when the front door bursts open a moment later with a jangle of the bell, and a perfect stranger hurries in. I say stranger but, by the shock of recognition on Josiah's face, the two are well acquainted. She has mousy brown hair and is petite and attractive with simple features. There is a tenacity about her that is manifest from the start. She closes the door as though a wolf is on her heels and fixes upon Josiah and Lizzy in his lap. The newcomer scowls. When she speaks, it is with a deep Loncaster accent and a threader drawl.

'Did you not swear I was the only girl for you till your dying day?' She seems serious.

Josiah stands briskly, just about ditching Lizzy onto the floor. 'Willow!'

For a moment nobody moves. We all stare at Willow and Josiah.

Well, this is awkward.

'What are you doing here?' asks Josiah.

Willow doesn't answer straight away. Now that she's over the shock of finding her old boyfriend with another woman on his knees, all her attention is on the street beyond the windows. She throws nervous glances up towards Rook's Bridge and down the road towards the sprawling houses of Crowlands before ducking quickly away from the front of the office.

'In here!' Josiah launches himself over to the case room door and ushers her inside, where the frosted glass shelters her from the street.

She gawps at the wall with the map and the grim imograph. 'Huh! What you got yourself into?'

Back in reception I turn to Lizzy, Penney and Mardon. 'Stay

here.' I enter the case room and close the door, disturbing Willow and Josiah as they embrace and kiss, long-parted sweethearts.

'Would somebody care to explain to me what this is all about?' I ask.

Josiah steps back from her and clears his throat. Pulls himself together. Straightens up. 'Mr Banyard, this is Willow, the girl I told you about. Willow, Mr Banyard is the silker who rescued me from the noose. The man who saved my life.'

'Michael.' I offer my hand but Willow defers into a curtsy, though I sense a degree of mockery in the gesture. It's quite possible that she would deem a handshake a far too familiar greeting between a threader and a silker. It's the kind of thing that lands you in trouble with your silker master, if he's the cantankerous sort.

She laughs, apparently at the thought of calling a silker by their first name. 'In that case, sir, I am deeply indebted to you, Master Michael, for saving my Silus.' She curtsies again and hugs Josiah's arm. She has a boldness about her, a rebelliousness.

'And now, I'm to save you, too, it appears. Am I right in presuming you are... a runaway?' I open the door an inch to spy out through the windows into the street. A man in a black silk topper has appeared and is snooping around. He has a large moustache and stands out from the other pedestrians because he's subtly searching while trying to look inconspicuous. He's certainly not shopping or on his way somewhere, like the others. But he is hunting. And so is his dog, its great long snout sniffing ever closer to our doorstep.

I close the case room door again for privacy.

'It's not her fault, sir,' says Josiah Mingle, or Silus Garroway – take your pick. 'I wrote to her. I had to let her know I was all right.'

'You did what?!'

'I wrote a letter.'

I'm dumbfounded. 'And you told her you were here. Do you realise the danger you've placed us in? You've jeopardised everything we've worked for!'

By the crestfallen look on his face, he didn't realise. Not fully. Not until this moment.

'Well, I didn't tell her to come here but now she has, we have to help her, surely.'

'Oh, Silus, you do sound funny!' says Willow, giggling at him. 'Like a proper gent! 'As 'e got you talkin' like this?' She jabs a dirty-nailed thumb at me.

For a while I'm beyond words. I turn away into a kind of circular pacing that lands me back where I started. A multitude of scenarios run through my mind and none of them ends well. He's right, of course. Now she's here, there's nothing else for it. We must help her and do what we can to limit the damage. Getting her to shut her big fat mouth would be a start.

'Very well. We must wait and hope that your pursuer, whoever he is, has not traced you to our door. As soon as he's gone, I'm putting you on a carriage straight back home. You can return to your master as though of your own free will, apologise and beg his forgiveness. Any other course would endanger Silus.'

Willow spins towards me in dismay. 'Please, sir, do not send me back to 'im. Anything but that! No apology will be good enough for 'im. Master Bletchley will hang me for running. That or he'll banish me to Mors Zonam.'

'Either way, she'll be dead,' says Josiah. 'Please don't do it, Mr Banyard.'

So here I stand. It's a lose–lose situation and I'm already guilty of aiding a threader criminal. Nothing new there, I suppose, but that alone could see me hanged. The longer I think on it, the surer I am. Like it or not, I'm already committed. 'All right. When all's clear, we'll get you back to the house and hide you there. But know this: I'm not happy about it.'

Back home I pace the floor. 'You just don't get it, do you?' I hiss. 'This could doom us all!'

Josiah shrugs. 'I'm sorry, Mr Banyard. I truly am.'

'Not sorry enough. You *must* start using your head or you'll get us killed.'

Our dampened conversation is taking place in the kitchen of 96 Bunson Street, away from Mother and the others. Willow is secreted quietly at the back of the house on the second floor, resting. She's been on the road for three days with barely a morsel to eat. She's survived by drinking water straight from rivers – it's surprising she's not already died of dysentery – and has avoided detection by travelling at night. It gets cold at night, even in the summer.

Penney is here for dinner. She's seated in the dining room with Mardon, Mother, Widow Blewett and Ebadiah. My home has already become a threader retreat. What harm can one more desperate soul possibly do?

Finding two glasses, I carry them to the green room, where we're alone, and pour the port. 'Here.'

Josiah takes a glass, which is like a thimble in his massive hands, and downs it in one.

'She's been tracked all the way from Loncaster. The man's called Harris. A real hardball. One of Gladlock Bletchley's lot, carries two pistols. He nearly had her outside the office but she lost him a few moments before finding us. Says back home he abuses all the master's threader women. He's filth.'

'She's lucky to have avoided him. May her luck continue, for all our sakes.'

'It'll work out. You'll see. Harris will hang out for a day or two, sniff around. When he realises he can't find her, he'll go back home to Loncaster.'

'You hope.'

'As do you,' he says quickly, prodding a finger at me.

'Yes, well… I don't like it, all the same. She can't stay here. Not permanently.'

Josiah looks horrified. 'So, where's she supposed to go?'

'I don't know. I haven't thought that far ahead yet because, believe it or not, this was never part of my plan.'

'But you *will* help her? *We* will help her…'

I look him in the eyes and let him agonise a while before admitting, 'Yes, of course we will. She'll need papers, silks, a new identity. The full works. It's going to take time. And a fair bit of money, as always.' I finish my port and Josiah refills our glasses. 'For now, this stays between the three of us. And Mother will have to know, of course.'

'What about Lizzy and the others? They all saw her arrive.'

'I don't know. We'll think of something to tell them, but Lizzy is a stickler for the law – as you're aware, she knows nothing of our crimes – and the fewer who know about Willow the better.'

He nods. 'Just the four of us, then.'

We head into the dining room to eat with the others.

Dinner feels like a disaster. Not the food – that's fine. It's everything else. I'm way too distracted by the Willow problem to focus on much else and Penney goes woefully unattended. If this is an attempt to woo her, it's a pathetic one. To make matters worse, she raises the subject of the mysterious woman named Willow, who made a brief yet startling appearance at the office. I'm not ready to answer questions yet and it shows. 'Ah, yes. Who is she indeed! I... She...'

As I stammer to a halt, Josiah swoops to the rescue.

'Oh, the girl, yes. She's one of Farringsgate's threaders up at the big house. I'm afraid she got entirely the wrong idea and came looking for me. Terribly unfortunate, you know. The poor girl was rather disappointed. Had to send her on her way. I'm not sure what she was thinking. A threader and a silker? Ha! Never going to happen. Tragic. No doubt she cried all the way home.' He's convincing. Quite the cad, in fact.

'It seems every girl in Camdon is falling for you, Mr Mingle,' says Penney. I suppose she's thinking of Lizzy's recent fondness for him.

'Oh, not every girl, surely,' says Josiah, with a knowing grin.

I'm not quite sure if Penney has suckered for it or not but *good effort, Joe*! As long as no one starts prying into his story, it might hold.

70

# 6

# Bunkin's Tea House

*In which Banyard meets yet another attractive woman*

When Penney has been collected by her father's private carriage, Mother finds me in the green room. She slaps a cream envelope into my hand in her pragmatic way.

'This came for you earlier this afternoon. You know you really might have been a little more attentive to Penney. She's such a sweet girl.'

I'm not listening because in the yellow lamplight the address on the letter looks green, possibly the second of its kind.

'I'd like to meet my grandchildren before I die, Michael.'

'What?' Looking up, I finally absorb her words. 'Oh, yes. I'll apologise in the morning. I've been rather distracted. Grandchildren? You may be waiting a while.'

'Don't keep me waiting too long, Michael. I'll not live forever.' She gives me one of her warmer forbearing smiles before climbing the stairs to bed, storm lamp swinging. She looks frail in the golden light.

I look again at the envelope.

M
96 Bunson Street,
Crowlands,
Camdon City

Carefully, I take a letter opener from the side table and slit the envelope. It is not from the green ink author. The hand is different, less fluid, and I decide the ink is actually blue, a far more common colour.

> *Dear M,*
> *I am writing, as promised, to tell you I am well and have encountered no hazards along the way. My new surroundings are grand and our mutual friend has ensured my well-being. I cannot thank you enough for your assistance in arranging my new position.*
> *Forever indebted,*
> *J*

A smile invades my face. I know who it's from before reaching the final initial. Jemima Gunn is a threader who used to serve under Maddox, an abusive silker and owner of a nearby butcher's shop. Jemima is now dead to Camdon, presumed to have drowned in the Tynne. She is free, living as a silker in my cousin's house in Loncaster. She has new silks and forged papers in the name of Ruby Shaw. In time, I may find her a more permanent situation elsewhere. I am glad to hear she is well, and pleased she kept her promise to write.

I hold the papers over a candle on the mantel and, when they're aflame, drop them into the cold fireplace where they blacken and curl before the embers fade and die. A trace of pale smoke snakes up with a gratifying aroma; the scent of another soul rescued from the cursed life of a threader. But it's no good, I remind myself; Mardon can't take them all.

The following day is another scorcher. I roll up my shirt sleeves, mop my brow with a handkerchief and reach for my stereoscope. It is essentially two sets of optical lenses bound together in a leather and brass casing. Small enough to slip into one of the larger pockets of my coat, it fits easily in my shoulder bag. It's in my bag today because of the heat; I wear no coat, only riding boots, britches, a shirt and waistcoat. I take the stereoscope out to spy on Gouldstone and his companion, the lenses working their magic, carrying me impressively close in an instant. It's remarkable, really. I wish it could amplify their conversation too.

I've spent an hour this morning observing Gouldstone's office from across the street and tailing him to Bunkin's Tea House where he now sits with a short man. At least, I presume it's Gouldstone. He seems to be the one in charge of things and he's been busy signing documents and ordering folk around. I'm intruding in a doctor's practice, standing at a window that overlooks Bunkin's from a small platform set between stairs. A flight of steps and a single turn separates me from reception on the ground floor and more stairs head up to the waiting room and surgery above. Here between I'm in limbo, unnoticed except by the occasional patient on his or her way in or out who, no doubt, has better things to worry about than a silker loitering on the landing. When anyone passes, I drop the stereoscope to my side, tucking it behind my leg and pretend to be taking in the view. No one seems to care and Gouldstone certainly has not noticed me. He's been focused solely on his companion, absorbed in deep discussion about what? I can only guess.

Behind this vast window of the landing in the glaring sun I'm sweating like a court-bound threader, though.

Gouldstone himself seems stern and yet has the look of a proper gent. He's on the tall side, of moderate weight, and carries a silver-handled cane, the wood of which is lacquered a glossy nut-brown. His suit is plain but new and smart; chocolate silk, with a topper to match. His façade is austere and he's not yielded a hint of a smile in all the time I've been spying. A vast moustache lends further gravitas to the severity of his features. All in all, he appears a man not to be trifled with, and I'd wager he's powerfully built beneath those fine silks.

His companion is of a shorter, heavier build and has a stubby, clean-shaven chin, set between bushy sideburns that fizzle into a thinning line of hair that encircles his crown. The peak of his head is bald and as shiny as Gouldstone's cane. His silks are russet and he carries a small leather case, which he guards closely. I don't know his name but I've already made a quick pencil sketch of his face in my pocketbook. All these physical traits, however, are surpassed in my mind by the overbearing sense of his nervousness. His mannerisms are quick and edgy. His small eyes flit here to there. There's something of the rodent about him and, in my mind, he is a fat rat.

Thirsty and increasingly frustrated that I can't overhear their words, I leave the landing and descend, exit the doctor's practice, cross the street and order a pot of tea in Bunkin's. The shop is well adorned with plenty of glass in its frontage, a dozen round tables draped in crisp white linen and a counter of hammered brass, where stands a collection of copper pots, cups, saucers and utensils, all gleaming like warm gold in the sunlight. Gouts of steam fog the air over several of the kettles.

There is an unoccupied table far enough from Gouldstone's so as to be unobtrusive and yet close enough, perhaps, to eavesdrop. I sit there and wait for my tea, find a folded newspaper on the chair next to me and pretend to read it, all the while straining to hear what they're saying. I catch the odd word, terms like marketeer, trade, evaluation, interest rate, profit, and something glints in the sunlight that is streaming in through the bullseye panes of the windows.

My tea arrives. It's strong and refreshing. When it's cooled a little, I down a cupful and pour myself another from the little copper pot provided.

Fat Rat checks his pocket watch every five minutes and throws frequent glances at the door. Once or twice I even feel his eyes find me and I bury my face a little deeper in the news sheets.

I see the glint again; a blinding golden flash catching my eye and, when my vision recovers, I search out the cause. There, on the middle finger of Gouldstone's right hand, is a heavy gold ring set with onyx. It's not clear from my position, but it's a frog ring.

It has to be.

To be sure, I take a stroll over to the doorway with the pretence of catching some air and, passing their table, steal a better look. It *is* a frog ring. Ebadiah was right: Gouldstone is a member of the Order. And what's more, so is Fat Rat. Two frogs for the price of one.

Facing the street, I linger in the doorway for a while before retaking my seat.

At length, Gouldstone's companion makes his farewells and leaves, clutching his precious case and waddling into the street, casting a string of nervous looks around him. I'm almost surprised to learn he has no tail. Gouldstone, however, shows no sign of moving. He takes out his pocket watch, checks its glassy face and holds it to his ear. Satisfied that it is properly wound, he returns it to his waistcoat pocket, unfolds a letter and reads.

Several minutes pass while we sit. Other customers come and go. Tea and cakes are ordered and consumed. The gentle hum of the tea house surrounds us. I finish my second cup of tea before emptying the dregs of the teapot.

A finely dressed lady enters the tea house and, folding a bottle-blue lace-edged parasol, walks to Gouldstone. Rising, he takes her white-gloved hand in a genteel manner and stoops to kiss it. He pauses long enough to say, 'Miss Avard, a pleasure as always.'

She smiles. They sit.

I do not catch her reply because she is softly spoken. Her face is soft, too, in a way. Smooth, pale skin – flawless but for a scattering of freckles around her nose and cheeks – rises and falls over the gentle curves of well-formed bones. Her cheekbones are notably high and prominent, so much so that they dominate her face. Her hair is long but tied up, a dark brunette, but it's the eyes that demand my attention. They are somehow inescapable, a deep hazel brown, large, absorbing all they touch with a quiet confidence. In her beauty she is intimidating. I spend the next few minutes trying to decide if she knows she has this effect on those who perceive her, but I fail. There is something untouchable about her and something vulnerable and cloaked behind her startling appearance, a quality I cannot place.

She orders tea and cake that is swiftly delivered by an attentive waitress.

Again, I find myself catching only the odd word as Gouldstone and Miss Avard talk and so, when they briefly glance away, dare to inch my chair closer.

'Mr Gouldstone, I do believe we have an agreement,' says Miss Avard, her accent an Amorphian twang.

'We do, indeed. In principle, if nothing else. I shall have my secretary draw up the contract this very afternoon. Tell me, when would be a good time for you to sign the papers? Will you come to our offices on Tall Street?'

'I will. Tomorrow morning at eleven.'

'Very well. Until then. If you'll forgive me, I have another appointment pending. Good day, Miss Avard.' Gouldstone rises. They shake hands amicably and with a tip of his hat he leaves.

Miss Avard is left sitting alone with a pot of hot tea and a slice of red velvet cake she has yet to touch. I am torn. It would be unwise to socialise with her in any way – after all, she is now part of my investigation – and yet I feel genuinely rude not offering my company to a woman who appears alone, vulnerable and in potential danger from a man who is likely a criminal and murderer. There is, of course, the added lure of her beauty that, as you know, has not escaped my notice. If nothing else, I feel an urge to offer some notion of warning about the man with whom she is consorting. In the end my valiant nature gets the better of me and, tentatively, I approach.

'My lady, I do beg your pardon, but I cannot help noticing

you are unaccompanied here and I find myself in the same unfortunate predicament. Would you care for company?'

There is a pause during which those large brown eyes turn upon me appraisingly. Her mouth forms a subtle smile.

'Why, yes. I do believe I would like that.'

'Then I shall sit with you a while.' I sit, folding the paper neatly and laying it on the table. 'Your accent, Western Amorphian?'

Her smile broadens. 'I am Londaland, born and bred, but I was out there for fifteen years with my father. Long enough to absorb a little of the culture.'

'How wonderfully exotic.' It's a stupid thing to say but it makes her laugh.

'Exotic? Why, Mr…'

'Banyard.'

'Mr Banyard.' She takes the hand I offer. 'You clearly have never been to Amorphia. Exotic is not a word I would use, though it is an interesting land, to be sure. My name is Clara Avard. Miss Clara Avard.'

'I'm pleased to meet you, Miss Avard. I would so like to visit Amorphia one day. I've heard marvellous tales of the place. The natural wonders of geology. The natives and the enterprising new world.'

'Indeed, it is marvellous. Though Camdon has its charms.'

'And what brings you here?'

'Business, like most.'

All this while, those large eyes have not left mine. To be honest, it's unusual and slightly unnerving. I let my gaze fall to the paper, the copper teapot on the table, the cake, the folded parasol – upon anything that might defuse their intensity.

'My, it is terribly warm in here.' She pulls the gloves from her hands.

'It certainly is.' I check her hands. She has several delicate rings of silver, gold and diamond. No frogs. Eventually, I look back into the unreadable depths.

'Miss Avard, may I be candid?'

'Please, be as candid as you desire.'

'Very well. Then I must warn you. The individual who occupied this seat before me is a dangerous man, a member of a secret society, guilty of who knows what horrors. I beg of you; beware Mr Gouldstone and anything he offers.'

Her eyes widen at this news. Her mouth opens and she presses her fingers to her cheeks. 'Not Mr Gouldstone, surely.' She gropes in her clutch bag for a folding fan, flicks it open and waves it to cool her face, seemingly unsettled.

'Oh, my dear, I've distressed you. I do apologise.'

'It's nothing, really. It's just... Are you sure? Why do you believe him dangerous?'

'I'm afraid I can't go into details. Suffice it to say he is under investigation for certain crimes.'

All of a sudden she appears more vulnerable than ever, her eyes imploring. 'But I have only this minute agreed to go into business with the man. Oh dear. Whatever shall I do?'

'Is it too late to rescind your commitment? What business is it that you have with him?'

She straightens up, dabs her face and eyes with a lace handkerchief and steels herself. 'Oh, it wouldn't be right to share that with a perfect stranger. I mean you no offence but, after all, that is what we are, strangers.'

I smile. 'Well, you know my name.'

'Yes, I suppose that's something.' She tucks her fan and kerchief back into her clutch and takes a sip of tea before offering her hand, which I shake. 'Thank you for the warning, Mr Banyard. And now, I really must be going.'

We rise together.

'You'll consider my words?'

'I will. I promise.'

'Then, farewell, Miss Avard, and good luck to you.'

Before leaving Bunkin's I make a quick sketch of Clara Avard in my pocketbook. She's not easy to capture – not at all – but I manage an approximation of which I'll never be proud.

During my walk home I ponder the women in my life: Mother, with her persistent nagging for grandchildren; Penney, the redhead I'd marry like a shot, if the chance availed, or so I thought until recently – I'm not so sure now; Lizzy, outspoken, with looks that would floor the coldest of men; Willow, a new arrival, and yet one who has already shaken my world and threatens it still; and now this delicate creature, Miss Clara Avard, a fine but vulnerable lady of culture, in need of protection. Can I defend her? I wonder.

The truth is, Penney has become an enigma to me. Yes, I love her and always have, but she's now a colleague and our working relationship has rather backfired. It's brought us closer, as I'd hoped, and yet we've become more like siblings than suitors. I fear Mother will be in for a long wait.

# 7

# Harris

*In which Mingle proposes a plan and an overseer calls*

Josiah has beaten me back to the office and is lounging in the visitor's chair as I enter. Lizzy has reverted to her usual prim and proper self, all business, flawless silks and tightly wound hair, her former flirtatiousness gone. There's a palpable tension between her and Josiah. She writes up notes on the Snarlton case while he contemplates her from across the room. All our other operatives are out.

'So, what are we to make of these other names on Ebadiah's list?' I ask. Josiah's job this morning was to research the names further.

'There's no mention of them anywhere,' he says. 'It's like they never existed.'

'You're telling me there are no ...' I check my notebook. '... Thomas Hiddlesworths or Jacob Mansvilles recorded in the annals of Camdon City?'

'Not one who's a silker.'

'Really? What are the chances?'

'I know.'

Lizzy peers up from her notes. 'I suppose you've considered the names Ebadiah gathered may have been false.'

'No. I don't think I have.' I toss my tricorn onto a hook of the coat stand, a game I play most days. One I've become rather good at. 'He got Gouldstone right. Why would people give Ebadiah fake names?'

'Well, for one thing, he was paying for the information,' says Josiah.

'Ah, yes. Invent a name. Earn a copper.'

'And then there's your notoriety among the threaders,' says Lizzy.

'Notoriety?'

She gives me one of her schoolmistress looks as though I'm being an idiot. 'You know for a fact the Drakers hate you. Do you think the criminals like you better?'

'You're not saying all threaders are criminals, surely.'

'You're right. I'm not.'

I consider this. 'We'll forget about the other names. The lad did well to get us a lead at all.'

'One name. It is a *very* secret society, isn't it?' says Josiah.

'Hmmm.'

Josiah rises. 'May I have a word in the case room, Mr Banyard?'

'Of course.' We enter, closing the door behind us.

'I may have found a way into Dover Palace. Is that royal enough for you?'

'Yes. It would be a start.' Dover Palace is the largest royal establishment in Camdon City. King Lychling Dover himself resides there more often than not. I sit at my desk, intrigued, while Josiah remains standing. 'How?'

'I've made a contact there, a threader, works in the kitchens. She tells me every fourth Thursday the toffs go out while some chimneys are swept. It puts a bit of soot on the air and they don't like it. Most of them make sure they're out of the way until the job's done. Well, there're so many chimneys in that old place it takes a whole host of sweeps and they're changing all the time. No one would question a couple of new faces.'

'Sounds promising. When's the next sweeping day?'

'Next Thursday.'

The doorbell jingles, soon followed by a knock on the case room door.

Lizzy calls from the other side. 'Mr Banyard, there's a man here to see you.'

Opening the door, I'm greeted by a slightly sweaty, unfamiliar face.

'Mr Banyard, I presume.' The man offers no hand. He's more than twice my age and large, though not as big as Josiah, and dressed in travelling silks the colour of sand – a less-formal attire than the general citywear we usually see. A dusty light coat falls to his knees, bulges each side marking the pistols on his belt beneath. His face has a certain squareness that his curling moustache fails to soften. The whiskers are oiled; his hair, dark but greying. His eyes are cold, hard and unwavering. This is Willow's pursuer, Mr Harris. I have no doubt.

'Yes. How may I help you, sir?' I ask the question while a hundred others jostle for a hearing in my head. A couple bubble to the surface, though. What has he already asked Lizzy about Willow? And what has Lizzy told him?

Out on the pavement his huge lantern dog lazes, awaiting its master's return, watching us through the glass. Lizzy has a concerned look that she's trying hard to hide.

'I'm an overseer, seeking a runaway. A Loncaster threader by the name of Willow Buxton. I've reason to believe she fled this way yesterday just after five o'clock. Have you or any of your fine folk seen her?' He glances at each of us in turn and raises an eyebrow, unsmiling. 'There's a reward for information leading to her capture.'

Lizzy parts her lips to speak so I cut in. 'No, we've not seen any threader runaways. Only clients.' I attempt an easy smile. 'They tend to be silkers on the whole.'

He looks around at the reception room and at what he can see of the pinboard in the case room through the adjoining door. 'What is it you do here, exactly?'

'We solve mysteries, Mr…?'

'Harris.'

I offer a hand which he takes in a sceptical manner, his grip crushing.

'I'm the proprietor of Mysteries Solved. We're private detectives.'

He studies me, stone-faced. I can almost hear his mind ticking. 'You find missing people?'

'Missing people, murderers, thieves, stolen goods. That sort of thing. We are the agency that recently recovered Doon's funerary urn. You may have heard...'

'Ah, yes. I read about that.' I'm surprised to hear he can read, seeing as he couldn't tell what we did despite the enormous sign outside that spans the full length of our premises. He continues. 'Then you might be able to assist me. Fifty guineas to the man who finds my runaway.' He turns to Lizzy, his gaze lingering a little too long on her cleavage. 'Or woman.' He hands over an imographed copy of a drawing, a fair likeness of Willow. 'You can keep that. Might help you spot the little wretch.'

'I shall inform all my agents. Tell me, Mr Harris, where might we find you, should we happen upon the girl?'

'Madame Rouge's,' he says, tipping his hat and heading for the door. 'You keep your eyes peeled, now.' And with that he leaves.

Madame Rouge's is one of those Southside places that need little explanation. Officially, it's a hotel but, unofficially, there are other less respectable services on offer, and everyone knows it. Even the Drakers, who – let's face it – probably make up a good half of the clientele.

Outside, Harris moves on to the next shop, his lantern hound trotting briskly to heel.

We watch him go.

'I'm not sure we want to get on *his* bad side,' I mutter, taking the imograph of the Willow sketch and pinning it to the wall.

'I could take him.'

I throw Josiah a look and scribble a note in large letters.

'I mean, if for some reason I had to.'

'I'm sure you could, Joe. I'm sure you could.' I pin the note above the image of Willow.

'What are you doing that for?'

'Harris is bound to return. When he does, he'll see we're keen to help. He'll be less suspicious of us.'

Lizzy taps on the door and enters the case room to point at the sketch. 'Michael, wasn't that the girl who came in, the one who knows Josiah?' She turns to Joe. 'You called her name. I heard you. Shouldn't we call the Drakers?'

'No, that was a different girl,' I say. 'One of the Farringsgate servants who took a shine to Joe. They do bear an uncanny resemblance, I admit, but then all these threaders look alike. Don't you think? What was the name again, Joe?'

'Widrow,' says Josiah, thinking on his feet. 'That must have been the name you heard me say.'

Lizzy looks puzzled.

I conclude. 'I swear, we haven't seen this runaway. No need for the Drakers.'

After that I send Josiah out for black bean soup and spend some time pawing over my pocketbook. There are so many aspects to investigate in this case that I can't keep it all straight in my head. I make notes, a list of things I must do.

Keep an eye on Fletcher Gouldstone and companions.

Research each of the supposed murder victims named in the green ink letter.

Decipher the list of nonsense capitals from the Philshaw letters.

Investigate the possible presence of the Order at Dover Palace.

Investigate the murder of Oliver Ingham.

Investigate the disappearance of Tillie Ingham.

I stop because that last item has me vexed. How am I to further Tillie's part of the investigation? Her trail turns cold at the Old Coach House.

We're in the green room at home with after-dinner drinks. Just Josiah and me. To our relief, the day is cooling and the house is quiet. I pull down the sash windows, turning the little brass catches to lock them in place and our whispers are quick, harsh sounds.

'She knows, Joe. There's no getting around it.'

He stands by the fireplace, looking tense. 'But you told her it was another girl.'

'I did but Lizzy's not daft. Or blind.'

'You think she'll peach?'

'I don't know. I don't think she would but there's no grey with Lizzy. All is black or white.'

'Then we'll have to stop her,' says Joe, his face so screwed up with torment that it resembles an enormous pale prune. He's stuck somewhere between the woman he loves and the woman he admires.

'What do you suggest?' I ask as Mardon walks in and casts us a dubious look.

'Good evening, chaps. What are we up to?' His brow snakes as he stuffs a pinch of tobacco into the bowl of his pipe and lights up. He drops lazily into a green-leathered armchair. In the silence the old house creaks.

'Nothing. Just talking,' says Josiah.

'Just talking, eh? About that girl you have holed up at the back of the house?' Mardon reclines, not a worry in the world, and exhales a long stream of sweet-smelling smoke.

'Shush!' Joe rushes to quieten him.

I envy Mardon. However does one manage to care so little? 'You're not supposed to know about her. Promise you won't say a word,' I demand.

'Say a word to whom? Widow Blewett? Pah! Do you think

she doesn't already know?'

'What?!'

'She lives here, Micky. Did you think you could hide someone under her very nose without her knowing?' Mardon waits for that to sink in before continuing. 'Who is this slip of a girl, anyway?'

'She's a threader runaway from… Never mind where from. It's probably best you don't know.'

'Guessed as much. You and your grand heroics. Where's it all going to end, cousin? On the end of a rope, I imagine.' Mardon hoists an imaginary noose around his neck.

'Not if you can keep your know-it-all mouth shut,' I say.

'Know-it-all mouth? Nice.' He chortles and puffs. 'Anyway, it's not me you need to worry about. Jinkers was out earlier, snooping around the wall of his back garden. I think he may have seen her at a window.'

'Not Jinkers, too,' mutters Josiah, sweeping a hand across his brow. 'So much for just the four of us. Now it's Lizzy, Mardon, the widow and, worst of all, that barmy neighbour.'

Mardon chuckles to himself. 'You boys and your secrets. Priceless.'

'What are we to do about Lizzy and Jinkers?' Josiah's in a state now, pacing and doing his utmost to ignore Mardon.

'Calm yourself, Joe. We'll figure something out,' I say.

'So, to summarise, everyone in the house knows about the girl except Ebadiah.'

Mardon laughs and shakes his head. 'You wish.'

Josiah scowls.

On the positive side, the entire household knowing about Willow isn't all bad. It means a lot less creeping around will be required and the girl can relax a little and hide herself away less.

I reflect on the inevitable nature of secrets. They're like water in a leaky cistern. If they can find a way out, they will.

Later that night I'm passing Josiah's bedroom door in dressing gown and slippers when a thought strikes me. I tap twice on the door and wait a moment before opening it. Josiah's already in bed. He sits up looking half asleep.

'Sorry to bother you, Joe.'

'That's all right, Mr Banyard. How may I help?'

'I was just thinking. I don't want you getting too attached to Willow right now. If we're to hide her for any length of time it will have to be somewhere else. We have enough issues to deal with. Do you understand me?'

'I do,' he says, though I think I might be too late. I leave, closing the door behind me.

The morning is bright and blessedly cool. Now that the pretence is over, Willow breakfasts with us, though the mood at the table is sullen and Josiah spends the whole time glowering like a storm cloud except in moments when Willow catches his eye – then his expression softens and a hint of a smile turns the corners of his mouth. Willow continues to be nonplussed by her less-than-enthusiastic welcome and I'm still brooding over Josiah's monumental and, quite possibly, fatal flunk, which has led us into this situation. Of all of us, Mardon is the most content. In fact, he looks perfectly happy among our sour faces, if not amused. I begrudge this power he has over me, the effortless way he irritates.

Josiah and I have not long arrived at the office when Harris' unwelcome form appears at the door. At one short command his lantern hound sits on the cobbled pavement while he enters. This time, Josiah is quick to show him into the case room. As an outsider, he really shouldn't be allowed in here at all, where details of our various cases are pinned to the wall and confidential documents lie scattered across the desks, but in our haste we don't care. Our only concern is preventing Harris from grilling Lizzy or Penney about Willow.

'Do come in. How may we assist you this fine morning, Mr Harris?' I begin.

Harris seems slightly bewildered. He's not used to people offering assistance. 'I wondered if any of you have seen this missing girl since my last visit?'

'Ah, of course. No. I'm afraid we haven't. Not a single trace,' I say. 'I will be sure to contact you if that changes.'

Standing to one side, Josiah stares at Harris as if he would enjoy butchering him on the spot.

'Isn't that right, Joe?' I prompt.

Josiah snaps out of his trace-like gawp. 'Oh, yes. That's right. You can count on us.' He forces a smile.

'Madame Rouge's, right?'

Harris clears his throat. 'That's correct, young man. The runaway came down this road, I'm sure of it. It was around here I lost her trail. Now, I've been up and down this whole stinking street and no one remembers even seeing her. I do find that hard to believe. Don't you?' He leans in close, his small eyes absorbing my reaction.

'Why, yes.' I inch away because his breath is a sour reek; bitter black beans and stale cigar smoke.

'Makes me wonder what may have befallen her?' He's less sweaty today but a single bead forms to run from his temple. He dabs at it with a road-weary handkerchief.

I think. Hard. 'Perhaps she managed to disguise herself, or might she have hopped onto a truck? There are always steam trucks running these streets, you know.' Right on cue a Clansly Haulage steam truck screams past our windows, belching smoke and throwing up fresh plumes of dust to spiral in the air. We see its hazy shape through the frosted glass. 'Presumably, your hound had her scent. Would that not account for its sudden disappearance?'

'I suppose it would, though there's little chance the girl has coin to pay for transport.'

'She must have stowed away, then. It's easy enough to hop on the back of a truck or carriage. She may have travelled miles from here without the driver ever knowing.'

'I suppose,' says Harris, stepping past me further into the room where he has a full view of the wall and the sign I wrote over Willow's image. He grunts at it. 'Well, just so's you know, if anyone is found to have sheltered the girl or helped her in any way, they'll wish they hadn't.' He stomps off to collect his hound.

Josiah watches him leave with a curl of his lip. 'There goes a wretch if I ever saw one. I'd like to snap his neck.'

'Indeed. Now, to business. I have it in mind to follow the illustrious Mr Gouldstone this morning. Care to join me?'

We find Gouldstone once more in his office, although it's not long before he collects his briefcase and leaves, heading deeper into Highbridge. We tail him at a distance as he visits a street stand to buy a paper and then another where he pauses for a street boy to shine his shoes. He tosses the boy a coin and turns into Orleon Drive, where he stops outside a familiar stately building with marble pillars bearing a pair of intricately carved climbing dragons. The surrounding buildings are just as opulently made, golden stone, polished marble and striped with tall arching windows.

'I don't believe it. Cullins has his offices up there.' I nod to the second floor of the grand façade as Gouldstone enters.

'Cullins? As in the lowlife Jacob Cullins who robbed the widow and bribed the courts, the murdering, fraudulent smuggler who hates our guts?'

'Yes, that one.'

# 8

# The Dress

*In which Banyard and Mingle spy on Cullins and Gouldstone*

We wait. There's little else we can do. The sun climbs higher, burning off the cool of the morning and shrinking shadows almost imperceptibly. When Gouldstone reappears from the building accompanied by Cullins around ten minutes later, there's not a cloud left in the sky. By their body language and mannerisms it's clear they are well acquainted. Further down the road they head into a black bean soup shop, find a table and order.

Mr Jacob Bartimaeus Cullins. Grand capitalist of Camdon City. Oiled black hair with a touch of grey, slicked back from his brow. Stony-faced with a thick beard, shaved only about the mouth and chin. Dark eyes that seem sometimes black and other times green, depending on the light.

It's too risky for us to enter the shop now because he would recognise us and likely inform Gouldstone that we're tailing them, so instead we find a spot across the street partially hidden by a threader's cart and mule, where we squat against a wall, tucked in behind one of five pillars that support a money lender's shopfront. I have the stereoscope with me and use it tentatively. We're not as concealed as I'd like but there's something I really need to know.

'That place I've seen the frog ring before? I've a sneaking suspicion it might have been on Cullins' finger.'

'Wouldn't surprise me to learn he's part of some high and mighty secret club. The man's no gentleman.'

I glance at Josiah. 'Is that the best you can do? He's *no gentleman.*'

'I rejected several less seemly descriptions before choosing that one. Thought you'd tell me off for being a threader again.'

'Tell you off?'

'Come now. You can't deny it. You're always correcting me. It's embarrassing. Humiliating...'

That gives me pause. I should apologise but something prevents me. I guess I've never truly considered Joe's feelings in all this. Is there room to consider them when him acting threader-like could get us killed, probably Mother, too? 'Well, Joe, I'm impressed.' I chuckle. 'No gentleman – I must say, I agree. He's a scoundrel of the highest order.'

'Oh, yeah. That's better. A scoundrel of the highest order. I'll remember that one.'

Through the lenses I glimpse a gold ring on Cullins' right hand and focus in for a closer look but it's no good. He's too far away. 'See the trays of cakes in the window over there?'

'I see them.'

'Think you can go take a look? I mean, pretend to be looking over the cakes but get a good look at the ring on Cullins' right hand? I think that's the frog ring.'

'Why me?'

'Cullins is less likely to recognise you.'

'What? On account of my petite stature?'

I must admit, Josiah's vocabulary is really coming on. He grunts and heads for the window where he gazes at the rows of cakes before entering the shop. When he returns a few moments later he's stuffing a large creamed sugar bun into his face and can't talk for some moments.

'The ring, Josiah. What about the ring?'

He gulps down the last fragment of bun, licks his lips and

wipes his mouth on his shirt sleeve. 'Ah, that was great! Oh, yeah. I forgot about the ring. Want me to go back?'

I check Cullins through the stereoscope. He and Gouldstone seem deeply absorbed in conversation. I wonder what they're discussing. 'Yes, and this time focus on the ring, not the cakes.'

Returning to the shop, he has a good long look at Cullins through the window – subtle as a blunderbuss – and saunters back across the street. I watch the whole thing despairingly through my lenses, though neither Cullins nor Gouldstone appear to notice him.

'He's not sitting close enough to the window. I can go and ask him, if you like.'

'No. Please don't.'

Joe seems particularly useless today. I guess Willow is on his mind. We're getting nowhere and Josiah's a liability when he's like this, so I decide to head back to the office. I need time to think, and some peace and quiet.

While Josiah fetches black bean soup, I grab my chance, slipping into the case room without pausing in reception to hang my hat on the stand. I close the door and, alone at my desk, take out my pocketbook to reread my notes, settling on the line reminding me to decipher the list of nonsense capitals from the Philshaw letters. Over the page the capitals are noted down and I stare at them blankly for a while. Several initials soon pop out from the paper as I realise they could be in pairs.

ASYOETFGMLJCWS

Could 'FG' be Fletcher Gouldstone and 'JC' Jacob Cullins? If so, the capitals might all stand for members of the Order. Quickly, I rewrite the list, spotting another anomaly.

AS
YO
ET
FG – Fletcher Gouldstone?
ML
JC – Jacob Cullins?
WS – Willard Steeler?

If this is to be believed, it seems a further four existing members of the Order may also have had a sinister interest in Tillie Ingham, and the author of the Philshaw letters was trying to warn her without naming them outright.

I recline, quite proud of my progress. Even Mardon failed to figure this out. Perhaps I'm not such an awful detective, after all.

By the time Josiah arrives with the soup, I've also convinced myself of a way forward because I want to know the other names on the list. 'Joe, I'm afraid there's an impossible task we must somehow perform.'

'Oh?' He sips the hot black soup as its bitter aroma fills the room. 'You want me to sack Lizzy or something?'

'Not that, though that would be challenging. No, this is something on another level. I need to get hold of the register that sits on the reception desk of Chantrees.'

'The goldsmiths? You'd have an easier time of it sacking Lizzy.'

'I know. We'd need a plan, a good one. Perhaps Ebadiah can help.'

'I'll call him in.'

I mull over the other aspects of the case, waiting for Josiah and Ebadiah to return, wondering what my father would have done.

His old hat is perched on the skull at the end of my desk. His old desk. 'What do you think? Would you have me drop the case?'

'*I* didn't,' says the hat. 'But look where it got me.'

'I know, but that's why I can't let it go. It got you killed and, somewhere out there, your murderer walks free, which means other innocents will die. It's not right. I just wish you could tell me who did it – give me some kind of clue.'

'Just watch your back, son.'

'Sound advice, I'm sure.'

A few minutes later, Josiah returns with Ebadiah in tow and we set about making a plan. I explain the situation. 'There's a register that's kept open on the service counter of Chantrees. It's very old and thick. In it is likely written every private commission Chantrees has ever taken. If my hunch is correct, it will contain the details of every frog ring made for the Order, including names. The problem is this: Chantrees is probably one of the most guarded buildings in the city. We won't be able to simply waltz in and pick the register up. The salesman wouldn't even let me take a peek.'

'Are there guards in the showroom?' asks Ebadiah.

'I didn't see any, only spy holes through which the guards must watch. But I'm sure it's heavily guarded at night.'

'So, who *was* in the showroom?' asks Josiah.

'Just a plumped-up salesman. A scrawny fellow.'

'Plumped-up?' asks Ebadiah.

'Full of himself. The self-important type.'

'One man alone,' says Josiah. 'Shouldn't be too much trouble. A good punch and he'll be out.'

'But the room is certainly watched. There has to be more wealth in that place than in any bank in Camdon. One wrong word – one foot out of place – and it will flood with guards quicker than you can fall off a stool. And anyway, I'd rather we were more subtle than a punch in the face. Wouldn't it be better if they were left wondering what had happened? If they didn't even know who stole the ledger?'

Josiah's brow wrinkles. Always an ominous sign. 'Or if they didn't realise it was stolen at all? Wouldn't that be better?'

'I'm listening.'

'What I mean is we don't need to steal the register, not really. We just need to borrow it and put it back without them knowing. It's the names we want, right? We'd need your camera and a replica of the register – well, not the full register, of course; only the open pages need to look right – and we'd need a distraction. A pretty lady should do it. A wealthy, pretty lady.'

'Well, we can't use Lizzy or Penney,' I say. 'They'd never agree to such blatant lawbreaking. Well, certainly not Lizzy, anyway.'

Oh dear. Is this another of Josiah's excellent ideas? I fear so.

We find Willow recuperating in the cool of the green room, one of Mother's folding fans in her hand, wafting air at her face. She's wearing one of Mother's old dresses, white with small embroidered flowers around the collar, cuffs and hem. It's a bad fit, too loose and baggy but it's clean and dry. Seeing us, she drops a glossy red apple back into the fruit bowl as though she's been caught stealing.

'It's all right, Willow. Help yourself.'

She doesn't move, is as yet untrusting and suspicious of me, but she smiles at Josiah and he grins back inanely, his eyes wistful.

'How are you feeling today?' I ask.

'Well, thank you, master.'

'Please call me, Michael, or Micky if you'd prefer.'

'Oh, I couldn't do that, master. It wouldn't be right.'

'Well, in that case, call me Mr Banyard. Anything but master.' I place an apple in her hand. 'Please, eat. No one is cross with you here. You are safe. No one is going to hurt you.'

She glances at the apple and back at me before tentatively taking a bite. A little juice escapes to run down her cheek and she quickly wipes it away with a sleeve, again fearing rebuke.

'If you've quite recovered from your journey from Loncaster, I think it's time you started to earn your keep...'

The same pinch-faced assistant stands aloof behind the counter. Other than Pinch-face, Chantrees is empty. It's a quiet afternoon because the banks are shut and it's too hot for people to be about the streets unnecessarily.

Perfect.

The entrance bell jingles to a halt.

Willow looks good. I mean, really good. Like a rich silker lady from noble stock. Like a gentleman's daughter. I'm still amazed at the way she has transformed. The make-up has worked wonders with her face, which I'm now forced to reassess. Where, before, it was plain and almost simplistic in nature, it seems now sophisticated and commanding, both striking and exquisite. She looks every bit a woman of power and influence. Her silk dress and hat are the finest we could source from the best shops Highbridge has to offer. With much debate, we decided violet would be an apt colour for her; after all, we are investigating the disappearance of Tillie Ingham, and Willow is supposed to be a distraction.

Her natural tenacity shines as she walks into the showroom with every confidence. She is a silker, will be served like a silker. She begins by demanding to view every diamond necklace in the shop. This grabs Pinch-face's greedy attention as firmly as a slap across the cheek. He's all oily and greasy around her, smarming up to her in the hope of a sale, or perhaps something more.

Beneath a carefully layered disguise, I open and close the door for her, carry her large suitcase and an armful of shopping bags from upmarket stores nearby, bow the knee at every chance like a good threader should. I'm dressed like a rich lady's servant: a cotton shirt, cream-coloured britches and polished shoes; a waistcoat with cloth of gold buttons completes my ensemble. My false beard and eyebrows do a fair job at hiding my face and the cotton wads packed along my gums distort my cheeks. I'm sure he won't recognise me but I keep my head bowed to avoid eye contact and do my best to maintain a convincing stoop.

Out front, Ebadiah waits, watching through the corner of a dazzling window display. I catch his eye and give him a wink before turning to search out the spy holes. There are two that I'm aware of. If there are others, they are well hidden so all I can do is deal with these two and hope for the best. The one to our left is the easy one. I plonk the suitcase onto the counter at just the right angle to hide the register from view.

Pinch-face raises an eyebrow at me and the case, frowning, and opens his mouth to speak, but at that moment Willow intervenes.

'Oh, I do like this one with the cluster!' She places her handbag onto the counter right beneath his nose, a handbag we've primed with as many bank notes as we could lay our hands on. It's stuffed with several newspapers beneath, but on top of those is a good thickness of one hundred guinea notes, each wad bound in a rubber band. 'May I, perhaps, try it on?' Her accent leaves a lot to be desired. It sounds like a stereotypical impression of a Loncaster silker, which is exactly what it is, although Pinch-face doesn't seem to notice. He's more interested in Willow's smile when it flashes his way and the contents of her purse.

He fixes upon the cash and tears himself away from it only to look back at Willow, his smile broadening. 'Why, yes. Of course, madam may try it on. I do believe it will suit madam very well. Allow me...' He takes the heavy necklace from its cushioned board and, skirting the counter, lowers it over Willow's head from behind to clasp it in place. He skips back behind the counter to brandish a silver, baroque looking-glass for her.

'Oh, no. It's too bulky. Perhaps the thinner one there.' She points to another necklace in the display. 'May I see it?'

This time, he lifts out the entire tray of jewellery, depositing it on the countertop. He unclips the narrow necklace from the cushion and hands it to her. This is more like it. She has him exactly where we need him, right in front of the remaining spy hole.

I glance towards the window and meet Ebadiah's gaze, give him a subtle nod. It's now or never.

Ebadiah rushes in, triggering the overhead doorbell.

Pinch-face turns, his face morphing into a sour expression when he sees the boy. 'Yes? What is it?'

'A message for the lady,' says Ebadiah. He wastes no time in delivering a paper note and Willow does an admirable job of fumbling with it and knocking the tray of jewels from the counter. Pinch-face lunges after the tray but is too late. It topples to the floor on the far side of the counter with a catastrophic clash around his feet. Priceless necklaces skitter across the marble floor.

'Oh, clumsy me! I do hope nothing is damaged,' says Willow. She bends to retrieve the note and, straightening, reads it.

Pinch-face is clearly irritated by the accident but swallows his annoyance to maintain a smile with Willow. The sale is everything. 'Never fear. Diamonds are the hardiest of things. I'm sure everything will be just fine.' He doesn't sound too sure.

He kneels to collect the valuables, once more exposing the spy hole, and Ebadiah sidesteps closer to the register. I hurry around the counter to help collect the necklaces, pausing in front of the spy hole as long as I dare while Ebadiah slips the camera out of his shoulder bag and takes an imograph of the open pages. There's no time for a tripod or for a long exposure but the room is bright with light streaming in from its many windows, all designed to show off the jewels with maximum pizazz. It should be enough for a decent image.

Pinch-face notices my feet next to him as he scrambles for diamonds. He glares up at me. 'What in the world do you think you're doing?'

'Oh, I er, came to help, master,' I say, attempting a Dockside threader accent. Ebadiah has finished and is walking to the door, the camera safely back in his bag. I drop to one knee and grab a necklace.

'Leave them!' screams Pinch-face. 'Leave them alone and get back to your side of the counter immediately!'

I obey, playing the humble idiot.

Behind the counter, a door opens between the spy holes and a guard pokes his head into the room. 'Is everything all right, Mr Poundsworth?'

I glimpse Ebadiah's ankle trailing out of sight before the main door closes with another jingle of the bell.

Pinch-face – Mr Poundsworth – rises to place the cushioned tray of jewellery back onto the counter. 'Yes, all is well. Thank you.'

Madam thinks better of looking for more diamond alternatives.

'I'm afraid I'll have to leave it for another day. I have a rather urgent matter to attend to. Thank you for your assistance.' She throws Poundsworth a rolling wave with the note in her fingers and saunters for the door. We leave the shop, phase one of our mission complete.

# 9

# Names

*In which disaster strikes*

Josiah meets us around the corner from Chantrees.

'How did it go?' he asks Willow before turning to Ebadiah. 'Did you get the imograph?'

'It went fine,' says Willow, dropping the silker accent.

'Yeah, I got the picture. Pah! Old Poundsworth's a sort ain't 'e?' Ebadiah hands me the camera and, with a wave, hobbles away. 'I'll see you later.'

'You did well in there, Willow,' I say. 'You seem to have a natural talent for this kind of thing.'

'Pulling a con? I should say,' she says. 'You don't survive as a threader for this long without learning a trick or two.'

'Come along, then. We have an imograph to develop.'

Nearing Bunson Street, we take precautions to ensure that Willow is not observed entering the house from the front. There's a lane, nothing more than a dirt track, that services the rear of the houses. We use that, checking for Jinkers and other neighbours, and take her inside where she can change back into the loose-fitting dress and hide away once more. We've not seen Harris since the office, but even if he has seen us with Willow in her violet gown, I'm pretty sure he won't have recognised her.

Josiah and I leave her with Mother and walk back to Mysteries Solved.

In the blacked-out darkness of the case room an hour later, Josiah and I watch a ghostly image emerge on an imographic print as it soaks in a tray of silver halide salts. A red-glazed oil lamp paints the room in deep crimson shadows by which we work. I agitate the tray to sluice the chemical bath over the paper's surface as the picture deepens into clarity and the open pages of the register appear before us. A third tray of chemicals fixes the image and a fourth rinses it clean. I peg the finished print up to drip dry from a string that's pinned tight across the corner of the room.

'Josiah, the blinds, if you will.'

He opens the blinds and I turn the switch to pinch out the flame of the red lamp.

In daylight the imograph looks even better. It's more than I'd hoped. We go in close to peer at the details. The open pages of the register show several columns detailing the dates, the customers' names and addresses, the commissions, the prices, the dates of payment received and the dates upon which the jewellery was collected. There is a slight blur, as you'd expect from an exposure without a tripod, but Mr Poundsworth's fluent pen strokes are legible.

There is a calculated risk involved in our scheme. Chantrees must surely sell mostly from existing stock. New and bespoke commissions are, by comparison, a rarity. The list of dates in the left-hand column confirms our assumptions, the most recent being two weeks ago, while the oldest is more than a year old. It seems reasonable then, as Josiah first suggested, to believe the register lies open at these two pages and is seldom touched. When it is used, it is to add a new commission on the next available row and, even then, the pages are not turned. That won't be happening any time soon, judging by the thirty or so blank lines that are waiting to be filled out on the lower half of the right-hand page. Our plan is to swap the real register for a fake, soon to be created, and once we have taken the information we need from the real one, we'll swap the original back in place, all without anyone at Chantrees knowing a thing about it.

It's a lot of effort for a few names, I know, but it is one of Josiah's more bearable ideas and, if it works, those names will give us the Order with nowhere to hide.

When the imograph is dry, I package it up with a payment, a letter containing instructions and a new gilt-edged register I bought that's a fair match for the old one at Chantrees except, of course, its pages are empty. This package I send with Ebadiah for delivery.

The forger I use for all my fraudulent silker documents is the best in Londaland. The man who crafted Josiah's and Jemima's papers – and all the others – lives in Holloway. It's a deprived backwater of Camdon that silkers avoid, which is why it's a perfect place for a forger to hide. Holloway's gutter-stinking streets run for leagues all around the city's south-westerly edge, hemmed to the east by Curlston Marsh, the last patch of wet ground between here and the inhospitable Borderlands. When strong winds blow up from the south, it's Holloway that gets the worst of the reeking toxic fumes of Mors Zonam. Not the most pleasant place to live.

But I digress...

The forger goes by one name alone and, let's face it, that's not his real name: Ranskin. It will take Ebadiah half a day to get there and back and another day or so for Ranskin to copy the open pages onto the new register so, for now, I'm forced to leave Chantrees' register well alone.

Instead, I turn my attention to the victims named in the green ink letter and, unfortunately, there's only one place to research them. Back to the City Registry Office.

Josiah and I spend the rest of the stifling day searching through old copies of the city newspapers for mentions of Zacchaeus Mandon, Foster Keen and Martha Judd. I'll spare you the details, for the memory of it is dreary enough, but suffice to say, we learn two things of note from our toil: Martha

Judd and Foster Keen both had connections with Dover Palace.

Martha, a dressmaker from Highbridge, regularly made dresses for Lady Dover, the Countess of Lockingshire, and so Martha's name features in several articles on the changing fashions of the highborn silkers.

Foster had, up until his death, been frequently called upon to drive carriages back and forth from the palace on royal occasions when the usual palace carriages were insufficient for the numbers of guests attending. As such, he was questioned by several reporters about various royal balls and ceremonies with the hope of digging up some print-worthy gossip. Mostly, I'd say they failed, though Foster's name made it into the news sheets and was, at least once, quoted as being an *ardent source of royal titbits.*

'What do you think?' I ask Josiah, wearily. 'Is this pertinent?'

'Could be, I suppose.' He yawns, not bothering to mask his cavernous mouth. 'If not, it's a mighty coincidence.'

'I agree. If only we could find a connection with Zacchaeus Mandon, I'm sure then we could be certain.'

'Aye.'

But we've exhausted the papers and ourselves, so we leave. That name, however, stays with me. I carry it all the way home, hear it for the rest of the day and it haunts my sleep.

Zacchaeus Mandon.

It's in the small hours of the night that I wake in a feverish sweat with the need to rise and shake off the grogginess of slumber. I splash my face with cold water from the wash bowl in my room, light a candle and, in my nightshirt, sit at my desk. I revisit my pocketbook to search out what little there is to be known about the man.

Zacchaeus Mandon, property developer, lived and worked in Tower End. Died twelve years ago, upon the 5th of Quartersmoon back in 1783. It's not much to go on, but I decide then and there to find more on Zacchaeus in the morning. Someone in Tower End must remember him – a son, a daughter, or a colleague, perhaps.

The tobacconist of Tower End is the twelfth place I try, the retailer a short, round fellow and, by the fleck of silver in his hair and moustache, he's old enough to have once known Zacchaeus Mandon. His shop is a pleasant arrangement of darkly polished mahogany, red carpet and age-worn shelves bearing every brand of tobacco leaf a smoker could ever wish for. There's a warmth to the place and there are smoky sweet tobacco flavours of cherries and maple in the air.

'Zacchaeus Mandon? No, sorry. I never 'eard of no Zacchaeus Mandon. I knows a Phyllis Mandon. Would she do?'

'Yes, she may do. You don't happen to have an address?'

'Not exactly. She lives down Lupin Road, far as I know. You could try down there. Left out the door, second road on the right.'

'Thank you. I'll try there.'

I follow his directions and find myself standing in a splendid street of grand houses on the side of the hill, overlooking the Tynne. Somewhere in this road may or may not live Phyllis Mandon, who may or may not be related to the deceased Zacchaeus. It feels thin but I reach for it anyway.

Before me on the cobbled path, a couple approach, arm in arm. I prepare to interrupt their love-gazing but bail at the last moment, choosing instead the boy in the flat cap, shorts and braces who ambles a short way behind them.

'Here, lad, I'm looking for Phyllis Mandon. Does she live nearby?'

'Old Mrs Mandon? Yeah, she's number 43.' He holds out his palm, reminding me of Ebadiah.

'Here you go.' I drop a penny into his hand and he snatches it away as though I might relent and demand it back. 'Looks like there's a good sweet shop back there.'

'Sweets? You must be blathered. I'm going for gin!' With a tug of his cap, he speeds away leaving me to find 43 Lupin Road. It's not far, a pale golden stone façade in keeping with the neighbouring properties. Whoever Mrs Mandon is, she's doing all right.

I climb five stone steps and rap three times with the elaborately studded brass knocker. The door is opened by a weary-faced woman in a full-length gown, a misty shade of blue. She wears no bonnet but her pale blonde hair is braided and tied up atop her head. Her eyes are intense and enquiring.

'Yes, may I help you?' Her teeth are a light shade of ochre, a certain sign of a smoker.

'Good day to you. My name is Michael Banyard. I'm looking for a Mrs Phyllis Mandon, possible relation to Zacchaeus Mandon.'

'Zacchaeus was my husband.' She looks me up and down before adding, 'It sounds like you'd better come in.' Opening the door wide she steps aside, inviting me into the high-ceilinged sitting room. Glancing out at the street, I sit in a fine chair upholstered with a tapestry of country scenes. Around the walls, large oils portray bold landscapes.

'I would like to know what has brought you here, enquiring after my late husband.'

She seems honest and forthright. I follow suit. 'I'm investigating a string of murders, and questions have arisen over the nature of your husband's death.'

'I see. You think him murdered, then?' She takes a narrow cigarette from a silver case, lights the tip and smokes.

I feel uncomfortable, that I've invaded a sacred space, a precious memory. 'There is a distinct possibility, yes. Can you tell me if he ever had dealings with anyone at Dover Palace?'

She thinks about this, taps ash into a brass ashtray. 'No, I don't believe so, although he moved in some high circles.'

'I'm right in thinking he was a property developer, though?'

'You are.'

'I see. In that case, would you mind if I were to contact you again, should further cause arise?'

'By all means.' On the way to the door she stops. 'Wait.' She pales, the blood draining from her face. She takes a hard drag on the cigarette as though to steady herself. 'I remember now – there *was* a connection with Dover Palace. Some years ago,

Zacchaeus handled a number of properties for the Earl of Lockingshire. He was charged to make improvements and to sell them on at a profit.'

I nod, wondering how much I should tell her about the case, but decide to say as little as possible. 'Thank you for your help. If I learn anything that may be of interest to you, I will return.' I doff my hat in a gesture of farewell. 'Goodbye, for now.'

The front door is ajar when I get home. That's strange. I pause. Look around, puzzled. There's no sign of Mother, Josiah, or Jinkers, or anyone else. I know instantly that something's wrong. Through the gap, I can see the empty corridor within. The street outside is quiet.

A hiss startles me. Jinkers' cat, nothing more. A streak of grey and black at my side, the animal leaps from a low windowsill and dashes away.

Gently, I push the door further open and step inside, listening, looking for anything else out of place. The kitchen is ahead of me at the end of this corridor. It's empty, everything tidy. In the alcove to my left, the coat hooks hold the usual coats and hats. I turn right into the sitting room and stop in my tracks when a low growl greets me from the other side of the room. I turn my head slowly. There, an enormous lantern dog sits, a length of chain tethering it to an iron candle sconce on the wall. It watches me and I it, as I creep through towards the door that leads on to the lower landing. A strand of drool oozes from the dog's jowls to the floor as it maintains the growl.

Raised voices reach me from deeper in the house, the green room, I think. The hallway is empty, everything in its place: the patterned rug stretches across the old worn floor of diagonal red and yellow tiles; the grandfather clock in the corner shows five to four, its pendulums swinging softly; the oaken writing desk stands against the wall. I follow the voices, sounds that make me picture Josiah and Willow, too muffled for words, too vague to be sure but, closing, I hear them in clarity.

Harris. 'There's a noose on Gallows Hill with your name on

it, my girl.'

Willow. 'No! Not that! Anything but that!'

Harris. 'Oh, don't you fret, lass. There'll be plenty of time for us to get acquainted on the road home.'

I ease open the door to the green room, and what happens next takes place so quickly that there's nothing I can do but watch.

Firstly, there are three people in the room. Willow stands by the fireplace. I can see her face but she's looking at Harris, who is facing her and shouting at her. He's gripping her upper arms tightly. Willow's right cheek is swollen and red and blood trickles from her nose. Behind Harris, Josiah closes in, a fire iron raised in his fist. He brings it down on the unsuspecting Harris with a devastating blow to the head, as I open my mouth to shout.

'Noooooo!'

But it's too late. Harris takes the hit, his eyes roll back into his head and he slumps to the floor, a dead weight.

# 10

# The Uninvited Guest

*In which Banyard and Mingle take a dog for a walk*

Willow whimpers before running to embrace Josiah.

'No! No, no, no...' I babble. 'This can't be happening. Josiah, what have you done?'

'He was going to take Willow!' Josiah looks from Harris' body to the iron in his hand and back again. Except he's not Josiah, he is Silus Garroway once more, the condemned threader in fear for his life. 'I couldn't let him take Willow! You don't know what they would have done to her. He was going to abuse her. He said it himself! Promised it! And we already know what happens to Bletchley's runaways if he catches them.'

'You've killed him!' I'm pretty sure Harris is dead but I kneel to check. Yes. He's as dead as they come.

'All right... So... This is really happening...' Some form of shock has overtaken me. It's debilitating. I can't think. My mind reels.

'You have to understand, Mr Banyard,' says Josiah, stepping closer. I marvel. He doesn't seem fazed at all. 'He found us out. He knew who I was, which means he knew someone had set me up as a silker. Which means he knew about you!'

I ward him away with a shaky hand. 'Don't come any closer,

Joe, or I swear…' I don't know what to swear. My words drift into nothing. 'He knew about us?'

'Everything. Well, maybe not everything, but he'd worked out enough to get us all hung.'

'You mean hanged.'

'Hang you and your petty correctness! It were him or us! There were nothing else for it!'

There's a groove across the top of Harris' head where his skull is caved in. A trickle of blood runs through his hair to the rug beneath. The certainty of it all startles me like a pail of iced water in the face. It's happened. This is real. And there's nothing else for it but to deal with the fallout. My brain finally kicks into gear.

'The rug has blood on it. It will have to go. Quickly, help me roll him in it! Where's Mother? Widow Blewett?'

Josiah makes the sacred sign and together we roll Harris in the rug.

'Shopping. The grocer's, I think. We're the only ones here.'

'All right. Let's get him down to the cellar. We can deal with him later. For now, we just need to hide him.' We try to lift Harris and the rolled rug but it's all too floppy and awkward until we both get a better grip on the ends of the matting. We hoist Harris up from the floor and take him out of the green room and through the hall, passing the stairs. Further on, there's a small passage to our left that leads to the cellar door.

A word flashes raw and red in my mind.

MURDERER!

My brain keeps throwing other words at my face. You killed him, Joe! Are we into killing now? There are plenty more along the same theme. I clamp my mouth shut, letting nothing escape.

From the other room we hear a deep bark.

'The hound!' says Josiah, remembering the lantern dog chained to the wall.

'Yes. Quickly now. There is much to do!' We pause. 'Willow, the door.'

Willow runs ahead of us as we turn a corner to the cellar

door.

'In there.' I nod towards the door. Willow opens it, and we descend foot-hollowed stone steps into the dark. The cellar is one of the oldest parts of the house and is cool and damp with a musty smell. Its floors are uneven flagstones, all rounded and pitted with age, its ceiling flaking with ancient whitewash and striped by wood-wormed beams. We carry our load past racks of wine, port and a few bottled spirits to the end furthest from the steps and deposit it by the wall.

'Now for the dog.'

This is going to be trickier. The hound will not leave the house willingly without its master. In the sitting room we watch it.

'His name's Baker, apparently.' Josiah appraises Baker.

'How are we going to do this?'

'I don't know. Got any steak?'

'Meat! Good idea.' I hurry to the kitchen, grab an aurochs steak from the icebox and return to the sitting room. The steak is a bluish purple, two inches thick, succulent flesh marbled with fine white veins of fat. Baker senses it immediately, sniffing the air and rising to all fours. He whines.

'Here,' I pass the meat to Josiah. 'You do it.'

'Come, Baker. Dinnertime!' He swings it a few feet from Baker's nose. Baker yaps, slobbers some more and runs a large floppy tongue around the wet edges of his mouth. 'That's it. Come on, now.' Baker pulls the chain taut. Josiah turns to me. 'Get behind him and unhook the chain. Slowly.'

I don't care that Josiah is now telling me what to do. This is his mess. He can get us out of it.

I cross the room and ease in behind the dog to lift the chain from the iron sconce. Baker doesn't seem to care, his focus solely on the steak. He barks and yelps, craving the meat. Josiah backs away dangling the steak and, jowls wobbling with drool, Baker follows. We work our way out to the hallway and Baker pads along after the meat. Once out in the street, I wonder what Josiah is thinking.

'Do you think he'll go away if we throw the streak and shut him out?' I ask.

'That's the plan. Ready?'

I nod.

'Here we go!' Josiah launches the steak with an underarm throw, sending it spinning twenty yards down the road. Baker strains on his chain. I release it from his collar and he dashes away. We race back into the house and close the door.

Moments later, Mother and the widow return laden with groceries.

'Michael, there's a lantern dog waiting outside our door. It tried to get in the house! Do something about it, will you?'

'Yes, Mother. Of course.' I roll my eyes at Josiah. 'But there's something I must do first.' I find Willow in the green room standing by the window. 'Mother and the widow are home. Josiah and I will get rid of the hound. Can I trust you to stay here and prevent anyone from entering the cellar?'

'You can, master.'

'Good. Oh, and stay away from the windows. And don't call me master.'

Grim-faced, I fetch my pistols. It's time to end this problem but I don't like what I'm about to do. In fact, I hate it.

The carriage ride out of the city is a solemn affair. Josiah gazes vacantly out of the window for most of the way while the heavens grimace with gathering cloud and Baker settles down on the carriage floor. Lantern dogs are tall, shaggy creatures with lengthy snouts. They're bred for their speed and size as hunting dogs. Baker's long legs are a bad fit for the carriage footwell but he manages to sprawl out, his muzzle lazing on his front paws, his gaze on Josiah and me. It might be all in my head but his eyes seem puzzled and sad.

The air feels thick and heavy, like the pressured steam of a boiling kettle. It starts to rain, the leaden skies bursting with a million violent droplets.

I feel perfectly horrid. There's a part of me that wants to

forgive Josiah and move on. There's another part that wants him punished. It's not a nice part. Even I dislike it, but it's there, nonetheless. I'm tormented by the entire situation, torn and disjointed deep inside. The thought of taking life in any way sickens me. It goes against every principle I live by and yet he *has* taken life and, on this occasion, I see no other way than for us to take another.

One glance at the dog and I join Josiah, staring from the window at the darkling world outside. We pass the last hovels of Holloway on the city's southern fringe as fields roll in to dominate the view, spotted with the occasional dishevelled cottage or barn. Gnarled trees and tall grasses sprout from the edges of the road and soon we pass through a solid tunnel of ashblacks, those black-barked hardwoods that grow in the poorest of soils and burn black, even in the hottest of fires. Our destination is Black Down Forest, a place remote and deserted enough for the foul deed we are about.

At the edge of the forest I rap on the ceiling to let the driver know we've arrived at a suitable spot. The rain stops as suddenly as it began and the remaining light sickens and sinks lower behind the trees, giving the forest an atmosphere to match its name. The sky flames with deep, angry shades of red while the trees lurk in pit-black silhouette, like a forest of coal and tar. Over Mors Zonam to the south there is a green aura, a haze on the horizon. The evening is warm and sticky. The driver brings the horses to a halt and we alight onto the wet grass at the edge of the trackway and pay him to return in half an hour. That should be plenty of time for us to find a suitable place in the forest to shoot Baker.

'I can just wait here,' the driver says, shrugging. He has no idea of our plan. 'It's no bother.'

'I'd rather you didn't, if it's all right with you.' I don't want him to hear the gunshot. Don't want anyone to know anything about it.

Throwing us a dubious look, he takes the hint without further question and flicks the reins. The horses set forth to draw the carriage away, leaving Josiah, Baker and me in the growing darkness.

'Come on, then. Let's get this over with.'

Josiah leads Baker on his chain and we trudge soberly into the deeper shadows of the forest, feeling last autumn's leaves moulder beneath our feet. We walk for ten minutes, our boots growing slick with the damp of the forest, neither of us truly wanting to stop. If we did, it would mean it was time to kill the dog, which we don't want to do. Fearing we might march all night, I slow when we reach a small clearing of grasses and rusting ferns.

'I suppose this is as good a place as any.' I look around, trying to shake the uncanny feeling that we're being watched.

Josiah stops and looks mournfully down at Baker. He seems every bit as miserable as I feel.

'I'll hold the chain, keep him still.' I draw a pistol and wad a shot into the barrel, check the powder is dry and prime the chamber. The moment has come. I pass the loaded gun to Josiah and take charge of the chain.

Josiah swallows hard and levels the barrel at a point between Baker's soulful eyes. I note the dumb dog seems oblivious to what's coming his way. He just looks up at Josiah with those large melancholy eyes, seeming a little confused. I think, he must be wondering why his master has abandoned him and why we've brought him here. Even if he's dumb, he must at least be thinking that.

Josiah tenses his arm, finger tightening on the trigger. A long moment passes. He looks at me, looks back at the dog and refocuses. Just when I think he's going to shoot, he relaxes his arm to let the pistol hang desolately at his side. 'Mr Banyard, there must be another way.'

I think for a moment. 'I don't see one.'

'Couldn't we just let him go?'

'We can't be sure the hound wouldn't come back sniffing around for Harris, or worse. What if he returned to Bletchley in Loncaster? A sure sign something has happened to his master.'

That feeling is still there. I gaze into the shadows of the forest, thinking there is movement, but see none. The faint wind stirring the leaves of the trees, perhaps a hag bat or a screecher owl.

'They'll know something's happened to Harris when he doesn't return anyway. Either way they'll come searching.'

'More than likely, but if both Harris and his dog vanish, we might trick them into thinking he's found a better position and moved on. I don't know. I need time to think but we don't have any. We have to get his things from Madame Rouge's and we have to get them tonight.' Pause. 'Please get on with it, Joe.'

He takes aim at Baker again. My teeth clench as he tenses the trigger. He spins sideways. 'I can't do it. I can't kill a helpless dog. Not even Harris' dog. I mean, look at him.'

Now Baker has grown more used to us he does seem rather harmless. He releases a small whimper, perhaps pining for his missing master. We had the odd growl at first, and he could certainly cause some serious damage if he wanted to – his canines are a good two inches long, his jaws massive – but once we had him back on the chain, he became as docile as a lamb.

'All right, Joe. Give me the gun.'

We swap, Josiah taking the chain, and I aim the pistol at the centre of Baker's forehead, feel the tension in the trigger as sweat beads upon my brow. I hold it there for what seems an age, as incapable as Josiah.

'Unclip the chain from his collar.' Blood beads on my brow as though forced out by the pressure in my head. I look into the trees to see two white points of light gawping back at me and think, *No, not here – not now.*

Josiah frees Baker and glances at me. 'Mr Banyard, you're bleeding!'

'We're being watched. A gawper, in the trees.'

The dog stands there, every bit as dumb as I thought he was. Finally, when the apprehension is too much to bear, I shift aim four inches to the left and send a shot into the ground. Baker jumps.

'Go!' I cry.

He barks, agitated, and lollops into the forest.

I look back into the trees, searching for the eyes before slipping the pistol into my gun belt, but the gawper has gone. 'We'd better get out of here before the mutt returns.' I mop blood from my brow with a handkerchief.

The hike back to the carriage is mildly less sombre but the previous tension is replaced by a fear that we've made things worse. We're also faced with the next problem on a growing list: how to extract Harris' belongings from his room at Madame Rouge's without rousing suspicion.

'It's not going to be easy,' I say, anger apparent in my tone. 'We can't just waltz in and take his things, although I suppose his room key is likely somewhere on his body.'

'It'll be in a pocket for sure, so we'll be able to get in, with luck.'

'Right. We'll need disguises.'

The carriage is waiting for us as we reach the road, and we're glad to get out of the night and sit for a while as it trundles us home. At 96 Bunson Street we hurry in. It's late evening and the house is quiet and everyone asleep in their beds, except Willow. She greets us with a tray of port and crystal glasses.

'Thought you might need a drink, Mr Banyard,' she says, pouring the port.

We accept it gratefully and down it.

'The dog?'

'Has been dealt with.' I take a storm lamp from the table and march through the sitting room. 'To the cellar.'

Harris lies as we left him, inside the rug. Josiah makes the sacred sign.

'Help me with this,' I say.

He assists me, unrolling the rug, and we search the body by the flickering yellow light of the lamp. The musty air down here has already become fouler with the presence of a corpse. Josiah is growing bolder in his dealings with the dead.

'Here! Told you so.' He draws out a small iron key from a

pocket in Harris' waistcoat, and holds it up.

I squint at it. 'Does that look like a key to one of Madame Rouge's rooms?'

He shrugs. 'How would I know?'

We search on but soon realise it's the only key there. I check my pocket watch.

'It's gone eleven. We must get ready and go.'

# 11

# Cadavers

*In which a body is discovered*

Josiah is easy to transform back into the likeness of a threader. Silus Garroway is never truly far beneath the surface. In these few moments it's like flicking a switch. The old clothes he wore to his hanging are still in the back cupboard of his room. He dons them and relaxes into his old threader stoop that, since his flight to Camdon City, he's had to work so hard to conceal.

As usual, I'm the challenge when it comes to a threader disguise. I do what I can, pulling on the simple, old clothes and trying to adopt a slouch. You know the drill by now: a bit of dirt rubbed into the face and hands; false beards and plenty of make-up for both of us; an unkempt grey wig for me. The details are everything – grime beneath the nails, our skin dusted with make-up to give the impression of sun-browned manual workers. I give Josiah dark bags beneath his eyes and make him look a good twenty years older. We find cloth caps and pull them low to overshadow our features.

Willow finds us and lowers her voice. 'Mr Banyard, why don't you let Silus and me do this? You're risking too much and it's all for us. It's my fault. I should go instead.'

I think, *If I let you and Josiah out alone, I've a mind I'll never see either of you again,* and try to shake the feeling that things have already sped out of control. 'It's quite all right, Willow. We'll be fine. You stay here. Keep an eye on Mother and our guest in the cellar. We'll be back before you know it. How do we look?'

'Like a right old pair o' threaders. Wait, your signet ring...'

'Ah, quite right.' I ease the gold ring from my finger and pass it to Willow. 'Keep this safe for me, will you?' I rub make-up over the pale band that the ring leaves on my finger.

'Yes, master – I mean, Mr Banyard.'

'Thank you. Now, let's be off.'

A muggy night greets us at the door and we slip away into the pale blue lamplight on foot. In general, threaders don't use carriages or ride horses unless accompanying their masters. Even then, they're usually made to walk, so this is what we do. We tramp all the way through Crowlands to Southside, where the streets become cluttered with industry. There are tanneries and the workshops of coopers, iron smiths and dyers, each befouling the air even though closed up for the night. There is dirt, too. The cobbles are strewn with waste, the trash the locals can't be bothered to deal with. Either that or they don't have the energy or time. In Highbridge these threaders would have been flogged daily until the lot was scrubbed clean. Not so in Southside. No one cares here. The kerbs are open sewers and we get the benefit of the accompanying stench. Treading carefully, we hurry along and I try to limit the number of dreadful breaths I take while Josiah doesn't appear to even notice the stink.

We enter Turner Road where the taverns are still alive with music and gossip. Here the night is just beginning and the ambiance spills into the street. A commotion in the Crown and Pudding boils out from its open door to become a full-blown brawl, tankards flying. We give it a wide berth and turn into Cloak Lane, where we are by no means the only visitors. Several hours will pass before Southside cools into slumber.

Madame Rouge's is no exception. Men come and go, weaving through the shadows, some lurking with heads down and collars up, others more candid in their purpose, heedlessly sauntering in and out. There seems to be every sort here: the seedy, the needy, the fat and the thin, the well-formed and the disfigured. No doubt there are lowlifes: thieves and vagabonds, haters, fraudsters, drunkards and abusers. There are those who seem well-to-do, perhaps silkers, even (they are the ones hiding their faces beneath broad-brimmed hats and high collars, sneaking in or out) and there are those who loiter, penniless, in the empty hope of a handout, though my impression is there are no handouts here. Everything is about money and everything has its price.

We enter through the door, stopped open with an old slipper to ease the flow of traffic, and head straight for the front desk to beg passage up to the rooms. A haughty girl of sixteen or so greets us with a gap-toothed smile and it seems Madame Rouge is absent or otherwise engaged. The freckled girl wears a frilly dress that must have once been striped with white and pink. Now it is more grey than pink and it carries a grimy hand-me-down look.

Josiah whispers in my ear. 'You'd better let me do the talking, Mr Banyard.'

I nod, though the thought fills me with dread.

We approach the desk and he leans in to address the girl with an exaggerated Loncaster-threader drawl. 'Good evenin', my dear. We're come for Master Harris' bags. He's been called away, sudden like, and he's sent us for his stuff. Can ya show us to his room?'

Freckles studies us down the length of her dappled nose. 'How do I knows you is who you says you is?'

'Ah! That's easy, miss. We have 'is key.' Josiah drops the words like a trail of breadcrumbs and holds the key up for her to see. 'Master Harris says this would be proof enough.'

She seems satisfied although irritated by our interruption. 'Right, then. Follow me.' Grudgingly, she leads the way and shouts, 'Big Martha! You'll 'ave to watch the desk.'

Aptly named, Big Martha clomps her way out from a room

in the rear as we ascend the first flight of stairs that are as old and worn as the rest of the house. The banister, spindles and the ends of the tread boards are all varnished dark wood beneath the dust, though much of the varnish has long gone. There's a landing at the top and this takes us around clockwise past a laundry chute to the second flight.

Five flights later – and as many laundry chutes – Freckles pauses before room number 54. 'This is Mr Harris' room. Between you and me, we won't be sorry to see 'im go, nor that monstrous dog of 'is.' Pause. 'Go on, then…' She steps away from the door and waits while Josiah fumbles to fit the key in the lock. He turns it until there's an audible click, opens the door and begins to step inside, but quickly halts, pulling the door closed again, causing me to collide with his back.

'Everythin' all right?' asks Freckles.

'Oh, yes. Everything's fine,' says Josiah, though I can tell it isn't. He forces a smile and waves. 'We'll just fetch the master's things and soon be out of your way.' Carefully, he inches the door open before sidling through, all the while keeping it as closed as possible so that his shirt buttons catch on the edge. I follow suit and see Freckles shaking her head as she heads back downstairs. When I'm sure she's gone, I peer into the room, wondering what Josiah saw that made him hide the interior from her.

Harris' room is a mess – looks like a robbery – but that's not the cause of Josiah's odd behaviour. Oh no. The cause is lying flat out on the rickety bed, half-naked and a deathly shade of white. She has a syringe still hanging from a vein in the crook of one arm.

'What do you think, Mr Banyard? One of his playmates who's played too hard?'

'It appears so, Joe. Is she…'

Josiah makes the sacred sign and checks for a pulse at the woman's throat. 'Stone cold. What are we to do now?'

In life she must have been beautiful.

We stand silently for a while, grieved and perplexed.

'Well, we can't leave her here. There'd be an investigation. The Drakers would hunt for Harris and that's – '

'The last thing we need.'

'Exactly.' I take the needle from her arm and sniff at the syringe. 'Morphic and horrowin. She got too greedy or Harris administered an overdose. Either way, there's nothing we can do for her now. I'm afraid she'll have to come with us.'

'How are we to do that?'

There is silence as we both think. Mostly I'm thinking, *I didn't think this could get any more miserable.* But it just did.

'She's slight enough,' says Josiah. 'Perhaps she'll fit into Harris' trunk.'

We try, dragging the trunk away from the wall and emptying it before carefully folding the girl inside. It's a tight fit but the trunk is large and we manage to cram the body in. The only problem is the lid won't close. Josiah is pushing it down and I'm trying to close the clasps when the door slams open and Madam Rouge stomps in, storm-faced.

'What's the meaning of this? You can't just march in 'ere and remove a guest's belongings. Who d'you think you are?' Madame Rouge was, no doubt, once a real stunner, but these days not so much. Her slender waist of youth has barrelled, life has not been particularly kind on the rest of her and no amount of powder and lipstick, or tightening of the corset, can redress the balance. As though to compensate, she wears a ridiculously tall wig of silver curls which clashes with the red of her face. There's a badly drawn beauty spot over the right edge of her upper lip.

Freckles cowers in the doorway.

Josiah stands, planting himself firmly between Madame Rouge and the trunk. 'We was hired to fetch 'is gear, I swears it! We have 'is key. What more proof do ya need?'

I back away from the trunk and surreptitiously search for something to drop. I quickly find a heavy glass ashtray, which I secretly grab from the tabletop at my back. The room is cramped and hot, the window already open. One more subtle step takes me to it. Madame Rouge launches into another tirade, aiming it mostly at Josiah as he's the one doing the talking and, while he keeps her busy, I steal a glance through the window at the street below. There, a man is leaning against the wall almost directly beneath me. I ease the ashtray behind my back through the gap and release. It plummets and explodes on the cobbles like a small glass bomb, shards flying all around. A shout goes up from the fellow nearby and other voices join the clamour.

I peer down at the scene and turn to Madame Rouge. 'Look at that! They're wrecking the place!' I'm on the cusp of adding, *You'd better get down there quick like, 'n' sort it out*, when she does exactly that, abandoning us and the room.

'Don't move,' she says, stamping her way to the stairs, leaving Josiah and me to get on with the job, which we do in great haste.

'Quickly.' I run to the trunk.

He sits on it and his weight is enough to close it. I latch it shut. There's no lock, so that will have to do. We cram everything else we can find into Harris' other bags and heave them out into the corridor, but making for the stairs we stop, for we both get the same idea.

'The laundry chute!' I say, as Madame Rouge's boots hit the first flight of stairs below on her way back up.

We hoist the trunk and let it slide down the chute. The chute door flaps back and forth as the body descends. Harris' other gear soon follows and then I start to climb into the chute. I pause, one foot in, one out, realising Josiah's massive shoulders will never fit in there. I climb back out. We'll have to find another way.

The stamping from the stairway grows louder. Madame Rouge's return is imminent.

Josiah opens the door to the room next to Harris' and strikes lucky. 'In here!' he hisses, peering into the gloom.

We slip inside, one of my boots clinking against a discarded whisky bottle littering the floor, and he closes the door gently so as not to alert Madame Rouge whose enormous hair is at this very moment breaching the level of the landing floor. Her footfalls paint a detailed picture of her movements as we listen at the door. She turns from the stairs and passes us, pausing outside Harris' room before entering. There follows a silence and I can only imagine she is standing there glowering at the emptiness of the room and seething at us for thwarting her so. She stomps back past the door and down the stairs.

In the darkened room, Josiah and I breathe easy. We've escaped the madam for now, but we still have to recover the 'baggage' safely and somehow get it out of the building.

At our backs a long snore emanates from a humped shape on the bed in the corner of the room. We leave the sleeping drunkard and, with trepidation, creep back out onto the landing to edge down the stairs, scrutinising the flights below that lie ahead.

I marvel at the situation in which I find myself: how did it come to this? Perhaps my decision to rescue Josiah from the noose was a mistake. After all, *this* is where it has led me! And what further foul deeds must I perform, perhaps even before this hideous night is through? We now have two bodies to lose and I'm no closer to knowing how.

We reach the bottom of the stairs without incident and find the front desk unattended. A disturbance in one of the downstairs rooms has drawn everyone's attention. Perhaps my glass bomb has kicked off a real fight. I'll never know. We skirt the desk and dash into the back, hunting for the laundry room. This, too, is abandoned and it seems at last our luck is changing. We grab the trunk and the bags and head out of the back door into a stinking, unlit alleyway, thankful for the shadows.

It's a long haul back to Bunson Street, where the house awaits us in stark moonlight. Jinkers and his fleabag are nowhere to be seen – another boon – and we're soon inside, collapsing into the sitting room chairs, exhausted. I'm sure it's a big mistake but for now the bodies will have to remain here. Until we have figured out a way to dispose of them safely, it's all we can do, anyway. We drag the woman's body down into the cellar and lay her alongside Harris in the rug before climbing the stairs to fall into our respective beds.

The following morning, we leave Willow defending the cellar and go to work as though nothing awry has happened. It seems vital to me that we are seen to act normally and so I give it my best shot, all the while my head spinning like a whirligig.

Our problem is never far from my mind as I greet Mardon, Penney and Lizzy. Josiah follows me into the case room and, although the room is already stiflingly warm, we close the door behind us to whisper.

'So, what are we going to do with the bodies?' asks Josiah.

'I don't know. I'm trying to run a private detective agency, not an undertakers.'

He purses his lips, unimpressed. 'I only asked. You know, it's not my fault. Well, certainly not the girl...'

'It doesn't matter who's at fault. The fact is we have two bodies to be rid of and no way to do it. What's more, we must do it soon, before they become malodorous.'

'We could go back to the woods. Dig a hole.'

'Not good enough. The grave could be discovered. Maybe even traced back to us.'

'Undertakers...' He's thinking again. Always a worrying sign.

'What about them?' I hang my waistcoat on the back of my chair and recline with my boots on my desk.

'Undertakers,' he repeats. The creases of his forehead dispel as his eyes widen. 'Why, Mr Banyard, I do believe I've had an excellent idea!'

'To be honest, I'm not sure I'll survive yet another of your ideas.'

'Do you want to hear it or not?'

'Go on, then.'

'Well, there's undertakers and then there's undertakers, you see?'

'Not really. Get to the point.'

'I'm talking about Mort and Jarvis, the undertakers down

Dire Lane. You know it?'

'Do you mean the place that handles the unnamed threaders?'

Unnamed threaders are the threaders who turn up dead, unknown and unclaimed. They frequently wash up on the banks of the Tynne having taken their own lives, or perhaps having been killed by their masters, or are found dead from unknown causes (probably malnutrition) in the backstreets of the city.

'The very ones. They get so many dead threaders through their doors that they'd hardly notice one or two more. They have to run night and day to deal with the numbers.'

It's a sorry accolade for our wonderful society.

'What about papers? Every body coming in is surely subject to documentation.'

'Ah, yes, but I reckon not so much once they're on the way out. Anyway, since when did you let a few documents get in your way?'

He's right, there. I'm probably one of Ranskin's most reliable clients.

'They all get loaded up on the same cart. The driver takes them to the Tobias Field at Digger's End and they're thrown in the same big hole.'

It's a grim picture I wish were not true. Although, as usual, I find myself actually considering Josiah's insane proposal. The thought of the poor wretch from Madame Rouge's being tipped into a nameless mass grave is sickening – just one more indignation for the hapless girl – but for Harris, on the other hand? It seems most fitting that he should be buried among the threaders he so mistreated. The idea's growing on me.

'All right, Joe, you may be on to something. We'd need to discover the exact procedure Mort and Jarvis employs when discharging bodies – Ebadiah can help with that – and we'd need a rush job from Ranskin.' As Josiah said, Mort and Jarvis is open at all hours because of the sheer number of threader corpses this city produces, and that means shift work. Perhaps if we can catch a consignment of corpses that straddles two shifts, we might somehow slip them in unnoticed.

Josiah's plan might just work.

There's a sharp rap on the door before it opens and Lizzy enters with a brown paper parcel. 'A package for Mr Banyard.'

## 12

# Mort and Jarvis

*In which Banyard and Mingle make an exchange
and bodies are moved*

I unwrap the package, already knowing it's the fake register back from Ranskin. He's done a good job. Turning to the two pages he's brilliantly copied in faded brown ink, I compare with the imograph, which he's also returned. I don't think I would be able to tell this from the real one.

'A talented artiste is our Mr Ranskin.'

Josiah nods. 'Fine work, no doubt.'

'We'll make the swap this very day and get a look at that register of names. Fetch Ebadiah.'

Josiah leaves and while he's gone, I draft a brief letter to Ranskin.

> *Dear R,*
> *We have a pressing need for two threader certificates of death and two coroner's reports, both for the recently deceased. One is an unidentified male of forty years or so, dark hair greying, moustache, blue eyes, and one an unidentified female of some twenty-five years, blonde with brown eyes. Both were found whole and cause of death is unknown. My messenger will wait*

*and return promptly with the documents.*
*Gratefully yours,*
*M*

If Josiah is correct, the forged documents will be more than enough to convince the cart driver the bodies are legitimate. It is certainly the case that before their final journey to the Tobias Field, any newly discovered threader corpse is scrutinised by law and science, but once the dead have been processed, they are handed over to others who are likely illiterate and care little for their jobs. They will be naturally disinclined to ask questions. With this in mind, I seal the letter in an envelope and mark it with an R in time for Josiah's return. Ebadiah follows him in and closes the door.

'Ebadiah, have one of your trusted lads deliver this to Ranskin and wait. Your fellow is to return with the papers Ranskin will produce. It's of utmost importance.' I pass him the letter. 'And then get yourself over to Mort and Jarvis, the undertakers on Dire Lane. Do you know it?'

'Where they send the threader dead, over Southside?'

'The very place. Do a little spying and see what you can learn about its procedures. We specifically need to know the protocol for passing the corpses on to the cart that takes them for burial.'

'Proto-what?'

'How do they take the bodies out onto the cart?' explains Josiah. 'Does someone sign for them? That sort of thing.'

'Right you are. Anything else?'

'Just be sure to report back by five o'clock. We're in rather a hurry.'

He holds out his palm and I pay him in advance.

'Don't you want to know why?' I ask.

He gives me a shrewd look. 'None of my business,' he shrugs. 'I ain't going near no stiffs, mind.'

'You should do well enough observing from a distance.'

He doffs his cap and leaves, the letter in his hand.

I turn to Josiah. 'Meanwhile, we can pay Chantrees another visit.' I tap the forged register.

'How do we swap it without that snot-nosed assistant seeing? We can't use Willow this time. She's minding the cellar.'

'Hmmm. Penney, perhaps?'

'What would we tell her?'

'As little as possible.'

'I'll call her in.' He heads for the door.

'Josiah...'

He stops.

'Let me do the talking.'

He leaves with a nod and returns a moment later with Penney. He offers her his chair and stands while she sits.

'You wished to see me, Michael?'

'Indeed. We could use your help. Can you spare an hour or so?'

'Of course.' She crosses her legs.

'We need to take a look at the register on the desk in Chantrees' showroom. It's to do with the green ink letter.'

'And what do you need from me?'

'A simple distraction. That is all.'

Less than an hour later we enter Chantrees, Penney first, resplendent in a deep-blue velvet gown embroidered with gold thread and armed with a matching parasol, accompanied by Josiah back in his threader guise.

Transformed into an elderly silker gent with a grey beard longer than King Lychling's, I allow a few seconds before following them in, pretending to take an interest in some jewellery well away from them on the opposite side of the shop.

Penney engages the irritating assistant while Josiah awaits her command, standing to one side and three feet behind, as befits a humble threader servant.

'May I see the sapphire choker?' She points to it beneath the glass top of the display cabinet.

'Why, yes, madam. One moment.' Poundsworth hurries to unlock the cabinet and takes out a red cushion bearing several chokers.

And so it goes on. Penney makes such a thorough job of it

that I'm convinced she truly intends to make a purchase (she probably has enough money in her purse to do so). I loiter around, perusing the diamonds in the rising heat of the shop, my briefcase heavy with the forged register.

It's hotter in here than outside because of the many tall windows at the front which intensify the light, and the lack of a breeze. I wouldn't want to work here, not on a day like today.

The moment finally arrives when Penney launches her ruse.

'No, I think the deeper blue. They'll match my dress.' She throws a hand to her forehead, wavers on her feet and faints to the floor.

'Oh, golly!' says Poundsworth and he calls for help, mopping his brow with a handkerchief. 'Alticus, Orius, some assistance, if you please!'

The two watchers behind the wall rush in through the central door of the panelling behind the counters and join Poundsworth, busying themselves around Penney, who's as limp as a smoked herring. In two steps I'm at the left counter where the register waits.

'I told her it was too hot for velvet, but would she listen?' I hear Josiah say.

With a glance at the stooping guards to check they're focused on Penney, I ease the fake register from my bag and make the switch. I double check the book is open on the one page with Ranskin's copied text and leave. The jingle of the doorbell informs Penney our task is completed and that it's safe to rouse from her faint.

In the case room, I slide Chantrees' register from the bag and spread it open on my desk. The earlier pages are so old that the ink has faded and here and there the handwriting changes, but I'm not interested in any of these details. All I want to know is who commissioned the frog rings and when.

The first is on the third page, in an entry dated 1735. A name we know well: Willard Steeler. No surprises there. A scan of my notes and a quick calculation tells me he was twenty-four years old when he ordered four of the rings to be made. Closing my eyes, I picture him, a zealous young industrialist with money to burn, the product of a thriving silker dynasty built on iron smelting, literally forging a way forward that would ensure prosperity for his lineage, but at what cost? And for whom were the other three rings?

I read the entire register line by line and note down two more names in my pocketbook. Both Assanie Strictor-Booth and Eadward Trent commissioned three gold rings bearing the same bullfrog motif cut in onyx. It's not what I had hoped for but it's better than nothing. I realise my summation was flawed. Why would each new member of the Order commission their own ring? What was I thinking? It makes far more sense that one member alone would be given the task. I only have the two new names because over the years the elected member has changed. So what of Assanie Strictor-Booth and Eadward Trent? Are they still members of the Order? Are they even still alive? It seems we will need to venture upon another of Josiah's dubious schemes but, before that, I turn back to my previous notes on the unnecessary capitals from the two Philshaw letters written to Tillie Ingham and add the new names next to the appropriate initials.

AS – Assanie Strictor-Booth
YO
ET – Eadward Trent
FG – Fletcher Gouldstone?
ML
JC – Jacob Cullins?
WS – Willard Steeler?

That leaves only two sets of initials unaccounted for: YO and ML. For now, they must remain an enigma.

Josiah, Willow and I meet at home briefly and plan a way to return the true register to Chantrees. Mother and Widow Blewett have gone to meet up with a friend on the other side of town and will be gone for several hours, so Willow has become available once more.

She wears the violet dress again and we each disguise ourselves as before. My costume has a crucial addition: I'm bulging with baggage that's hanging from my back and shoulders. The load is so cumbersome that Josiah has to help me pass the entrance when we arrive. We find two customers already in the shop. This bodes well: two more people Mr Poundsworth and his guards, behind their spy holes, will have to watch. Willow has two servants in tow also: Josiah follows her every step over at the counter to our right, while I linger on the other side before the open register. The other customers view glass cases sparkling with diamond-encrusted gold.

Clutching her bag bulging with banknotes, Willow resumes her browsing of the Chantrees display cases, engaging Poundsworth in a pointless quest for the right necklace. I give the ruse a few seconds until I'm sure Willow has his full attention before making a quick half-turn, making sure that my baggage sweeps the fake register clean off the countertop and into my shadow. It falls to the floor, hidden at my side beneath the counter and Poundsworth flies into an instant rage at the mishap.

'What are you doing? You imbecile!'

'I'm sorry, master. I shall put it straight,' I say in my best threader drawl. Before anyone can near me, I stoop to collect the fake, slipping it into one of my bags beyond view. From another bag, I take the real register and then rise to place it on the counter. 'There, no 'arm done.' I open the register to the usual page and turn it so that it sits just as before.

Poundsworth scowls suspiciously, scrutinising me.

Willow loses interest in the jewellery.

We leave.

The sooner these bodies are in the ground, the happier I'll be. Hours inch by with sluggish petulance. I want, with all my heart, for this sorry mess to be over with, but there's nothing I or anyone else can do to speed things along. By three o'clock I can stomach it no more. I grab my hat, leave the office and, with Josiah at my shoulder, ride out to Southside. On the corner of Dire Lane we hitch the horses to an iron hoop set in the wall of a tavern, and walk from there.

Dire Lane is one of those places that has an almost forgotten feel. There are houses – though poorly kept – and a scatter of low-end silker-owned businesses much like Cloak Lane, but there is more space between buildings here, scrubby patches of overgrown, unkempt land. It has an unloved air about it. Old news sheets and other detritus lie in the gutters and collect in corners, blown on the wind. The road is unmetalled and filthy, rutted by carts and steam trucks. Mort and Jarvis is situated towards the southern end of the lane in such a way that it appears others have distanced themselves. There is a good piece of waste ground on all its sides where dust and weeds prevail.

We find Ebadiah at the edge of one such area, leaning casually against a tree, watching the back entrance. The place seems quiet, so we join him.

'Any movements?' I ask.

'It all happens round 'ere. The bodies come in. The bodies go out. A cartload left a while back.'

'You watched the whole procedure?'

'Sure as y'nose. They bring in the empty cart there, right up to them doors.' He points to a set of double doors that lead out from the undertakers into a rough yard area. 'The bodies are brought out and dumped in the back of the cart. The driver's mate checks the documents and signs for the load. Then they take 'em.'

'So, how do we get our documents in with the others?' asks Josiah. 'And how do we get the bodies on the cart without anyone seeing?'

'I don't know.' I'm out of ideas.

Ebadiah looks at us in turn. 'You could always catch the driver down the road and bribe him to take the bodies.'

I shoot Ebadiah a warning glance and ask, 'What bodies?'

He shrugs. 'Say, for example, someone did have a couple of bodies they needed to lose – through no fault of their own, I'm sure – that might be a way to make it happen.'

'The driver and his mate might blackmail the briber later at their leisure. No, we need something safer.'

We watch the undertakers a while longer in silence without finding an answer. The only thing I'm sure of is that however we choose to approach this, we will do it under the cover of night. At least that gives us a few hours to solve the problem.

I think, *I wish this was someone else's problem*, and that's what gives me an idea. 'Wait a minute. You say the driver's mate checks the documents and signs for the consignment?'

Ebadiah nods. 'Aye.'

'What happens with the documents after that?'

'The driver's mate takes 'em. I guess they have to stay with the bodies until they're buried.'

'So, the driver's mate keeps the documents and gets on the cart. They drive away with the bodies.'

'That's right.'

I smile. 'I wonder, how many taverns must they pass between here and Digger's End?'

We hire a cart from a man on Brittling Street and park up outside home. The white mare is also hired (you cannot go penny-pinching when it comes to the clandestine disposal of incriminating bodies).

We find Willow in the green room polishing the mantel. It's the room closest to the cellar door so she's been spending a lot of time here recently. If she keeps the door open, she can hear when someone approaches and is close enough to quickly intervene, should anyone near the cellar. She hands me an envelope.

'The boy delivered this for you.'

I take it and open it to check over the forged documents from Ranskin. They're good.

'You'll be pleased to hear we're taking the bodies out tonight.

Where's Mother?'

'She's back, upstairs with Widow Blewett. The old girl's taken a turn. She's laid up in bed.'

'Right. We'll do it now. Willow, kindly watch the stairs. Josiah and I will bring them up.'

Josiah and I hurry down into the cellar while, around the corner, Willow takes her place at the bottom of the stairwell. The bodies are where we left them but the air in here is foul. We'll have to do something to sweeten it before Mother comes down again, though now is not the time.

We take Harris first, hoisting him in the rolled-up rug and toeing a path through the hallway, the sitting room and entrance hall. We slide the whole bundle into the back of the cart and unfurl the rug beneath an oiled tarpaulin, which we leave to cover the body. We roll the rug up again, slide it out of the cart and carry it back inside to repeat the process with the girl. We climb the cellar steps and are halfway across the landing when Willow coughs loudly. A warning: Mother is coming.

We speed onwards but not quickly enough. Descending the stairs, she catches a glimpse of the rug and the back of Josiah as he follows me into the sitting room.

'Michael, is that you? What are you doing with that rug?'

We rush through the sitting room.

'We're just taking it for cleaning, Mother. Back later. Good evening.'

'At this time of night? Michael? Michael?'

Into the back of the cart it goes. We hitch up the tailboard, hop up onto the driver's bench, release the brake and whip the reins. The mare sets off.

'Do you think she believed us?' asks Josiah.

'I sincerely doubt it.'

A voice reaches us from the neighbouring doorway ahead. 'Here, Banyard, what are you about?'

Jinkers. That's all we need.

'Nothing, Jinkers. Nothing at all.'

'I see.' Jinkers leans out and taps the side of his nose

knowingly as we draw level. 'Secret, is it?'

'Something like that.'

We pass him at a swift trot.

'I'll tell you later,' I shout back over my shoulder.

We drive, but not far, because next we need to call at the office to make use of the secret room, a recent installation I commissioned to make better use of a wasted backyard area on the Mysteries Solved property. In the case room, I press the concealed button at the end of the mantelpiece to open the hidden door, which hinges away from me into the wall. We walk into the small chamber and search among the many and various garments that hang on racks against the walls. Everything needed for a multitude of disguises is here in this chamber and, once dressed in our chosen outfits, we use the dresser and mounted mirror to work on our wigs and make-up.

It's five minutes past ten in the evening. There are few watch lamps in this part of town but pale yellow light glows from windows and doorways. Our disguises are complete. This time we're both threaders again, though I've a pocket full of cash most unfitting for the outfit. In another pocket I carry the forged documents. We've also dressed Harris' body in threader rags. The clothes we forced awkwardly over his limbs are ill-fitting but convincing enough.

A little legwork revealed that there are four taverns on the stretch between the undertakers and Digger's End. We drive the bodies to the Mutineer's Head – one of the quieter ones – and stop at the edge of the road.

Now Josiah plants his feet to one side of the cart, braces his massive shoulders against the side boards and lifts two wheels clean off the cobbles. I tug out the linchpin and ease the rear wheel from its axle. Josiah lowers the cart to rest unevenly on its remaining three wheels.

We wait as occasional drinkers come and go. Seeing a problem with the cart, one of them approaches. He's a whiskery fellow, his skin wrinkled and heavily tanned.

'Need help with that wheel?' he asks.

I smile. 'No, thank you. It's all in hand.'

He moves on, an eyebrow sceptically raised.

Ebadiah knows the undertakers' cart by sight and from his position further up the road he signals its imminent arrival with a wave of his cap. It turns the corner into view, the portly driver and his thinner mate nestled up high on the driver's bench. Josiah waits until they're closer before stepping out into the road to halt them.

'We've a wheel worked free. Can you lend a hand?'

Their eyes narrow with suspicion but the driver slows the horses enough for Josiah to take hold of one of their bridles and he helps bring them to a halt.

'That wheel don't look broke,' says the driver's mate, a spindly threader with narrow eyes, a thin silver earring, long sideburns and a small, pointed beard.

'"Tis well enough,' says Josiah. 'We must lift the cart to slide it back on. Will you 'elp?'

The driver and his mate lean in to consult in whispers.

'There's a drink in it when we're done,' says Josiah.

'Two,' I add. 'Apiece.'

That clinches the deal. The driver pulls their cart over to the side of the road, draws up the brake lever and they hop down to help. We soon have the wheel back in place and I slip the linchpin in, hammering it home with the heel of my shoe.

'Shall we?' I nod towards the Mutineer's Head, from where the jaunty notes of a fiddle spark up as though to welcome us in.

'We shall,' says the driver with a nod from his mate.

'What about your cart? Will your load not vanish while we partake?' asks Josiah.

The two exchange a glance and laugh.

'I very much doubt it,' says the driver.

'That load ain't going nowhere,' says the mate. 'In we go.'

The four of us enter the tavern. It's gloomy inside, lamplit and smoky. The bar is a rough plank of wood thrown over a line of barrels, behind which are more casks, these full of ale or wine. That's the choice: cheap ale or cheap wine. We go for the ale, which is cool, dark and surprisingly good. We take our tankards and find benches around a cold fireplace; four work-worn threaders in a threader tavern, in a threader part of the city.

Josiah and I don't try too hard with the talk. There's not a lot we need to say – the offer of free beer is lure enough – and soon our tankards have been drained and two pairs of thirsty eyes turn upon us again.

'Sirs, another round?' I raise my tankard.

'Aye, another round!' says the driver, whose name we've learned is Hawkins. He's balding, strongly built – if a little overweight – and has a crooked nose.

'I don't mind if I do,' says Tox, the driver's mate. We learn that the two of them not only collect the bodies from Mort and Jarvis but also dig the graves in the Tobias Field. ''Tis thirsty work digging those graves. The ground is baked hard and the day hot.'

'Grim, too, I'd venture.' I rise to fetch the drinks. 'Ain't you afeard of ghouls an' such?'

'Not any more. You gets used to it after a while.'

When I return, Josiah, Hawkins and Tox are talking animatedly like old friends. I catch another rare glimpse of Silus Garroway in his natural habitat, for here he is at ease, at home, and it's a reminder that the Josiah Mingle I know and work with is but a veneer, wafer-thin and fragile.

'So, you collect the dead and bury 'em,' says Josiah. 'Don't you need some kind of paperwork for that? I mean, not just anyone can go out and bury a body, surely?' He laughs.

'I deals with all the papers.' Tox taps the left side of the waistcoat over his chest. 'Keep 'em here, all safe an' sound till the job's done.'

'What happens to them then?'

'I sign my name to say they've been buried and the papers go back to Mort and Jarvis for filing.'

'What papers are they, exactly?' I ask, trying to sound nonchalant.

'Oh, the usual – certificates of death an' notices of interment,' he says.

'You can read, then.' In any other circumstance this might sound like a rude or condescending thing to say, but among threaders, many of whom are illiterate, it is acceptable.

'Enough to get by,' says Tox, proudly stroking his pointed beard.

'Notice of interment?' asks Josiah, trying to mask his concern. We have no notice of interment for either of our two.

'Aye, you can't go burying folk without a notice of interment,' Tox chortles. 'That could land you in a whole heap of trouble.'

# 13

# Notice of Interment

*In which Banyard and Mingle visit Digger's End*

Several rounds later, Hawkins and Tox are rolling merrily in their seats. Josiah and I grab the chance to talk privately at the bar while waiting to order. We throw glances over our shoulders at the contentedly drowsy pair of gravediggers. A few more ales and they'll be too drunk to know where they are. Free drinks will do that to a poor man. Josiah and I have watered down our beer and spilt much of it onto the thresh when their eyes were turned away.

'What are we going to do?' asks Josiah. 'We don't have any notices of interment!'

'We'll just have to create some. Smile. You look too sombre, as though you're trying to solve a problem.'

'I *am* trying to solve a problem. We can't just magic up a pair of documents. It would take a day to get more forgeries from Ranskin.'

'I know. We need to change the plan. I'll have to forge them myself.'

'How are you going to do that? You don't even have paper or ink.'

'I'll ride back to the office. Buy them a few more drinks. I'll go and copy out the documents. All that's needed is a master to work from and Tox has plenty of those in his waistcoat pocket. I just need to take one when he's not aware. When they're good and drunk, drive their cart to Digger's End and I'll meet you there as soon as possible.'

Josiah grunts. 'Right. I'm to take a cartload of corpses to the Tobias Field in the witching hour. Alone. Can't wait.'

'We can switch places, if you like. How are you at counterfeiting documents?'

He shrugs and throws me a resigned look.

'I'd choose another way if there was one, believe me,' I say.

We order drinks and carry them back to our companions, keeping our empty tankards.

'Listen,' says Tox, his voice slurred. 'We best make this the last one. We still got four bodies to put in the ground before we're to bed.' He takes a fresh tankard and sups.

'As you wish.' I smile. There's not a chance these boys are going to turn down more free ale in this state.

It takes another two rounds before they reach the desired level of witlessness. Josiah and I take one each, supporting them with an arm under their shoulders, and steer them to the door and out into the street.

'... got to ... bury these folk,' slurs Tox, managing a feeble gesture towards the back of their cart. He's the more wakeful of the two. Certainly, Hawkins seems incapable of stringing a coherent sentence together. They're drunker than I imagined so I adapt the plan.

'It's all right, Mr Tox. We're going to finish the job for you. It's the least we can do,' I say, delving into the inside pocket of his tatty waistcoat. 'Here, let me take these. We'll deal with everything. Don't you worry.' I take the papers, stuffing them into my pocket.

For a few moments we loiter until the street is empty before quickly helping them up into the back of their cart where they can rest alongside the dead. They don't seem to notice the other bodies and they're asleep almost before their heads hit the boards. Josiah and I transfer the two corpses from our cart into theirs and drag the tarpaulin over the lot; eight sleepers lying shoulder to shoulder, though six shall never wake.

'Up you go, Joe. I don't think we'll need those documents after all.'

'Right you are.'

He clambers up into the driver's seat and takes the reins.

I climb up to drive our cart. We release the brakes, flick the reins and move the carts off down the road as the darkness swallows us.

The Tobias Field is quiet as we approach, hooves marking a staccato heartbeat upon the baked surface of the dirt road. It takes us a while to locate the black shape of the spoil heap where Hawkins and Tox have dug out a long grave pit earlier in the day. Josiah huddles in the driver's seat of his cart, silhouetted against the velveteen blush of the sky. There are stars out tonight – thousands of them – and away from the city watch lamps, they shine all the brighter.

There are lanterns hanging from hooks on the front of the carts but we don't bother lighting them. Our eyes have already adjusted to the gloom and we're in a hurry to end this, and to do so without attracting attention.

Josiah peers around the Tobias Field and shivers before making the sacred sign.

'It's all right, Joe. There's nothing here that can harm you.'

'That's what you say.' He descends to join me at the rear of the grave diggers' cart.

We throw back the tarpaulin, releasing a foul stench, a toxic cocktail of alcohol vapours and the fumes of decaying flesh. Stepping back, we wait for the air to clear. We carry the bodies out one after the other and lay them carefully, side by side, in the mass grave, starting with the four legal burials from Mort and Jarvis. In silent accord we treat them with as much respect as we are able and take a moment to stand over them. There seems no reason to rush now. Hawkins and Tox are snoring, slumbering deeply. The city is a soft glow of lamplight at our backs. It feels like someone should say something but we remain silent, observing the neat row of frail bodies, each a tale untold. Each an undervalued soul of great worth. The night hangs about us like a gentle cloak enfolding us in sorrow.

Next, we take Harris and, swinging his body to gain momentum, fling him into the pit to one side of the others. He lands awkwardly, one arm beneath his side, the other sticking out at an obscure angle along with one leg. He looks a complete mess and I consider repositioning him, but don't. It seems fitting because of the mess he's left behind; the mess he's made for others with his life. We leave him and return to the cart for the poor threader girl from Madame Rouge's. For her, we reserve the most care. We are sombre as we carry her to the grave. When we're done, she lies with arms crossed over her chest, feet and ankles neatly together, her face gazing peacefully up into the speckled heavens above.

Again, we wait, simply looking at her. I'm not sure why. It just seems right. Respectful.

I fetch the spades from the cart and toss one to Josiah.

'One moment,' he says, thrusting it into the ground at his feet. He climbs down into the grave and tears a large square portion of grey linen from the shirt we put on Harris. With this he reverently shrouds the girl's face before scrambling back out of the hole.

'There. That's better. I couldn't bury her like that.'

For such an ox-headed lump of muscle, he's a gentle soul at heart.

We dig into the spoil heap and cover the bodies, working until the mound is gone and the grave is noticeable only by a hump in the ground. I take out the paperwork, along with the forged documents.

'We must wake Tox. He has to sign the notices of interment.'

We look doubtfully at the two sleeping in the back of the cart.

'How's he going to do that?' asks Josiah.

'I'm not sure. Give me a hand to get him up.'

We climb up and lift Tox into a sitting position. His head lolls and he continues snoring.

I slap him lightly about the face, left and right. 'Wake up, Mr Tox. It's time to sign the documents.' A few more slaps and his eyes roll open, unfocused and glazed. I find a pen and a vial of ink from his pockets, unstopper the vial and dip the tip, ready to write. Persuading Tox to take hold of the pen is a different matter. He's most uncooperative but eventually his spindly fingers close around the stem, his eyes focus on my face and I guide his hand to the first notice. 'The bodies have been interred. Here, Mr Tox. Can you sign?'

His hand moves slowly across the page, scrawling his name. Painstakingly, we work our way through the four notices of interment and Tox signs them all, his work suitably shaky. That should help him and Hawkins to reach the right bleary-eyed conclusion in the morning: We got blind drunk, buried the bodies, signed the notices, fell asleep, all is well.

They'll never know anything about the two extras we slipped into the mix.

We lay Tox down and I tuck the documents into his waistcoat pocket and, leaving the gravediggers sleeping with the tarpaulin drawn up to their chins like bedsheets, we climb up onto the driver's bench of our cart and head home, hoping with all our might that the entire sorry episode is now behind us.

A new day dawns and it's another hot one, perhaps the hottest this summer. The wind is driving northwards up from Mors Zonam and the Borderlands, bringing a toxic sulphurous taint.

During our walk to the office, a crowling drops to the ground at my feet like a bad omen. Jinkers gets hysterical if any fall near him. On days like these we often find crowlings and burmas – those tiny fast flitters that join us for the summer – and even sea larks fall from the sky, sickened and perishing from the fumes carried high overhead. I stoop to cradle the fragile crowling. It tries to move; the faintest flick of a wing. I stroke its sleek head and it expires in my hand.

'Poor bird,' says Josiah.

We walk on only to meet Miss Clara Avard, shaded beneath her lace parasol a few paces from Mysteries Solved. Today she is in a striking deep-red. She offers her hand.

'Why, Mr Banyard, I do believe you may be following me.' She smiles beguilingly, her eyes alighting on Josiah.

From the corner of my eye I see him smiling back with great enthusiasm. 'Miss Avard, I swear I would never do such a thing. Please, may I introduce my business partner, Mr Mingle?'

Her delicate fingers look ridiculously small in his great paw as he bows. He stops short of kissing the back of her hand.

'Charmed,' he says.

Try not to drool on your shirt, Joe. He holds on a moment too long.

'What brings you to this side of town?' I ask.

'I'm meeting a friend for breakfast.'

'Not Mr – '

'Gouldstone? No, you needn't worry. Well, I really must be going. It was nice to meet you, Mr Mingle.' She walks on, but stops and turns.

'Mr Banyard, I'm holding a masked ball at Steadholm House on Saturday. Would you and dear Mr Mingle care to attend?'

'Why, yes. I'm sure we'd be delighted,' I say.

'Very well. I shall have an official invitation delivered to you. Your address?'

'Ninety-six Bunson Street. Or you may use the office.' I hand her my card.

'Mysteries Solved. My word, you're a detective! How very quaint. Goodbye for now, Mr Banyard, Mr Mingle.' She lets the words trail like bait in water, waves a gloved hand and saunters away towards Rook's Bridge.

We watch her high heels sidestep another moribund crowling as she leaves and Josiah shifts focus to me. '*Dear Mr Mingle*? You didn't mention her.'

'There was not much to mention. She met with Gouldstone.

145

I warned her about him.'

'I'm sure you did.'

'That was odd.'

'What was?' asks Josiah.

'Meeting a friend for breakfast in Crowlands? Old Camdon or Tower Bridge would be more her scene. I'd expect...' I notice Josiah is staring at me as though I'm bonkers. 'Never mind.'

At the office we're greeted by a scowl from Lizzy. 'You're late.'

'Late for what?'

'For work. Really, Mr Banyard, you're supposed to set a good example when you're the boss.' She's serious.

Josiah laughs so I glare at him.

He sobers up. 'We're late because we were out working into the early morning on a case. We've barely slept.'

Good answer. I think, *There's not much she can say to that.*

'Out working? Where, exactly? And on what case? The green ink letter?'

I realise I've failed to update the others on the case. They must be wondering what's been going on. It's easier to work a case between Josiah and myself because more people means more people to manage, but I did include the others earlier, so I feel obliged to call another meeting.

'Lizzy, please gather everyone for two o'clock tomorrow. We'll talk about everything then.'

'Ebadiah included?'

'Yes, please.'

'As you wish, Mr Banyard.'

We hide ourselves in the case room.

'Was that wise?' asks Josiah. 'We've barely made any progress on the case because of Harris and his stupid dog.'

'I know, but I think it prudent to keep them in the loop with the little we *do* know.'

'You do realise tomorrow is Thursday...'

'What of it?'

'Sweep's day at Dover Palace.'

'Ah! Then we must prepare. The disguises won't be a problem. Have Ebadiah gather the gear. We'll need a map. I'll source that. For now we should get back on to Gouldstone and Cullins. With everything that's happened, we've lapsed and they could be getting up to anything.'

We split up, Josiah taking Gouldstone while I look for Cullins. I find him, rather unfortunately, when we run into each other on the corner of Orleon Drive and Mason Street. He's carrying an armful of legal folders which our impact scatters like leaves of the wind.

'Oh, it's you.' He glares. 'I might have known.'

We race to collect the folders and the papers that have spilled. He snatches them from my hand as I return them to him.

'Mr Cullins, I'm sorry.'

'Pah! Sorry? You should be. I know you're watching me, Banyard. Your oaf was most indiscreet the other day at the soup shop. You should find yourself a smaller lug-wit to do your bidding, one less notable.' He shuffles pages into place, tucking them back into a folder. 'It's strange – your man – doesn't look much like a silker. Built more like a labourer, I'd say.' He stoops to grab a stray sheet. 'Anyway, the point is, keep him away from me or there'll be consequences. Understand?'

'Watching you? Why, what a ridiculous notion. I can assure you – '

'I care not one jot for your assurances, sir. You're a threader-loving embarrassment to the silker name. You're a traitor to your own kind, boy!'

'Mr Cullins, I must – '

'Want to know why I hate them? Why they should be kept well and truly suppressed?' He continues before I can answer. 'There was a time when I wondered of them, liked them, even.' Here he slows, a shadow of melancholy creeping in to mingle with the coldness of his eyes, which seem to darken. It doesn't last long. 'When I was younger, I befriended one of them. Let

147

him join me in my games. Back then I saw no reason for the chasm between us and them. He soon disabused me of that notion.' His eyes flash emerald. 'I was rather keen on a girl, you see. He knew it, of course, but that didn't stop him. He stole her from me. A firmer stab in the back I've never felt.'

'And ever since you've judged the entire threader population as worthless cheats because a friend of yours happened to fall in love.'

Cullins turns purple with rage and looks as though he might explode.

'Why, you threader-loving dog! I knew you wouldn't understand, you scoundrel.' He wags a finger at me aggressively. 'You crossed me once and I was most lenient on you. I shan't be so a second time, mark my words. You should be worried, Banyard. I have people. I'm watching you.' He points in my face, spits on the ground at my feet and narrows his eyes before stalking away. 'Just keep out of my way, Banyard. You've been warned.'

# 14

# Secrets of Dover Palace

*In which Banyard and Mingle sweep chimneys*

In the hidden room of our office we dress as sweeps. We carefully glue on false beards and don unkempt wigs, pinning them firmly in place. We darken the skin around our eyes to give them an unhealthy, sunken appearance and, with the same make-up, add hollows to our cheeks.

We're finishing up when Ebadiah arrives, arms loaded with sweeping rods and brushes.

'Here ya go. Tuppence for the day. Half a crown for the week. The sheets are outside.'

'The day will suffice.' I toss him the coins and we set about collecting soot from the brushes to rub onto our clothes and skin.

'So, you're sweeps today, then? How's that gonna work?'

'What do you mean?' asks Josiah.

'Sweeps have boys, don't they? The ones what go up the chimneys. Where's your boy?'

Josiah turns to me. 'The lad has a point.'

We hire the same cart as before and drive out to Dover Palace with around four hours to spare before our meeting back at the office. That should be enough time to infiltrate the grounds and have a good poke around inside. It's a risky business and I figure the longer we hang around in there, the greater the chance we'll be discovered. Ebadiah rides in the back of the cart with the rods, brushes and soot sheets, whistling a tavern song. It's one of his favourites. The words are something like *Oh, Mary-Lee, Oh, Mary-Lee, Come home now, I won't beat you no more.* Dressed in rags with his limp and his bad eye, he'll add a certain look to our ensemble that I think must now be wholly convincing.

Other sweeps have already made a start when we arrive in the expansive circle of road before the tradesman's entrance. The loop encircles an exquisite fountain where stone maidens gather fish in baskets. Beyond this, the west wing adjoins the main house with a large arched door that looms over a broad, central set of steps. It's a smaller door to one side at ground level that we and the other sweeps use. Josiah shoulders the rods and brushes while Ebadiah and I split the soot sheets between us. We leave the cart in a line of other carts out on the road and enter, nodding merrily to anyone we meet along the way. Inside we find a pasty-faced butler directing sweeps to their designated rooms and it's easy for us to join the line and receive orders. He looks us up and down, a brow rising. For a moment I think we've been rumbled, but rather than question us, he directs us in a haughty voice that would suit a high-born silker.

'Third floor. The Nave Corridor. All twelve rooms.' He waves us aside. 'Next.'

We shuffle off, wondering where the servants' stairs are, and follow the sweeps ahead of us until they turn into a deep-blue carpeted passageway ending in steep, narrow steps. We pause.

'Are we actually going to sweep the chimneys?' asks Josiah.

'Yes. Once we've settled in, we can investigate if things go well.'

'Third floor it is, then,' says Ebadiah. 'Just so's you know – I ain't goin' up no black hole stack.'

The next hour is hard, dirty work. The air is heavy with soot as we shove a brush up chimneys and add the rods one at a time.

A servant pokes his head into one of the rooms we're working to check on us, but soon leaves. We collect soot in sheets, knotting their corners together to make bundles.

In each room we search for anything that may be pertinent to our investigation, but the Nave Corridor seems to be full of guest bedrooms and drawing rooms, all vacated and, on the whole, cleared of personal possessions. Now and then we find a hairbrush or a chest of clothes, drawers with more garments and trappings, but nothing of real interest, and it feels like we're in the wrong place. We begin to run low on sheets.

'What now?' asks Josiah, glowering, his face blackened. I can tell he feels the same frustration. He's only not complaining because this was his idea.

'We can take these down and dump the soot in the cart,' I say, gesturing to the bundles. 'Whoever goes will have a chance to snoop around along the way, report back.'

'Fine. I'll go first.' He seems keen to take a break from sweeping.

'Did your contact give you any idea where we should search?' I take a map of the palace from my pocket, unfold it and flatten it for us to study. We gather round. 'There must be hundreds of rooms. We can't search them all.'

Josiah nods. 'Well, the servants' quarters are on the highest floors so I guess we can forget about those. The kitchens, laundry rooms and such will likely be on the ground floor but towards the edges. Yes, here and here.' He points to areas on the map.

'And these wings look the same as each other, all guest rooms.'

'So, what we want is here in the middle,' says Ebadiah, placing a sooty finger in the centre of the ground floor plan. 'That's where the king lives and, all around him, the rest of the nobs.'

Josiah exhales a long puff of air. 'I say we finish up here and get down there. No one's going to check on us now. There must be fifty sweeps working. Who's going to check on them all when

151

the nobs aren't even in?'

I have to agree. 'All right, take some bundles. If anyone questions you, tell them you're lost, that you're looking for the west wing.'

'We're splitting up, then,' says Josiah.

'We'll cover more ground that way, but you take Ebadiah, work together. I'll see you back here in an hour.'

Josiah and I consult our pocket watches.

Ebadiah and Josiah grab two bundles each and slip out into the corridor. I pocket the map, collect an armful of bundles and, after a few moments, open the door to peer both ways down the empty corridor. Assured that no one is around, I step out and walk quickly deeper into the palace. It's a maze of blue-carpeted corridors, vestibules, stairs and landings. After an age of wandering, all the time working my way down and towards the centre of the palace, I reach the first of several grand halls where the carpets change to red. The high vaulted ceilings are elaborately decorated with geometric mouldings and striped with lines of gold leaf. Footsteps in a nearby passage grow louder. I run across the hall and enter another corridor. At the end there's another elegant hall, this one painted with naturalistic forms stretching up from the floor all around the walls, patterns of woven branches and sprays of leaves. It's as though I'm in a forest of tall trees. A most impressive room, but I'm not here to admire the surroundings. Pressing on.

In the next passage I hear people approaching and poke my head into a room to check it's empty before slipping inside. This room is an extensive library and it's hard to not get lost in the wonders it holds. I allow myself several minutes to scan the first few stands of books. The shelves reach all the way to the ceiling and cover every inch of wall, as well as the twenty or so stands that protrude in rows from the walls out towards the middle of the room. I walk to what I hope is a cataloguing system in a central cabinet and open drawer after drawer, stopping only when I find G and a section titled *Gawpers*.

There's a comprehensive collection on the subject – books

I've never seen before, books I didn't know existed. I could spend several contented days, if not weeks, in study here. One edition in particular catches my eye: *Of Kings and Gawpers*. I climb a wheeled ladder to find the book and bring it down to read, delving into its pages. In the list of contents there's a chapter titled 'King Osbert', a name inextricably linked with gawpers.

I check my pocket watch again. Fifteen minutes has flown by already. My eyes rest upon the filing cabinet. No time to lose. I rifle through the *Gawper* listings and pull out a handful of the most interesting catalogue cards before hurrying around the shelves, collecting as many as I can carry. Most are leather-bound and comprise parchment pages. Several appear to be ancient and are in danger of disintegrating. They are heavy, but wrapped in the soot sheets and tucked under my arm, they're easy to carry and well concealed. I'm not convinced this is the part of the palace we're looking for. Every room is devoid of personal possessions. Onwards.

A passage takes me straight out and to the right and there, at the end where another corridor transects, stands a single sentry guarding a door. This must be it, surely, the entrance to the royal residences, the Dover apartments included. I tuck myself into the nearest recess, a closed doorway, and wonder how I might pass the guard. Coming from a doorway almost opposite mine a short way further down the passage, a hiss startles me. There Josiah hides, placing a finger to his lips.

I frown, and gesture with my palms out: *What now?*

In answer, he takes the chain of his watch and lifts it from his waistcoat pocket. He regards me with a blank look, which I return.

Oh, charades! Good, because that's just what this situation needs.

He swings the watch gently from side to side.

Now I'm unsure. Is it charades, or is he trying to hypnotise me?

He jabs a finger towards the guard at the end of the hallway, a gesture that leaves me none the wiser. He holds out his palms as though to stop me. All this he does within the shadow of his recess so as not to alert the guard to our presence.

I suppose he means 'Wait', so I wait, though I don't know what for. Not until Ebadiah walks out from the transecting passage at the end and, in full view, approaches the guard. The lad speaks to the guard, who then leaves his post with Ebadiah, gesticulating and pointing down the hallway. They walk out of sight.

'Now!' hisses Josiah, and we head for the door.

We're through in no time, our new surroundings sumptuous. The walls are panelled in dark oiled oak, huge paintings of old royals in grand costume watch with leaden eyes from the walls and crystal chandeliers gleam high overhead. The carpet is plush velvet.

'This is more like it,' says Josiah, checking around and knocking softly on another door before opening it to peer inside.

'What's the story with Ebadiah?'

'He'll meet us outside later. The lad did good. Told the guard about a broken window.'

'Did *well*. Was there a broken window?'

'There is now.'

I follow him in. The room is much smaller than the grand halls and the library, though for a bedroom it's still enormous. We make a quick search but find nothing of interest, except there's enough jewellery in a ruby-encrusted box on the dressing table and elegant gowns in the wardrobe to say with certainty that a woman is staying here. We leave the jewels and the box.

The opulence of this place is startling, even for a silker like me. It's bedazzling and my mind plays tricks. For a blink, I see a royal child, clothed in splendour and feasting at a fine table overloaded with all manner of delicacies. Another blink and a very different child cowers in the corner of a broken-down shack, malnourished and sickly, dressed in rags and sobbing for a crust of bread. Here is a joyous scene: a group of ladies and gentlemen join in song around a grand piano beneath sparkling chandeliers. They quaff wine, dance and laugh. When I look again, I'm on a street in Southside where the crowd is a drunken threader mob jeering around a bloody fistfight. A fighter lies dead on the road, his hard-earned wager null and void.

Next, we enter a gentleman's room. There are a few books about the place, mostly botanical journals and studies. He's a whisky drinker, a connoisseur to be sure, but other than the expensive liquor, there's nothing much of interest.

And so, it goes on. Room after room.

I'm beginning to think we're wasting our time when we find a door bearing a name engraved into a golden plate.

'Earl of Chathamshire,' says Josiah. 'Sounds royal.'

'Let's take a look.'

Chathamshire's door opens into a splendid study with many fine books and a pair of grand Wexfords. Dark wood and green leather greet us wherever we look. We survey his belongings and search the other rooms that lead on from the study, but again find no artefacts or anything that might suggest a connection with the Order of Lithobates or anyone pertinent to the case.

Earl of Westmarshton. Baroness Longarton. Duke of Buckingfenshire. The royal quarters go on and on, and time is slipping away.

'We're stretching our luck. We should go.'

We halt before a door that reads 'Earl of Daggonshire'.

'Just one more,' says Josiah. 'I've got a good feeling about this one.'

And so we knock and, when there's no reply, enter.

Daggonshire's study is perhaps the richest we've encountered. There's a marvellous collection of books, and one entire bookcase is devoted to gawpers. Perhaps Josiah is right. Perhaps this time we'll hit upon something of real interest. I dump my library books onto a claret-red grand Wexford that sits behind a broad mahogany desk with a matching leather inset.

The dark wood panelling around the room is luxurious. There are several doors leading to other rooms: a bedroom, a bathroom and a sitting room. Josiah searches these while I peruse the books, paintings and drawers. There's a lantern at one end of the desk and a case containing a fine pair of pistols, Charlemagnes – collector's pieces, no doubt – and a rack of equally desirable rapiers crossed on the wall. At the other end of the desk is a collection of crystal flasks, brandy, whisky and the like, presumably. I unstopper one to take a sniff. An exquisite cherry brandy. I take a large gulp. It's every bit as delicious as I imagined. I steal another slug before replacing the stopper.

A walnut writing bureau in the Morracibian style catches my eye. Correspondence, perhaps? It's locked but I soon find the key on a hidden ledge beneath the lower drawer on one side. The drawers hold all the usual writing paraphernalia: quills, pencils, paper and parchment, several penknives, blotting sand, a variety of inks in their respective bottles.

There. Green ink! A whole bottle of the stuff.

This focuses my mind and I realise I was not truly expecting to find anything. I'd already decided this was a wasted venture. But here it is. Green ink. I wonder how relevant it is, though; after all, there is also a bottle of blue ink, one of black, one brown and one red. Why, then, should I find it at all notable that this one is green?

I take a blank paper from another drawer, dip a pen in the green ink and write my name. I fold and pocket the paper for later analysis. What else is concealed within the desk? I find letters, around a hundred or more, certainly too many to study here and now. Oh, for an entire day in here so that we might do this properly! And for time in which to check all the other rooms of this royal warren.

There are letters from other royals, letters from politicians and city bigwigs; the list is copious and impressive. I rifle through, checking only names and titles, hoping to strike lucky with a connection to the case. After fifty or so I hear the brandy calling and cross the room for another taste and, feeling heady, lean against the panelling at my back. There's an audible click and the sound of a hidden weight falling, the whir of a mechanism, and to my right a panel of the wall recedes to reveal a Logg & Farrow safe. I press the wall where my shoulder touched and the mechanism stirs again, concealing the safe. A further touch and the wall reopens. These safes have a single large dial at the centre of the door which, with the correct application of a six-figure digit, releases the lock. I press my ear to the door and turn the dial, hoping for an audible click when the correct number engages, but each click is the same as the last. A good safe, is the Logg & Farrow.

It's pointless. I close the secret wall panel and return to the letters but, halfway through them, have a thought sparked by the hidden safe. It seems Daggonshire is a fan of secret doors. I begin searching immediately, knocking on walls, around the fireplace, testing every lamp and ornament to be sure it isn't a lever or trigger. It's the wall lamp to the right of the fireplace that does it. Without a sound and, with the gentlest of touches, the lamp swings downwards, pivoting from a hidden hinge at its mount. There's a click, the whir of a mechanism, and a panel before me opens to reveal a new passageway.

'Josiah.'

He appears in the entrance to the bedchamber. 'I didn't find any... Oh.'

The passage is dark. We light the lantern and, with trepidation, enter.

# 15

# The Passage

*In which bad things happen*

Our lantern lights the way, more carpeted floor and panelled walls. Ahead, a door stands closed at the end and, with ominous footsteps, we approach. Tremulously I test the doorknob, open the door and walk in. Cast in the soft yellow light of the lantern, objects reach out to us from the gloom, from the corners and planes of this hidden chamber. They are strange and obscure in the shifting shadows, both monstrous and macabre. We search but find no gas lamps.

Why would someone construct a room so? A clandestine space that may be viewed only through the dim cast of candle or lantern? It seems peculiar. There is a smell in here also, an unhealthy, stale smell that reminds me of something dead, like the dusty tang of stuffed animals. Josiah finds a second lantern and we light it to better see. Paintings spring from the walls. I close on a large dark image in a black frame: a gawper, eyes of white flame glowing, its body partially obscured by a spray of spindle trees. Its form is tall but hunched, its arms poised as though in preparation for some deadly deed. Other details are vague, painted with clever dabs of light that hide what cannot be shown in certainty: its outline, its facial features, its lower half. I hold the lantern up close, hoping to discern a pair of feet, a stump, tentacles, anything that might inform me of what is there, hidden in dark, time-cracked oils – yet see nothing of substance. It's as if the gawper simply dissolves into the tuffets of the ground.

Josiah mutters close by. 'He sure likes his gawpers, this fellow.'

I turn, wondering what else he's found, and recoil. In front of Josiah a gawper reaches out from the corner to my left, grasping to take a hold. This one is not painted and flat but sculpted from hardwood, glossy and polished, perhaps a half-sized figure with white glass for eyes. It, too, has been cut in such a way as to obscure the lower details.

'What is this place?' asks Josiah.

There are shelves of books and heraldic crests on the walls, niches with odd ornaments and relics. We check them all in turn. The books appear to cover two subjects only: the ancestry of the royal lines, and gawpers. The only subject I'm aware of that connects these two is King Osbert, the man who was king when the Order of Lithobates was created.

On a plinth at one side up against the wall, another gawper statue, this one smaller, takes centre stage flanked by a dozen candles. Rising up and over it, enshrining it, is an intricate arch carved from dark wood. Around its sculpted vines and leaves, niches hold more of the unusual artefacts. There is a piece of something that looks like blackened seaweed. There are small bones, engraved stones, teeth that are too long to be human, clay pots and bowls patterned with incised lines and earthy tones of paint. All of them appear ancient.

Stepping back to take it all in, I think aloud. 'It's a gawper shrine.'

I make a quick study of the crests along the wall and find one each for the Daggonshire line, the Dover line, the Hardlangate line. The rest are of other noble houses, though less royal. Notably, set in the middle of the wall and glowering over all else, is a portrait of King Osbert himself.

I open the drawer of a side unit and take out documents, squinting at their secrets in the lantern half-light.

'Listen to this. It's a letter written about the king's brother, Nathanuel Dover, from a Dr Wickfield. "Dear Lawrence" – presumably the Earl of Daggonshire – "Further to my previous notes, I must report an escalation in the mental decline of the patient. Indeed, the increased instances of psychosis are a sign for great concern. Many patients who exhibit a decline of this nature have been subsequently observed to develop a secondary cognitive disfunction leading to a morbid sensibility and violent outbursts. It is my diagnosis that Lord Dover is suffering from schizophrenia, a condition commonly termed the shattered mind, in which an individual may exhibit two or more contrasting personalities. I cannot state the following strongly enough. The patient must be committed to a mental institution immediately."'

'Sounds like ol' Dover's got some issues.'

'Yes, and the Order was created to protect the king. I think that perhaps they are still doing so, and to protect the royal name they would need to keep Dover's illness quiet. There are more letters here.' I paw through them. 'Lots of them. All from doctors and surgeons.'

'Are they all about Dover?'

'It appears so.'

The musty odour grows stronger.

'What is that? Do you smell it?'

Josiah sniffs at the air and follows the scent over to a tall cabinet. 'It's coming from here.'

We raise our lanterns and discover a morbid object, the severed hand of some long-dead creature. Creature? Perhaps it was a man at some time, but now it is shrivelled and leathered, the skin dry and splitting like that of an ancient mummy. But then again, perhaps it was never part of a man, for the withered fingers seem too long to be a man's, the whole hand is overly large, despite its state of decay, and it is tipped with thick claws rather than nails.

'I don't like it.' Josiah takes a step backwards.

'It's the hand of a…'

'The hand of a what?'

I catch a movement in my peripheral vision, feel a sudden impact to the back of my head. The world rolls black as the floor rushes to greet me.

# 16

# Bones of Mors Zonam

*In which Banyard and Mingle find themselves transported*

Darkness. Firstly, I'm aware of a hot, parched sensation in my mouth and throat. There is sand or grit on my tongue and between my teeth. My tongue feels swollen, my lips cracked. I can feel cloth fastened tight across my face and drag my head against my shoulder to dislodge it. The blindfold falls away. Opening my eyes, I blink and squint. The light is extreme, like the heat. A roiling sun glares low in the sky, blindingly bright over the orange-reds of desert stone and dunes. Shadows are long and there's a sulphurous reek in my nostrils. I feel it in my lungs.

I am not alone. At the edge of my vision a shape moves with a groan. I lift my head for a better look. Who is it? And why can't I move my hands? I try to push against the sand to rise, but realise they are tied behind my back. The effort of moving does something unpleasant to my head. It pounds. My vision blurs. My consciousness falters. Darkness enshrouds me once again.

I wake a second time. Josiah's close face, slick and hot in the orange glow, peers down at me. He has me in his arms, lifting my shoulders from the sand.

'Wake up, Mr Banyard. Wake up.'

'Joe... Josiah, where... What...'

'Mors Zonam, I'm guessing. Wherever we are, it's melting-hot, hotter than anywhere I've ever been before. And it stinks. Here, let me untie you.' On the shirt around his neck and armpits are vast patches of sweat.

He leans me on my side and reaches behind to loosen the rope that's lashing my wrists together. With my altered view I can see the rope he has already worked free from his hands lying discarded on the sand. I notice our feet are also bound.

I spit the grit from my mouth. 'Water?'

He shakes his head solemnly. I close my eyes and let my head rest on the wind-rippled dune.

He finishes freeing my hands and we both work on releasing our feet.

'They've left us with nothing,' he says, staring at a pair of cart tracks that must surely lead back to the Borderlands and, beyond, to civilisation. Already the granular surface is absorbing the depressions and I realise in an hour or two, half a day at the most, there may cease to be any visible sign of the cart's passing. The Toral wind might have obliterated all. There's a faint breeze now, but not a cooling one. Rather, it is hot, like the air from a furnace.

'They must have knocked us out and drugged us.' I scan the surrounding hellscape. 'We must mark the way. Make an arrow, a line or something to help us find our way back.'

'We have the ropes.'

'Good. We'll use them until we can find something better.'

'Who did this to us, Mr Banyard?'

'The Earl of Daggonshire and his cronies, I shouldn't wonder. Them or someone else from the Order.'

We scan the terrain. There are stones littered here and there, and a few sandstone bluffs that break the monotony of the dunes. 'Quickly. The longer we remain here, the less chance we have of escaping.'

We mark arrows with the ropes, one on each of the wheel tracks.

'Now gather some stones. We'll make the arrows more permanent.'

We do this and pause to assess our handywork.

'Won't the sand swallow the stones?' he asks.

'Quite possibly. A sandstorm could cover them in a matter of minutes. More stones!'

We gather more and deposit them on top of the first layer until we've built two low, arrow-shaped walls.

'That should give us a day or so, I would think. If we get lost, we can try to find these rocks again.'

'There,' he points to the nearest high intrusion of rock. 'We should make a sign on that also. Somewhere where the sand will not cover so easily.'

'Good thinking, Joe.'

We make a pile of stones in the shape of an arrow on top, pointing in the same direction as the cart tracks. It's a high point in the landscape. Hopefully it will remain so.

'What next?' asks Josiah, surveying our bleak surroundings.

'Shelter from this hideous heat, and water, if there is such a thing.'

There is no real refuge to be found as even the sand in the shadows is hot to the touch. It feels like we're being slow-roasted. 'We have to move.'

Nodding, I check to see if our executioners have left my pocket watch. They have. It could make all the difference, I think. I pull it from my waistcoat, give it a wind and take a bearing. It is nearing eight o'clock. Aligning the hour hand with the sun, I estimate south to be the direction of the ten on the dial. That makes sense because the cart tracks lead off in the opposite direction, which should be north. I wonder how long we've been out. Half a day? A day and a half?

'We're dead men, Mr Banyard.'

'Oh, come now. We mustn't give up, Josiah. One must never give in. It makes sense to search in the direction of home.'

Josiah nods sullenly.

'This way, then.'

We set off, following the tracks.

Half an hour of walking brings us to a pitiful sight. To one side of our path lies an old sand-blasted cart with a ruined wheel. One side of the cart is half swallowed by the dunes. The once-white canvas canopy is tattered and grey, flapping on the breeze, but it provides the biggest patch of shade we've seen so far. We walk to it only to find the ragged bones of the driver still huddled inside. Ahead of the wreck lie a scatter of horse bones.

Josiah makes the sacred sign.

I take the old canteen from around the driver's neck, check inside. It's as dry as his bones. All the same, I take it in case we find a water source.

Who was this man? A threader, paid to bring men out here to their deaths, caught out when the wheel broke? A short way beyond the cart are the scant remains of yet another poor soul. The skull sits alone, its empty sockets forever watching the way.

To say that nothing grows in Mors Zonam would be, strictly speaking, untrue. There are stumpy desert trees sparingly dotted around the sandscape, most of them dry and brown or dead and grey, without a single leaf or spine. Now and again we pass an exception to the rule, a spiny tree with touches of green, small but undeniable signs of life. Eventually we're driven to pause from our exhausting trudge to investigate, for where there's life there must surely be water. That's the theory, anyway.

We dig in the heated sand, follow the scrawny roots down and down until they disappear through a crack in a layer of rock.

'There is water below,' I say. 'The roots must go deep beyond the strata to an underground stream or lake. To a patch of damp sand, at least.'

'I'm sure you're right, Mr Banyard, but we can't dig through solid stone. Not with our bare hands.'

The sun closes on the horizon.

'Twill be night soon. Let's hope we'll get some shelter.'

'Indeed.' It's the only positive thought between us so we let it rest there for a while, floating in the hot vapours.

Thirsty and exhausted, we watch the sun drop slowly beyond view and, without thinking, we fall asleep.

I wake in near darkness to unsettling sounds around me. The heat has diminished but is still unbearable. The moonlight is strange, altered by a green glow in the air that intensifies on the horizon, the same sickly light we often observe in the south from the streets of Camdon, although now it's stronger than I've seen it before.

I take bearings, feeling sluggish. Our tracks are still dimly visible in the sand. We were foolish to fall asleep. We could have lost our path. I scramble for stones to mark an arrow before sitting next to Josiah, whose snores sound ragged and dry.

My arrow points north. It must do, because everybody knows Mors Zonam is in the south and we've followed the cart tracks faithfully this far. The sky is clear enough for some stars to shine through. I note them now, finding the Barrow and the three Brightling Stars, and burn an image of their orientation upon my mind. Good. With clear skies, I should now be able to keep us roughly on track day and night. It's small comfort: without water we won't get far.

The animal noises rise and fall, some distant, some not. They chatter and howl, snarl and whine, so many that I'm bewildered. I picture dogs. And monsters. Where were all these creatures during the day? All we saw was shimmering sand, stone and an occasional twig.

A growl close by alerts me. 'Josiah!' I hiss, shaking him awake.

He sits up, peers at me, hears it. 'My head hurts.'

'Mine too, though I fear we've bigger problems. Whatever that is, it's close.'

We rise and arm ourselves with fist-sized stones, before backing away. The sound shifts as though the creature is circling, weighing us, watching. One moment it's on our left, the next, our right. We strain to see it, catching only a flicker of shadow in the murk.

'There!' Josiah points into the night where a pair of jade eyes glower in our direction. The eyes are probably not green. This unnatural glow gives everything the same ghostly hue. The sand is green. The rocks are green. Josiah is green.

Ultimately, it's not the eyes that worry me. It's the teeth.

The beast growls again, its shadowed form stepping towards us.

Josiah makes a sudden run at it, raising a rock in his hand. Gaining speed, he releases a thunderous roar and hurls the stone at the eyes. There's a thump and a whimper, the patter of the stone coming to rest and the creature's retreat. The eyes vanish.

'Come on, Mr Banyard. We'd best go before it comes back. There could be others.'

'We need shelter, Joe, or we'll be devoured long before we die of thirst.'

'Agreed, Mr Banyard.'

For a while we run, stopping only to catch breath, drained of energy, our heads pounding.

'Wait. Where are the cart tracks?' I search for them fruitlessly in the eerie half-light.

'I think we've lost them.'

'Never mind. I can set a rough bearing from the stars.'

Josiah's not listening. He stares into the gloom. 'Look.' He nods towards a dark patch off to one side where the ground appears to roll into a void, as though it's the edge of the world and the land is a liquid that's pouring away. The glow touches nothing beyond this final line of sand but more details emerge as we approach. The dunes drop between slabs of rock, flowing downwards into a deep valley.

Our eyes meet in anticipation.

Caves? Shelter? Water? Perhaps all three!

We hurry down the slope, slipping as it shifts, tripping and rolling until we reach the bottom and the ground flattens. There are a few more of those dried, twisted trees here and the surface is harder, like baked dirt beneath a layer of sand. I take it as a good sign and check our bearing against the stars.

'It seems to run northwards. This way, I think.'

We turn right, which, if I'm correct, should bring us back in line with the tracks we've followed. The banks of the valley undulate with the rise and fall of the dunes and frequent outbursts of rock. We hunt for a cave, for even the slightest cleft in the rock that might offer respite. Often, we spy tracks, strange patterns made by a creature's movements and, frankly, it's terrifying. There are bones down here, too, some scattered, others grouped; the partial remains of unnameable beasts.

I feel liquid run from my brow and, wiping it away, discover I'm sweating blood. 'That's all we need, the scent of blood in the air.'

'But doesn't that – '

'Yes. It only happens when a gawper is near.' And it dawns on me: this is a valley of death. It's more likely to kill us than help us. 'Maybe we should climb out of here.'

Not all the bones are unrecognisable. We pass clusters of human bones, presumably those of condemned threaders who made it this far. A glimpse of our future, perhaps. You swallow hard in this place. Fumes burn your throat and irritate your lungs, and there's a quiet desolation that slips with ever-increasing spirals over your soul. The longer you stay, the deeper your sense of desperation, of desolation, of inescapable doom.

If we're going to die down here, there's something I need to say. 'You know, Joe, I never did apologise for the way I've treated you.'

'What do you mean?'

'The constant corrections. You said it was humiliating. I'm sorry. It's just – '

'I know. I get it. I'm sorry I don't make a better silker.'

'You're better than most. I – '

A shriek rises in the night, high and aggressive. Not a shriek of horror or pain but an attack cry.

'That sounds jolly. Where did it come from?' Josiah searches for the source.

'Close. From over there.' I point ahead.

It sounds again, echoing from the sides of the valley and we turn full circle but find nothing.

'I thought it came from this way.' Josiah points in the opposite direction.

'It sounds hungry. Do you think it's hunting us?'

'I hope not.'

We move on, but following a bend in the valley floor, stop. Up ahead is the shrieker, a monstrous creature the size of a coach – its skin a mottled grey-green, its powerful hind legs hunched – crouching over a second smaller figure that's trapped beneath it on a fall of rocks. The shrieker snaps and lunges at its prey but is hampered by a staff that its prey is holding tight to its throat, keeping it at bay, so that the two creatures are locked in a stalemate.

Josiah tugs my sleeve to draw me away.

'No.' I pull free. There is something happening here that I'm compelled to see. More blood trickles from my temples as I approach.

The shrieker has its victim pinned to the rocks with one of its forelimbs, a bulky arm with an extended claw several feet long that has pierced flesh. The impaled figure turns its head and stretches out a black-clawed hand towards a nearby rock, which jostles unaccountably on the sand. Although beyond reach, the rock rises into the air as though in the hand's thrall and, with a flick of the wrist, dashes against the shrieker's face. The shrieker yelps and rolls its head about, trying to bite, snapping huge jaws that are full of lengthy teeth. I glimpse two sets of eyes over this vicious mouth, one pair close together above the teeth and another higher and set more widely apart. Its head broadens towards the back and ends in a splay of curved horns.

Another pair of eyes focuses my attention, these like white flame that fix upon me now as the pierced creature gawps, its face seemingly black and featureless.

I stare back, leaking blood, as before me the stand-off continues: a gawper fighting for its life, a shrieker for its supper.

The decision rushes straight to my lips as though bypassing my brain. 'Hurry, Joe. We must help!'

Bewildered, he complies.

We scavenge for stones and edge in to throw them. Our aim is good. We pelt the shrieker and the missiles rebound from its head and side, drawing more of those hideous cries and, as we close, it reels and withdraws its long claw from the gawper's shoulder before retreating into the night. We watch in disbelief as its form dissolves into the darkness.

'We did it!'

In a moment, the gawper rises to drift towards us, its full height imposing.

'Run!' says Josiah, but we both feel it: the gawper's power, like a terror that urges you to flee while freezing your bones.

We're going nowhere.

On it comes, staff in hand, the strange fringes of its ragged outline oscillating in the air, and before us it halts. It turns to gaze down at me. I feel its eyes burn into mine, invading, like lances tearing into the very depths of my soul. I stumble on the ground, my body tensing. The blood is flowing now, running from my brow to drip from my jaw and chin. I hear a strangely distant voice, wailing, and realise it is my own. It only lasts a few moments and yet they feel like an eternity.

At last, as though satisfied, the gawper disengages, leaving me to slump back onto the sand. It moves on to Josiah, who drops to his knees, his back arching involuntarily as a look of horror contorts his face. His mouth falls open to release a prolonged cry. The gawper holds its position for several moments, doing what? Deliberating? Judging? I cannot say, but it appears so, because soon it withdraws as though decided and the verdict is damning. It raises a clawed hand ready to strike, a limb that is larger and more powerful than even Josiah's.

'No!' I shout. 'Don't kill him! He helped save you!'

It pauses, turns its terrible gaze back upon me.

*This one has taken life*, it thinks.

I know it thinks this because I hear the words as clearly as if they'd been spoken. I hear the words in my mind. They come like a thought.

'I need him,' I say. 'He's a good man. Please do not destroy him. He is my friend.'

*Out here, your words will get you killed. Only think what you want to say. I will hear.*

'But –'

*Only think, Michael Banyard. No talk.*

I try it.

*Please spare Josiah. Do not kill him!* I think it, good and hard, while wondering if the heat and exhaustion have driven me insane. Is this really happening, or am I suffering some kind of stress-induced delusion? Could it be the fumes, or simply dehydration?

*I cannot*, thinks the gawper. *This one is shrivened and has taken life. This one must die.*

Again, the gawper prepares to strike.

*But he only took a life to save others!*

*A life is a life, Michael Banyard. It is written.*

*Is it?* I think. *He was defending an innocent woman. He was protecting her. And he did not mean to kill.*

The gawper hovers there, thinking, only now it has shut me out of those thoughts, has closed some kind of invisible gate. Rather than striking Josiah, it gawps at him again, closing so that their faces almost touch and, releasing another involuntary sound, Josiah's body crumples to the ground where it stays, unmoving. The flaming eyes turn upon me once more. There's a searing white light, a jolt of pain and everything goes dark.

When I awaken, the sun is breaking cover on the horizon and the temperature already rising. Sweating, I lie on my back looking up at a crimson sky. My head pounds and I'm dying of thirst. Dried blood encrusts my face and has made dark hard patches on my shirt. Rising slowly, I glimpse a pile of grey objects on the sand between Josiah and me. He's still sleeping off the gawper's gaze – that or he's dead. I kick him to see.

'Ahh,' he mutters from his dream. 'You can't have it. It's just a penny dreadful.' He rambles on with a few incoherent dreaming words.

'I wish it were.' My throat is so dry and swollen I can barely speak. It's burning from this acrid air.

I study the grey items and my surroundings. We're still in the flat-bottomed valley, near the tumble of rocks where the gawper was pinned, but now we are tucked in to one side, hidden between the inside corner of the bend and the fallen stones. There are trails in the sand leading from the place where we fell to our current position.

The grey things are rounded, each one roughly the size of a human head. They are stitched from the hide of some shaggy beast I cannot place and they have rough cords made of the same material, like the straps of a bag. Tentatively, I prod one with my finger. It wobbles like a wineskin and I realise – or rather hope – that inside there is water. I rush to lift it and search for a stopper, find one carved of wood, tug it free and sniff at the liquid. It smells of nothing. A good sign. I dip a finger. It feels and looks like water. I put my finger on my tongue.

It is water!

I drink greedily, only pausing to kick Josiah again.

He stirs and looks up. I tip up my waterskin to down another few gulps of sweet liquid. He grabs one and rushes to drink, eventually lolling on the flat of his back, sated.

'We're saved.'

I stopper my waterskin and sling the strap around my shoulder. 'By a gawper, no less.'

Loading ourselves with the other skins, we pause. Beneath the waterskins are two more objects. These are black and made of something else. Taking one, I feel its texture, a rubbery organic material like something cut from a plant. I quickly realise they are shaped to fit snuggly over the lower half of the face, and try one on. They are masks. Pulling straps of the same material into place, I feel an instant relief as the mask filters the air and I take several deep lungfuls. I toss the other mask to Josiah. 'Here, put this on. It helps.'

Refreshed and masked, we set off.

'The sun rises in the east, Joe,' I say, my voice slightly muffled, 'which means north is this way. Perhaps we can persuade some outlaws from the Borderlands to give us a wagon ride to the edge of the city.'

Josiah gazes towards the Borderlands. 'If we make it that far. And if the outlaws don't kill us first.'

# 17

# Green Ink

*In which the ghost writes again*

We walk for three long days until finally the Borderlands lie before us, and stark planes of dusty soil and dry grasses have never looked so good as we trudge the last miles of sand. We are sunburnt, starving and thirsty again, our water having run out several hours ago. Our heads ache with skull-splitting pain. Our lips are dried and cracked, while our minds mock us with conjured images of lakes in the shimmering heat haze that hovers over the land. In a barren gully, still miles south of Holloway, we collapse and rest for a time. The inhabitants here are outcasts from the city, mostly threaders who have chanced a living in this desperate place. We raise ourselves and force our legs to trudge, devoid of energy.

'People,' mutters Josiah, his eyes squinting into the distance.

I look up from my broiling feet to scan the horizon, thinking he's seeing things, but I see them too, a gathering of figures moving slowly across the plane. Yes, they may kill us, but they might as easily choose to help us. We must reach them to find out.

A while later we meet, facing up on a dust road that cuts through a tangled sprawl of stunted trees and brown grass. They stop and stare, a ragtag group of rough folk in ragged clothes: men, women and children. One of the men drags an old battered handcart piled with their meagre belongings, which he lets drop to the ground. He stares at us oddly until we remove our masks.

'Help us!' I call out to them across the space between. 'Do you have water? Any food?'

'We are dying of thirst,' adds Josiah.

'There's a stream two miles north,' one of the men replies with a voice full of distrust. He points in the direction we are travelling. 'You'll see the trees. There's a stream and a small pool. You can drink there. The folk nearby will not harm you.' He seems to be the one in charge of the group. Perhaps they are a family. They keep their distance, nervous of strangers.

'Thank you,' I say.

He ushers the others away from us as they walk on, possibly because we appear to have nothing worth stealing. If his words prove true, I must amend my opinion of Borderlanders. They seem harmless, more amiable than many a silker I've met.

'You think you can walk another two miles?' I ask Josiah.

'We're about to find out,' he mutters.

The truth is he's doing better than I am.

We first notice the distant patch of ashblacks rising from the plane ahead and then the small huts of the Borderlanders away to one side. Venturing nearer, we find the stream and pool just as the man said and hurry to plunge our faces into the cool, clear water, gulping it down. We splash it all over ourselves before Josiah leads the way with a better idea. He throws himself in and floats on his back, sighing. We refill our waterskins, drink until we're bursting and stay at the pool's edge for the night.

At daybreak we gather our freshly loaded waterskins and set off again, giving the modest settlement nearby a wide berth as the low sun cuts pink ribbons across the sky to the east. The air is fresher here, the sulphurous taint almost gone. We walk through the day, happier in the knowledge that we may make it home. We begin to believe it.

It isn't until we skirt Curlston Marsh and reach Holloway that we are able to beg a carriage ride with the promise of payment and we sit in the cabin, relieved to be resting our feet, excited by the thought of the food we may eat when we finally reach home.

We stagger into the house and collapse into chairs while Mother, Willow and Widow Blewett fuss around. Mother deals with the payment and the driver goes on his way.

It feels surreal to be in the luxury of the green room after enduring the horrors of Mors Zonam. Ebadiah brings port and glasses. The grandfather clock chimes 6.30. And I think, *What a comfortable place this is!*

After some dubious explanation as to what befell us – by which I mean we do not tell the honest truth about our sortie into the palace – we down water and several glasses of port followed swiftly by a hearty aurochs stew and half a dozen honey cakes. Josiah devours the food like a half-starved wood hog and the sustenance hits our ravenous bodies like a drug.

Our feet are sore. We are exhausted. We stink. We are a mess, our sweeps' clothes even more grimy and tattered than when we set out for the chimneys of Dover Palace. I'm glad Penney is not here to see us. Or Lizzy, for that matter.

Ebadiah lingers as Mother, the widow and Willow leave us. 'Master Banyard, I have something. Something I learned at the palace.'

'Yes?'

'After I distracted the guard, I got talking with a servant who remembers that missing girl.'

'You mean Tillie Ingham?'

'Aye. The servant told me she thought Tillie was with child when she vanished. Said she hid it well, like, but she could tell all the same.'

'Tillie was pregnant?' I wonder aloud.

'Perhaps that was why she upped and left,' says Josiah, settling back into his chair and closing his eyes.

'Wait a minute. How did the servant know?' I ask.

'Tillie used to work at the palace as a seamstress.'

I'm stunned. This is a revelation. 'Another link to the palace, then! Thank you, Ebadiah. That could prove vital to the case.'

He nods before turning to go, but pauses. 'There's another thing, Mr Banyard. I think men have been watching the office and the house these last few days.'

'What men?'

'A thin fella in a cloth cap. He's been loitering across from the office. There were one or two others hanging around, rough sorts. I can't be sure.'

'Was there a man in a black bowler hat?' I ask, recalling my library tail.

'There was! He's been watching the office, too.'

'No matter.' I thank Edabiah and as he leaves, I wonder who is observing us and why. It could be Cullins, or the Order, who by now must know we are investigating them. Or could it be the ghost? Perhaps it's all of them.

When the hubbub of our return has settled and the others have retired for the night, Josiah and I are left alone in the green room and my mind returns to the palace. I recall taking a sample of the green ink from Daggonshire's study and search my pockets, only to find it's gone. Either they took it from me when we were drugged or I lost it somewhere in Mors Zonam.

'That hand we saw in the secret room,' I say, dabbing ointment onto the smarting skin of my arms and face. 'It was the same. Did you see? It was the same as the gawper's.'

I turn to Josiah but he's already asleep.


Mother wakes me the following morning. I've slept in the armchair and my back feels disjointed. I stretch and try to focus on what Mother is trying to tell me as she waves something blurry in front of my face.

'A letter. Came for you two days ago.' She gives up, ditching the letter on my lap and turning away. 'You need a bath.'

I take the letter and open it, coaxing my bleary eyes to focus.

Green ink. A flowing script. A pristine creamy page.

Josiah shifts next to me in his chair.

'Wake up, Joe. There's another letter.' I read aloud as he stirs.

*Dearest Michael,*

*I see that you have found the industrious Mr Steeler. Kudos to you.*

*By now you must realise who we are dealing with and, I trust, will manage the situation with the gravity it so demands. I write to warn of an impending death. On the third night of Sixthmoon, Eadward Trent will leave the Global Traders Club at midnight. He will leave the steps of the entrance and take a carriage but will not reach his destination alive. Forgive my presumptuousness in passing this charge – unfortunately I am quite powerless to do more than guide a quill upon a page and grow increasingly convinced that I am being watched. There are men in shadows. I fear our common enemy will find me soon. Will you intervene to save a life? Good luck to you, sir. I wish you every success.*

*Yours truly,*
*Demitri Valerio*

Surely I must act upon this news!

'The 3rd of Sixthmoon…'

'That's today,' says Josiah.

'Unless someone prevents it, this Eadward Trent fellow will be murdered this very night! I'm taking this straight to Bretling Draker.'

'Why?'

'Honour demands it. And there's another very good reason: if Eadward Trent is murdered and it's later revealed that we were warned but failed to act…'

'We shall be blamed. Who *is* Eadward Trent, anyway?'

I've heard the name before and I'm pretty sure where. 'One moment.' I hurry to my room, retrieve my pocketbook and quickly return to the green room. One glance through the notes confirms my suspicions. 'I took his name from the Chantrees Register. Eadward Trent is a member of the Order of

Lithobates; at least, he ordered three of the Order's gold rings.'

'But I thought they were the ones doing the killing – them or that Dover fellow.'

'Yes. It's peculiar. Yet I must act, all the same.'

'What's the Global Traders Club?'

'A gentleman's club where the rich like to congregate, an exclusive establishment in Old Camdon.'

'You want me to come?' asks Josiah, looking sunken-eyed and haggard.

I check my pocket watch. It's already approaching eleven o'clock in the morning. 'No. I'll do it. You go to bed. Rest. Eat. We may have another long night ahead.'

Josiah turns in his chair and closes his eyes. 'Right you are, Mr Banyard.'

Washed and dressed in clean clothes, I ride Blink hard to Rook's Bridge with the letter safely stowed in my inner waistcoat pocket. His hooves thunder across the old wooden sleepers of the iron bridge and we're soon racing westwards, through Old Camdon and on to Tower Bridge. The stone bridge there is wide and we cross it swiftly despite the heavy stream of clockwork cars, steam trucks, carriages, and threaders driving pack mules and pulling loaded handcarts. We pass City Hall and bear south, slowing in the street outside the Draker City Headquarters around noon. Inside, I approach the stocky Draker on desk duty in reception.

'Good morning. I must speak with Lord Bretling Draker at once. Kindly tell him Michael Banyard is here on an urgent matter.'

The Draker peers at me with distrust but mutters begrudgingly, 'Wait here,' before disappearing through the rear of his office. He looks mildly surprised when he returns. 'Lord Draker will see you now. This way.' He leads me down a corridor and through various departments to Bretling's office, then raps twice on the door with his knuckles.

'Yes,' calls Bretling from within.

The Draker opens the door and announces, 'Michael Banyard to see you, sir.'

'Very well. Come in, young man. What's all this about?'

It's not the first time I've seen his office and little has changed since I was last here. The walls and cabinets are adorned with his watchman awards and framed imographs of his crime-busting triumphs. The air is blessedly clear this time, the windows wide open, although he seems to take my arrival as an excuse to prime his long curving pipe with a fresh pinch of Old Beauty, which he lights with a Sulphur and smokes as I enter to explain.

'Lord Draker.' I make a brief bow and take the envelope from my pocket. 'This letter was delivered to my address in Crowlands two days ago. It contains a clear warning, telling of a murder that the author believes will take place at midnight tonight.' I hand the letter to him.

'Take a seat, Banyard. Whatever happened to your face?'

I sit opposite him. 'It's just a little sunburn.'

He grunts. The brass buttons of his uniform gleam in the intruding sunlight, bright against the black of his jacket as he unfolds the page and reads to himself.

'Well now, Banyard,' he says when he's done. 'Tell me, why did you wait until now to share this? You say you received it two days ago?'

'It was delivered two days ago but I was delayed and only opened it this morning. I came directly to you.'

'I see. And who is this Demitri fellow? Do you know him?'

'I do not, sir. I rather think it's a pseudonym. Demitri Valerio was a renowned judge of the fourteenth century. Perhaps it has meaning.'

'Indeed. Now you mention it, I do recall the name.'

'What are we to do about Eadward Trent? Surely, he should be warned.'

'Quite. I'll see to that and I'll arrange a Draker escort. See that Trent gets home alive.'

'Very well.' That wasn't too hard. I quite like Bretling.

'I'll have him watched for the next few days and if this supposed murderer appears, we'll take him by the scruff. Banyard, why is this person writing to tell *you* this?' He takes a long drag on his pipe and peers at me through a great cloud of smoke that smells of liquorice and cedar.

For a moment I'm torn, wanting to tell him both everything and nothing about the green ink letters. If Bretling and his Drakers were in part responsible for quashing my initial investigation into my father's death, why should I share details with him now that would bring it all back to mind? Surely, he'd instruct me to drop it again. I sidestep the issue and redirect. 'I really don't know. Do you know this Eadward Trent?'

'Of course. He spends most evenings at the Global Traders Club.'

'What can you tell me about him?'

He watches me with suspicion. 'Why do you ask?'

'Because I wondered why someone would plan his demise and why the author of this letter would choose to warn *me* about it.'

'Trent is a businessman, well connected in the city. He's dabbled in politics. There could be any number of reasons why someone would be out for his blood. Men like him don't rise to greatness without collecting a few enemies along the way.'

'I'm sure you're right.'

'Well, if that's everything, Banyard...'

'Yes.' I rise. 'May I keep the letter?'

'Whatever for?'

'For further study.'

'Very well.' He hands me the letter. 'But don't lose it. I may need it back.'

'I understand. Thank you and good day.'

'Good day, Banyard.'

We shake hands and I leave the office. I'm halfway through the building when I glimpse a storeroom with its door ajar. Through the gap, shelves of boxes are visible. The lettering on the door reads *Unidentified Decedents, Tobias Records*. It's too good an opportunity to miss. I poke my head into the room. No one there. No one to prevent me from taking a quick look.

For the first few minutes I search tensely for files relating to females who fit the general description of Tillie Ingham. It would save considerable time if I could establish that she is, in fact, dead and the condition and whereabouts of her recovered body might reveal much. I begin to relax. It seems no one is returning to the room and I work without interruption for a while, losing track of time. I pay particular attention to the clothes adorning the bodies in the files. As well as the ghastly imographs, there are reasonable descriptions in most files and a scattering of cases where the bodies were recovered naked. I collect the files and the few where violet, pink or purple dresses are mentioned. Perhaps Tillie is here among them. In all, there are ten files that pass my selection process – approximate age of victim, date of discovery and relevant clothing – ten unnamed bodies that could be her. I tuck them into my belt and button my waistcoat over the top to conceal them. I look plumper but I don't suppose the Drakers will notice. Usually they don't notice much at all.

Opening the door, I about turn as Bretling makes a sudden appearance striding down the corridor. He doesn't see me, so I hide behind the door, leaving a small gap to peer through until his footsteps have gone. When the passage is quiet I leave, heading straight for reception. I throw the Draker on the desk a cursory wave farewell and head down the outer steps without pause.

Blink bears me back to Bunson Street where I tether him outside the Mysteries Solved office before entering.

Lizzy greets me with a heavy stare. 'Michael, your face!'

'Yes, I'm a little sunburned.' I suppose I'd better get used to this.

'Where have you been? You've been gone for days!'

'Josiah and I were waylaid. We're both fine, though, apart from the burns. Have you seen Penney or Mardon?'

'They're out in the field.'

'Very well. Is there anything I should know?'

'I don't think so. Investigations are progressing nicely. Our clients seem content for now.'

'In that case, would you fetch us both some black bean soup? I have much to do and little time to do it. If no one else is around I may require your assistance.'

'Wait, there was something. It was Ebadiah – '

'Ah, yes. Thank you. He found me.'

Lizzy leaves to buy the soup and I settle in the case room to thumb through each of the borrowed Tobias files in detail. A pang of guilt hits me. What if a Draker investigation is hampered because of these missing records? Unlikely, but I make a silent promise to see them returned within a day, and continue reading. I open Tillie Ingham's casefile and dig out her picture. Holding it next to each of the imographs from the files, I work through them, narrowing them down to two individuals whose faces and physiques appear similar to Tillie's.

Lizzy arrives with the black bean soup and I call her in.

'Take a seat.' I receive a steaming copper cup and sip. I haven't had black bean soup for several days and it enters my system like a speeding fire, enlivening my senses. 'What do you make of these?' I gesture towards the files that I have laid out on my desk.

She puts her cup down. 'What are they?'

I explain and when I'm done, she takes the first of the two files and opens it, her eyes widening at the dead face that greets her inside.

'I'm sorry, it's an unpleasant task, but I'd like a second opinion. Do you think either of these women may have been Tillie?' I hold the second file open next to the first for us to compare.

However hard I stare at the two decaying faces, I can't be sure. They are changed, distorted by death, one bloated and swollen, the other already disintegrating when the imograph was taken. 'The first was drowned, found naked floating in the Tynne near Southside. The second was wearing a deep pink dress when discovered, according to the Draker account. Enough of her flesh survived to retain the cut to her throat listed as cause of death. There is no comment on the type of fabric, but we know that a threader from Holloway who was out collecting bog-wood stumbled upon her at the edge of Curlston Marsh.' I study the putrefied face and pass the imograph to Lizzy. 'Here, take a closer look.'

'It's impossible to be sure, but with the pink dress...' She grimaces. 'The face *could* be hers. Does the file say anything about her hair? It looks too dark in the picture.'

'I thought the same at first but she was in the marshes. It would likely have been damp if not sodden and so may have appeared darker.'

'Then I think this one is the closest match.'

'There's also the fact that she was last seen alive waiting outside the Old Coach House, late in the evening on the 6th of Doblemoon. She could have easily taken a coach south from there and for whatever reason ended up at Curlston Marsh.'

'Why on Earthoria would she want to go there? And at night? It would have been dark by five o'clock at that time of year.'

'I can't answer that.'

'When was the body with the pink dress found?'

I consult the file. 'On the 16th of Thripplemoon.'

'Three months later, in the summer. Would she look like that after three months out on the marsh?'

'She might. The state of decay fits well enough.'

'What about the woman from the river? When was she found?'

I check the file. 'Over a year after Tillie disappeared. If she is Tillie, she must have been in hiding somewhere during that time before she drowned.'

'It's not impossible.'

'Indeed.'

'I still think the Curlston Marsh woman is more likely.'

I thank Lizzy and she returns to the front desk.

I spend the next half an hour taking imographs of the two files' contents before bundling everything up, ready for return to the Draker Headquarters.

Next on my agenda is the new letter. Taking it from my pocket I unfold and reread it. There is an oddity, a disjointed narrative as though the writer is trying to tell me too many things at once. After much rumination I fix upon the following lines:

> *... and grow increasingly convinced that I am being watched.*
> *There are men in shadows. I fear our common enemy will find*
> *me soon. Will you intervene to save a life?*

Is the green ink ghost asking me to save Eadward Trent, or himself? And how does the ghost know about the attempt on Trent's life? From these sparse phrases it appears the ghost is hiding from the Order and fears imminent discovery. My gaze flits from the letter to the imograph of Tillie, to the picture of the dead woman in Curlston Marsh and back to the letter, as a thought forms in my weary mind.

Was Tillie Ingham's throat cut by the same blade that cut her father's?

Or is Tillie Ingham the green ink ghost, as yet alive and well? Did she learn of my father's search for her and decide I might now help in his stead? Is she, even now, still fleeing from the Order? If so, it is not only Eadward Trent who needs saving. And I am running out of time!

# 18

# Questions

*In which things get complicated*

Josiah wakes me in the case room that afternoon, where I have fallen asleep at my desk with the door closed. He shakes me by the shoulder to deliver these ominous words.

'Mr Banyard, Baker is back.'

'Baker?'

'Harris' lantern dog. He's returned.'

'To the house?'

'Hmmm.' Josiah watches me as my sleep-addled brain works to catch up.

'Oh.' This is bad. *Very* bad.

'He's roped to a post in the back garden. Won't stop howling.'

I check my pocket watch. Just gone three in the afternoon. 'That's a complication we could do without.'

'Back to the forest?'

I think hard for a better solution but come up with nothing that would be as quick and easy, seeing as we're incapable of killing the creature. 'Yes. Though it will be a temporary fix. If he's found his way back once, he can do it again. And we need to act fast. If the Drakers find his long snout pointing our way, we're in trouble.' I grab my hat on the way out and we hail a carriage, pausing at 96 Bunson Street to collect the hound, before heading south again to Black Down Forest.

Baker seems docile, settling on the compartment floor as we bump along over the cobbled road.

'He's stopped howling. Did you feed him?' I ask Josiah, accusingly.

'I may have done.'

'Wonderful. Now he'll never stay away.'

'He looked thin. Anyway, *you* fetched him steak last time.'

There's not a lot I can say to that, though from memory it was Josiah's idea. 'Yes, I suppose that's why he returned.'

'That and because he saw his master go into the house but never come out.'

Stopped on the rough trackway by the forest, we pay the driver to wait while we walk Baker out into the trees and let him wander. He seems reluctant to go far so we loiter until he's sniffing around twenty or so yards into the undergrowth and turn back at a brisk pace. Reaching the carriage, we hurry aboard.

'Bunson Street, with all haste!' I instruct the driver.

We set off at a good speed, bouncing along the rutted surface. Peering from the window I see Baker appear on the road behind us, a forlorn creature. He stands there bewildered, watching us go, and I can't help but feel sorry for him.

All the same, I hold my hat on my head and lean out to call up to the driver. 'There's an extra guinea in it if you can lose the dog!' Back inside the cab, I turn to Josiah. 'We'll have to think of a better solution. How long do you think it will take him to reach home?'

'This time he'll be quicker. A few hours at most, I'd say. We *could* keep him.' He seems keen on this idea.

'And have a permanent signpost about the place: Harris Died Here!'

'Surely one lantern dog looks much the same as another.'

'Perhaps. I'd still rather keep him away for a while. The

Drakers will be investigating Harris' disappearance. Willow's master will have his people look into it, no doubt. They would know the hound. And the hound would know them. It would be obvious if they found him. And then there's Cullins and his spies…' I've harboured a concern that Jacob Cullins might know all about our stint with Harris ever since our last encounter. In which case, it's only a matter of time before he uses the information against us. I dread the knock of a Draker at our door.

'Well, then, we have a few hours to think of something,' says Josiah.

We ride the rest of the way in pensive silence.

*Eadward Trent will leave the Global Traders Club at midnight.* That is what the second green ink letter says.

And so, we wait across the road a few minutes to midnight, sheltering miserably from a sudden downpour beneath the awning of a closed milliners. We watch the grand entrance of the Global Traders Club, which comprises two large, dark wood doors with brass fittings and around ten steps that drop down to the cobbled pavement. Handrails descending outwards from the top, also of polished brass, glimmer in the wet light of the watch lamps. My pocket watch is open in my palm as the seconds tick down to twelve.

There's a cheerless Draker posted on the corner of the street, sodden in the rain.

'Why's he standing there?' asks Josiah.

I glance at the hapless Draker. 'He's been told to watch, doesn't dare deviate from his instructions, even if that means a drenching.'

'Fool.'

'At least he's doing his job.'

'How long now?'

'Two minutes.'

We've been waiting a while because I wanted to get here early enough to check over the area. Before that, we visited the City

Hall where we were able to view a large portrait of Eadward Trent so that we might recognise him on sight. I also did a little digging. It seems Trent is a man of strict habit, and those who know him have confirmed his regular attendance of the club.

Josiah frowns. 'How does the ghost know Trent's going to leave precisely at twelve?'

*Precisely?* That's a fancy word for Joe. 'Because that's kicking-out time. He always leaves at twelve, apparently.'

'This ghost sure knows a lot about Eadward Trent.'

'Yes.' Josiah's incessant questions are irritating but have made me think. 'Yes, he does. That's a good point. I imagined the ghost as somehow removed from us, from reality or from the city, even, but he or she can't be far away. How else would they know this level of detail about Trent's movements? They may even be a member of the Global Trading Club.' I peer up and down the street, wondering if the ghost is also here, hiding somewhere, observing from a distant doorway. Or is he watching the drama unfold from inside the club?

'How's the killer going to do it, then? I mean, if all Trent does is get into a carriage and, somehow, he's dead before he can get out...'

'I don't know.' I say, thinking, *a mechanism, a trap? Poison? A bomb?* But then light dawns. 'Of course! Why didn't I see it before?'

'What do you mean?'

'The killer is already inside the carriage. He's paid the driver to carry him here on the stroke of midnight!' As I speak, a carriage drawn by two black horses turns into the street, hurtling towards the club. I consult my pocket watch as the second hand ticks on to the twelve: Midnight. 'And here he comes. Stop that carriage!'

Across the road the double doors open as Trent and a Draker guard step out of the club.

# 19

# Silver

*In which death comes to town*

Josiah and I dash into the road, putting ourselves precariously between Trent and the horses thundering towards us.

'Stop that carriage!' I shout and wave my arms frantically at the driver, who tugs on the reins. His face is hidden, shadowed by a coachman's hat pulled low against the rain, his lower face covered by a knotted scarf.

The horses rear and whinny, their hind shoes clattering on the cobbles, their front hooves reeling perilously close to our heads as the driver battles for control.

Shaken into action, the Draker leaves his corner, running towards us, blowing his whistle.

Josiah reaches for a bridle, but a hoof catches him on the side of his head. He falls. The skittish horses balk. The driver fights to curb the pair and the carriage swerves past us, almost tipping.

'Halt that coach!' I cry, chasing it.

The Draker joins the pursuit.

As the carriage draws level with Trent, a pistol appears from the cab's window.

'Look out!' I scream at Trent. His face is bone pale and terror stricken, but there's another aspect to his expression: a glimmer of recognition.

The pistol flares. The horses race on, spooked by the gunshot. Briefly, Trent stands statuesque before crumpling at the foot of the steps.

I run.

Racing, the carriage clatters into the next street and is soon nothing more than a fading sound. I stop, breathless, seeking another carriage to hail with thoughts of pursuit, but the street is empty and by the time another appears at the end of the road, it's too late. The assassin could be half a mile away. Grudgingly I trudge back to the steps.

When I reach him, Josiah is sitting up in the gutter, rubbing his head and gazing down the road. We are all wet now, soaking in the rain.

'Are you all right?' I ask, stooping to inspect his wound. The hoof has left a gash that is not deep but the flesh around it is already badly swollen. He looks dazed.

'I'm doing better than him.' He points to Trent, who lies motionless where he fell, a bullet hole in his forehead, as rain washes a stream of blood. Trent's Draker guard crouches at his side. The other pipes to call more watchmen to the scene. He stops as I approach.

'What are you doing here, sir, if you don't mind me asking?'

'The same as you,' I say. 'Trying to prevent a murder. I'm the one who warned Lord Draker of the threat to Trent's life.'

'But why try to stop that particular carriage?'

'Because moments before it's arrival I realised the killer was aboard. Where's Lord Draker?'

'He'll be along, no doubt.' He huffs and turns away to greet an incoming Draker.

I rejoin Josiah and help him up. 'Come on, Joe. I need a drink. Can you walk?'

He flashes a half-smile, seemingly cheered by the thought of a pint. 'I think I might just make it to The Dog.'

The Lantern Dog tavern is usually open into the small hours and we find it so, as bustling as ever. I order two pints of Ruby's and marvel at the leaning timbers of the walls. I think that of all the taverns in Camdon City, this is my favourite. It's surely the oldest. We find a plank-topped barrel table, sit, clink tankards and drink.

'It's been an *interesting* few days, Joe.'

'It certainly has, Mr Banyard. I'm sorry about Eadward Trent.'

'It's little consolation, but we were one step ahead of the Drakers.'

'Again.'

'Eadward Trent,' I murmur, reaching for my pocketbook and flipping through pages to the one with the list of initials.

> AS – Assanie Strictor-Booth
> YO
> ET – Eadward Trent
> FG – Fletcher Gouldstone?
> ML
> JC – Jacob Cullins?
> WS – Willard Steeler?

'ET: *Eadward Trent.*'

'It doesn't make sense. Why would the Order kill one of its own?'

'A good question, Joe.' I scratch a cross next to the name in pencil.

We sip our ale and watch the other patrons go about their business. I feel a pressing need to forget the day – the week, in fact – to escape and let my mind wander. It doesn't go far though, nor for long, because half an hour later, when we're edging closer to the bottom of our tankards and a melancholy calm has settled over us, a man in dusty travelling silks, wearing a long coat over a pair of pistols, enters the tavern. He orders ale and moves systematically around the room, questioning people. He draws my eye, for he doesn't look like he's from

Camdon City and he's clearly not here for the common banter or the ale. Notably, he's alone and he reminds me of someone else, which focuses my attention: He reminds me of Harris.

Josiah notices him, too. 'Who's that?' He sounds worried and I conclude he's thinking the same thing.

'I don't know. Have you seen him before?'

'He looks familiar.'

I place my tankard on the table and stare at Josiah. 'Where do you know him from?'

He frowns, presumably trying to recall the face. 'Loncaster, possibly.'

'We need to find out what he wants. Joe, I think you'd better leave. Go and find that dog.' Why on Earthoria did we let Baker go?

Josiah drains his tankard and, with an eye on the stranger, slips out of the tavern.

The newcomer works his way around the tavern, questioning and moving on, so I sit tight and wait for him to reach me, and eventually he does. His face is hard, long and clean shaven, his hair short and his shoulders broad.

'Evenin', sir.' His accent is northern and would certainly fit with Loncaster.

'Good evening,' I say. 'Can I help you?'

'I seek a runaway from Loncaster and an overseer who came here searching before me.'

'Oh?'

'The runaway's name is Willow Buxton, a slim girl with drab-blonde hair. Have you seen her?'

I pretend to consider that for a moment. 'I'm sure I have not.'

'The overseer, then? A large man, name's Harris. Keeps a big lantern dog at his heel.'

'No, I don't recall – '

'We know he came to Camdon City. I've tracked him to that filthy Rouge place over on Southside. Apparently, a pair of threaders collected the baggage from his room but that's the last trace of the man.'

I fight to contain my reaction. 'I'm sorry, your name?'

'Mr Silver.'

'Mr Silver, I shall certainly look out for these characters. Where should I find you if I learn of anything?'

'I'm keeping a room here.' He points upwards to the rooms overhead.

'Very well.' I drain my tankard and rise to leave. 'Good hunting, Mr Silver, and goodnight.'

Making a quick exit, I hurry after Josiah, hoping to catch him before he's lost in the night. I search for him for an hour or so before we meet a mile south of our house on Bunson Street. It's the road we took out of town when we transported Baker to the forest and so it follows the hound may pass this way.

'Anything?' I ask, though the answer's pretty obvious.

'Nothing. I've searched for miles. Went right out to Holloway. On the positive side, if we can't find him, I doubt anyone else can. Perhaps he's gone for good this time.'

'I only wish I could believe that.'

It's not true. We find Baker when we return home some two hours later. He's standing in the glow of the watch lamps, sniffing at our front door, on a rope, the other end of which is gripped firmly by the hand of a smug-looking Mr Silver.

# 20

# Shades of Black

*In which Banyard and Mingle fall out*

We spy him from the shadows further down the road. Fortunately, we see him before he sees us.

'You can't be here right now,' I whisper to Josiah. 'Hide yourself and let me handle this.'

'But… What will you do? Willow…'

'You'll just have to trust me, Joe. We can't have another corpse on our hands.'

He glares and points one of his huge fingers at me. 'You let him take her and her corpse will be on your hands.' He stalks away and I watch him turn into the next street, well beyond view. I embrace the inevitable and approach Silver, for I know he will stand there until someone comes to the door. Mother's concerned face watches from an upper window and I don't blame her for refusing to answer the door in the middle of the night to a stranger with an enormous hound.

'Hello again,' I greet Silver.

'Where's that large fellow you were drinking with?' asks Silver.

Did he recognise Josiah? That might complicate things. I frown. 'Large fellow?'

'The big man I saw you with. In the tavern.'

'Oh, *him*. I barely know him. I see you've found a lantern dog. Is this the hound you mentioned?'

'The very same.'

'My word! That's quick work! Another clue to the whereabouts of your missing man, then.'

'Yes. A trail that ends at this door. I presume *you* live here.'

He tilts his head to one side, glancing up at Mother and tipping his hat in what he may think is a friendly manner. In truth, it's just menacing.

I see no point in delaying things. It wouldn't take him long to learn that I do live here and, if I've denied it, *that* would look all the worse for me. 'I do.'

'And do you know of any reason why the hound might lead me here?'

I look at the dog, at Mother beyond the glass, at the door and then back at Silver. His face is stern. Words evade me for a moment as I reluctantly face facts. We've been caught out. There's no escaping it. Nonetheless, I lie as best I can.

'I don't know why the dog brought you here, but I did realise after our first meeting – I may be able to help you.'

'Oh?' He looks surprised.

'I think my mother may have recently taken on a maid who fits the description of the girl you seek. What was her name again?'

'Willow Buxton.'

'That's the one. Though our maid's name is Mary, or so she told us. Either way, do come inside and I shall rouse her for you. You can see her for yourself and say if she is the one you seek.'

Silver offers a tight-lipped smile and doffs his topper. 'Why, I'd be much obliged.' And it seems to me that the more affable he tries to be, the more intimidating he becomes.

This has become an exercise in damage limitation. I ask, 'Are these two people connected, the runaway and the man? Perhaps the dog has sensed the girl's presence here and that is why he lingers.'

Baker's not helping. He wanders over to me and licks my fingers. His eyes implore: *Any more steak?*

Silver simply looks at me, neither agreeing nor denying my theory. I can almost see his mind turning, like a clockwork contraption spooling over and over.

There is a palpable tension in the air as I unlock the door and open it for him. No one mentions the fact that it's approaching four in the morning, which is most peculiar, and I'm sure Silver doesn't trust a word I say.

Inside, I light lamps and make a great deal of offering him a seat in the sitting room and pouring him a glass of port. I fetch Baker a bowl of water before heading to the hallway where, beyond view, I unlock a cabinet and take out a loaded pistol, tucking it into the belt beneath my coat. I do not plan to use it but feel better knowing it's to hand. With it well hidden, I return to Silver.

'I'm going to fetch Mary down. No point in waking the whole household...' I take a lamp to light my way.

Silver seems happy enough with this suggestion, nodding. His hands are never far from the guns on his belt. I leave him sipping port as I climb the stairs to knock on Willow's door. She answers, wide awake, as I imagine she has been ever since Mother warned her of the man's arrival.

'Don't let him take me,' Willow whispers through the crack of the bedroom door, eyes pleading. 'They'll kill me.'

'I have to let him take you, but I will not abandon you. I promise.'

She draws away. 'No. They'll hang me as soon as they have me back in Loncaster. I can't go.'

'They won't get that far. You have to trust me. There's no other way. I refuse to kill him unless in self-defence.'

'Then stop him from taking me. He is sure to pull his guns.'

'No. I'm done with hiding bodies, and they'll send other hunters if this one also disappears. I have a better way. Come. Let him take you. He seems a little kinder than Harris. I doubt he'll hurt you. And it will be for a short time only.'

She searches my eyes as though for confirmation that I'm speaking the truth. 'You swear? You swear you will come for me.'

'I will die before I let them take you back to Loncaster. I can promise no more than that.'

She edges closer. 'Josiah will kill you himself if I die because you gave me up.'

'Then let that be your guarantee. I mean what I say.'

'Where is he?'

'Josiah? I sent him away, to prevent him from killing Silver.'

She nods pensively but then says, 'Very well. I will come.'

'You will have to play your part – say you came to me, telling me your name was Mary and that your master died and left you without shelter. Understood?' All this we whisper.

She nods and leaves her room to follow me downstairs.

Silver rises from his chair as we enter the room. 'Well, look who it is.'

'Hello, Master Silver.'

'This is the girl, then?' I ask, feigning anger towards Willow. 'Your runaway?'

'It is, indeed. Tell the gentleman your name,' says Silver.

'My name is Willow Buxton,' says Willow, peering at the ground between her feet.

'I see.' I muster an aggrieved face. 'You told us your name was Mary. You lied to us! Took advantage of my mother's kindness!'

'I'm sorry, master. Please don't punish me. My true master will take care of that.'

'You can be sure he will,' says Silver, fetching rope from a deep pocket of his long coat. He turns Willow to tie her hands behind her back.

She complies but asks, 'You will not harm me, nor abuse me?'

Silver huffs. 'Don't worry. You're not my type.' He takes Baker's rope and marches Willow out into the night, turning to me at the door to tip his hat. 'Much obliged...'

'Banyard. Michael Banyard.'

We shake hands.

'Much obliged, Mr Banyard.' And with another tip of his hat, he leaves, taking Willow and Baker with him.

I'm left alone, startled by the events of the last twenty-four hours. I sit and pour myself a port, drain the glass in one shot and rest my head against the chair.

Ebadiah creeps down the stairs and into the room. 'You all right, Mr Banyard? He took Willow, then.'

'He took her, but I shall take her back. You should be in bed.' I rethink. 'Are you up to a task?'

'I am.'

'Good. Get out there, quick smart. Follow them back to The Dog and have your friends set a watch. I need to know the second they leave the tavern.'

Around five minutes pass before Josiah arrives home, his face thunderous.

'Willow? Willow!' He pushes past me as I rise in an attempt to calm him. 'Willow!' He bellows, waking Jinkers next door, I imagine. He stomps towards the stairs.

'She's gone.' My words fall like stones to halt him.

He turns, strides purposefully back to me.

I raise my palms. 'Let me explain – '

He punches me hard in the face. I collapse into my chair, but he grasps my collars in his massive fists and lifts me into his face as blood streams from my nose.

'You let him take her? You've killed her!' He shakes me for good measure, holding me there as I droop. I don't like being this close. It makes the crazed look in his eyes seem all the greater. I'm dazed, feeling like I've run headlong into a brickworks, but manage to force out a few pathetic words that dribble towards the floor. 'I have a plan.'

He drops me, preparing a left hook. 'A plan...'

'Yes.' I try to focus but there are two furious Josiahs towering over me and a pain cascading around the inside of my skull like a marble rattling in a can. 'Hear me out.'

He pauses. 'It had better be a good one or you're dead, Mr Banyard.'

I take a moment to appreciate his formal approach. Nice one, Joe. 'We're going to take her back.'

He's listening, calming. I continue, wiping blood from my mouth. 'I've sent Ebadiah to watch them. When they leave for Loncaster we'll be ready.' I stagger to my feet and walk unsteadily to the desk in the hall to take out a map of Camdon City and the surrounding area. 'Look.' I point. He joins me. 'See, this road here, running north from Highbridge? That's the way he'll take when he leaves for Loncaster. There is no doubt about it.'

'So?'

'So, it would be terribly unfortunate if a pair of highwaymen were to waylay their carriage and demand the girl be delivered along with their other valuables. Unfortunate, but not unheard of. Nor even unusual.'

'Wouldn't he see through our disguises?'

'Not if I can help it.'

He grunts, pacified to a degree. After a pause he says, 'I'm sorry about your nose. I think I might have broke it.'

'*Broken*. Don't worry. I'm taking my doctor's bill out of your wages.'

'Once a silker, always a silker,' he grumbles.

It's early the next morning when Ebadiah knocks at my bedroom door.

'Master Banyard! Wake up!'

I open the door, still groggy from the night's events. 'Yes?'

His one good eye fixes upon me with purpose. 'They set out from The Dog in a carriage. My watcher saw them cross Rook's Bridge a few minutes ago.'

'They're heading north, leaving town. Thank you, Ebadiah.'

I'm startled into action. Firstly, I rouse Josiah and we both hurry to dress. We then collect our pistols and rapiers, don our disguises from my collection – taking scarves to cover our faces, long wigs of curling hair that are all the fashion among the wealthier silkers, long coats that are different from our own – and ride as swiftly as our mounts can carry us. Once across the bridge the city opens out and there are many roads running north. It doesn't matter which they take – though we must avoid using the same one if possible – because they all eventually lead to the northern road I pointed to on the map, the one that runs to Loncaster. It's upon *that* road that we must apprehend them.

### The Good News
As single riders we are faster than any coach.

### The Bad News
All coaches leaving major cities in Londaland must have, by law, a coachman's guard posted on the rear, armed with a blunderbuss or a snub-nosed carbine, so there's a good chance that someone is about to be shot.

### The Worrying News
It's likely to be me.

We tear through the streets of Camdon, our coattails flying, and join the northern road where I slow Blink and coax him through a gap in a knoll of trees that the sunken road bisects. Here we could surprise the coach from above, having an advantage on the higher ground and the cover of the trees. We wait, fixing our scarves across our faces and pulling our hats down low to shadow our eyes. Josiah has a coachman's hat, squat and black. Mine is a flamboyant Dragoon's hat from Amorphia, wide-brimmed with a long feather to one side, a dark grey. We're mostly in shades of black and, with long gloves to cover our hands and wrists, it is only the thin strips of our faces around our eyes that are exposed. If I can alter my voice convincingly, I see no reason why we should be recognised, especially with my nose swollen and my eyes as blackening as they are from Josiah's punch. The weakness in my theory is that his unusual stature may give us away. It is my intention, therefore, to keep him beyond view as much as possible.

'Are your pistols loaded?' I ask him.

'They are.'

'Your powder dry?'

'Aye.'

'Good. Stay behind the trees and only come out as a last resort. Keep hidden and be ready to fire a shot into the air upon my word.'

'I'm ready, Mr Banyard,' he growls.

'Be ready to ride and,' pause for effect, 'try not to kill anyone.'

'Right.' He's unimpressed, slouching in his saddle and viewing me with his head cocked. 'What are *you* going to do?'

I spur Blink onwards. 'I'm going to rob a coach.'

The coach comes into view ten minutes after we've settled in. We watch it rattle along the country track at an easy pace, the driver holding the reins lazily on the front bench, the guard scanning our trees with distrust. There are many patches of woodland along the road, though, so there's no reason for him to be particularly nervous of this one. The carriage is drawn by two chestnut mares, shaggy of hoof and sleekly muscled.

The driver may have a pistol, but he will not be as keen to resist as the guard. After all, that is the guard's job. No driver would give his life defending another man's treasure; at least, this is the mantra I keep telling myself.

My only hope of preventing a killing is to somehow get up close to the guard, close enough to turn the barrel of his gun when he decides it's time to fire. I see it now through the trees, a carbine with a broad muzzle. Getting close to *that* is not going to be possible without a degree of deception. Before the horses turn into the vale beneath me, I slip from my saddle and climb down into the trackway, where I lie as though thrown from my horse and knocked witless, with my hat askew and obscuring my face. Blink is faithful enough to idle where I've left him on the bank above.

I hear the coach approach and hold my nerve. The driver will curb the horses when he sees me, I hope. He does. I hear it rattling to a halt and a voice call from the rear.

'What is it?'

'A man in the road,' comes the reply, presumably from the driver.

There's a pause and then the small sounds of someone descending from the coach.

'Oye, you there. Get up!' The voice is surly and aimed at me.

'Is he dead?' I hear the other man say.

A few heartbeats later I feel the hard muzzle of the carbine prodding my back. This is my chance. Probably my only chance. I throw my left arm around to catch the barrel and grip it as I turn, in an instant forcing it past my side. The guard fires lead into the ground. The barrel flares hot beneath my gloves as I rise, drawing a pistol with my right hand and shoving the muzzle up under the guard's chin and holding it there. He's a burly fellow, all whiskers and hair. I smell brandy on his sour breath. I hold the carbine's barrel, clamped tight, locking us together.

Behind the guard, the driver makes a sudden move.

'Another inch and your companion here will die!' I say, deepening my voice. 'Cooperate and you have my word, you shall both live.'

The driver stills. He's a wiry man, wearing a coat that reaches to his ankles and a hat similar to Josiah's. His face is thin, pale and full of fear.

From the corner of my eye I see movement at the cabin window and glimpse the barrel of a pistol. A warning shot goes up from somewhere in the trees and lead thumps into the carriage roof a few inches above the emerging pistol. Birds scatter into the sky. Thanks, Joe! The pistol withdraws into the carriage.

'Move and my friends will shoot you,' I say loudly enough for them all to hear. 'Take out your guns and toss them. All of you.' The driver obeys. To the guard I hiss, 'Release the gun or

I'll blow your brains into the sky.' He obliges. Holding my pistol snug beneath his chin, I toss the carbine into the trees and with my freed hand make a quick search for other guns under his coat. It seems he has none. 'Now remove your boots, all of you. Slowly. No sudden moves or my friends in the trees will shoot you dead. You two, lie face down between the horses. You in the coach, throw your boots out of the window.'

'Between the horses?' says the guard.

'Aye, between the horses. It will give you a reason to lie still.'

'You'll hang for this and I'll be in the front row.'

'Then I hope you enjoy the show, sir. Now, down you go.' I prod him with my pistol and draw a second, keeping one on the guard and one on the driver. I shout to the trees, 'Keep your eyes on these two, my friends!'

The driver and guard remove their boots and crawl into place between the harnessed mares.

Now to tackle the cabin.

I walk to the window and aim a pistol at Silver. 'Open the door and throw out your guns.'

He opens the door and Baker lopes out.

From his seat, Silver fixes a pair of pistols on me, unperturbed. 'Why should I give up my guns? I could kill you as soon as you could kill me.'

'You might shoot me first but my friends in the trees would finish you. I swear, if you want to live, you should do as I ask.'

He holds his ground, his two guns pointing at me while I keep one on him and the other aiming at the two beneath the horses. For a moment I think, *I'm a dead man,* but then he relents, tossing the pistols out onto the trackway at my feet. Baker pads around and sniffs at the ground before setting off into the trees. I let him go, presuming he will return again to 96 Bunson Street. Willow watches from a cabin bench opposite Silver, her hands bound at her back. 'Untie the slave and release her.' Silver unties her and she climbs out to stand behind me. 'Now, sir, you will surrender your money or your life.'

# 21

# The Willow Problem

*In which Banyard is summoned*

I take the hat from my head and hold it out like a bowl. Silver complies. He doesn't have much to hand over, which is perhaps why he is complying, but that's not the point. The point is, he needs to believe he's being robbed and that this is not about Willow. When he's emptied his pockets and handed everything over, I step away from the cabin and call to the men who are lying face down.

'You two, up you get. Place your valuables in the hat.' They do so. 'Now take your boots and ride on.'

Willow and I watch as they gather their boots and climb aboard.

'What about our guns?' asks the driver. 'There are thieves on these roads. Rogues who would murder us! We can't ride unprotected!'

'Tell them you've already been robbed. If I see you returning this way, I'll have my men shoot you.' I give the nearest mare a hefty slap on the rump and the horses set off with a start, jerking the coach into motion.

At 96 Bunson Street we sit around the dining room table,

Willow, the widow, Mother, Josiah and me. I'm weary from recent events and wish things would slow down for a moment so I might get my bearings, but there seems little hope of that.

Baker has followed us home and now lounges in the corner of the room, gnawing on a ham bone.

'Willow can't stay here,' I state for the fourth time. 'I'll arrange a place for her, somewhere permanent. With a new wardrobe and the right papers, she will live well and be safe. She will live the life of a silker. In the meantime, Mardon has agreed to escort her to Rochington. I have friends there who will hide her.'

'But I won't be with him.' Willow plucks at Josiah's shirt.

'No. At least, not for a while. We must let things settle. Let your master forget about his missing man. Given time he may even forget about you. *Time* is what will make you safe. Time and being away from Loncaster and Camdon City.'

'Then I'll go with her,' says Josiah.

'No. I need you here.'

'Why? You can find another stooge. Any threader will do. You made do with me.'

I'm crestfallen and stunned. 'Is that all this means to you? You think I saved your neck to make you my *stooge*? You think I *make do* with you?'

In awkward silence, Mother and the widow watch.

'I need you here, now more than ever. We have work to do.' I meet Josiah's gaze vehemently. 'I saved your life! Does that count for nothing?'

He considers this, scowling, but there's a touch of surprise in his expression. 'I thought after I hit you, you'd want me gone. You actually want me to stay?'

'Of course, you fool. And you *will* stay. You must stay. And Willow *must* go!' I glare at them both. 'What do you think will happen if Silver decides to return? If he wasn't fooled? He'll bring the Drakers and we shall be overrun. Willow must leave this very hour before Silver comes to his senses, or we'll all suffer the consequences.' I address Willow. 'Get your things.

Mardon is waiting.'

The day is a mess and it's not even ten in the morning. I brood in the green room for a time, trying to think of ways to redeem the situation, though with little success. There's a wounded part of me weeping in a dark and distant corner of my mind, grieving over my deeds. I have conspired to conceal manslaughter. I have failed to report the death of a woman, one of society's neglected, abused and forgotten. I've buried two bodies unlawfully. And, only this morning, I have lied, threatened, bullied and committed highway robbery.

Whatever has become of me?

Where is Michael Banyard, saviour to the downtrodden? Michael Banyard the kind? He is gone or has become a monster. I am racked with guilt at my own shortcomings. Surely my own father would not recognise me if he were here.

I gaze at my old tricorn and hear his voice in my head.

'Ah, Micky, what have you become?'

'I'm sorry. I could see no other way.'

'There's always another way. You just need to seek it out.'

'I couldn't. There wasn't...'

'I know not all choices are easy.'

'Some are impossible.'

'Ah, you might be right, there. You might be right. Look forward, lad, and think on. No point in looking back. You can't go there.'

I try to follow my father's advice. I can't do anything about my past, so what can I change about my future?

What *will* Silver do now? I wonder. And what action will Bletchley, Willow's Loncaster master, take? Will he send more men to search for Willow, Harris and Baker? Will Silver shortly return to my door? I begin to dread the sound of a knock.

My focus falls back on to the case, considering the day ahead, prioritising and planning, but around 10.15 there *is* a knock at the door and Mother calls me.

'Michael, there's a Draker at the door asking for you.'

I check the pistol on my belt and with a sense of dread drag myself to the door, in no mood for civilities. 'Yes?'

The watchman blinks at me. 'Mr Banyard?'

'What?'

'You are Mr Banyard?'

'I am. What do you want?'

'Lord Draker requests your presence, sir. You are to visit him at his office in the Draker City Headquarters as soon as you may. Says you are to bring the letter.'

'Thank you.' I close the door in his face and grab my pocketbook and hat. It's just as well. I still have those Tobias files to return.


'Ah, Banyard. Come in, take a seat. I'll be with you in a moment.' Bretling Draker finishes reading the report in his hands, shuffles papers and stuffs them into a tray on the desk before giving me his attention, lighting his pipe as he talks. 'Well, now, it seems your mystery informant was right about Trent. A pistol shot right between the eyes – dime of a shot. I want to hear what you have to say about the matter. You were there, by all accounts.'

I breathe a sigh of relief. 'I was, though I realised too late that the killer was likely to arrive in a carriage. When the carriage turned into the street, I tried to stop it.'

'Did you, perchance, glimpse the culprit?'

'I did not. The horses bolted. I merely glimpsed a hand holding the pistol.'

'Shame. I'll need that letter, of course.'

'Here.' I take the second green ink letter from my pocket and hand it to him. 'It's all yours.'

He unfolds and re-examines the letter. 'It's mighty strange that an unknown person or persons should choose to warn you of this attack. Why not inform a Draker? Any Draker? But, no, they chose you. Why was that?'

Perhaps because of Draker incompetence. I keep my thoughts to myself. 'I cannot say, Lord Draker. It remains an enigma to me. What do you know about this Trent fellow? Was he involved in some underhand business that might have soured?'

'None that I know of.'

I nod.

'I'm intrigued by this note, Banyard. How do you imagine your informant knew the killer would strike?'

'I don't know. They may know the killer, I suppose. I think they probably knew Trent. Could you gather a list of his acquaintances? It might be a place to start. I think Trent recognised his killer. Saw it on his face.'

'Did he, now? Indeed, I shall do so. What about the driver? Did you see *his* face? Was he in on it or merely a pawn used by the gunman?'

'I wish I could say. He wore a scarf, had his hat pulled low. Not unusual for a driver in the rain and cold of night. I certainly couldn't name him and wouldn't know him even if he were here.' I feel we're both as exasperated as each other.

'Hmmm...' Bretling draws on his pipe, thoughtfully.

'If the driver is innocent, he might be persuaded to come forward.'

'I'll have a man visit the Old Coach House. See what we can find.'

'Good.' Again, I fight the urge to share details of my investigation with Bretling. Instead we sit blankly for a moment. 'Is there anything else I can help you with?'

'No, Banyard. I think that's it for the time being.'

'Very well, Lord Draker. By your leave...'

'Yes, yes. On you go. I may send for you again.'

'Then farewell for now.' I make a cursory bow, leave Bretling's office and, unattended, head directly to the Tobias file room. Finding it empty, I swiftly replace the borrowed files, which I've carried hidden as before. It's not until filing the last one that I notice a simple door in the corner of the room. It has no title printed on a sign, no window, only a plain brass doorknob, and is painted the same drab colour as the walls, which is perhaps why I have not noticed it until now. While the corridor outside is quiet, I test the door.

Locked.

Now my curiosity is roused. There's nothing else for it. I *must* discover what is on the other side, but how? There is a keyhole but no outer lock or catch so a key is needed, or something that may act as one. I search my person and find my own keys. There are several for the house doors and cabinets and around the same number for locks at the Mysteries Solved office. I try them each in turn and for some minutes work to unjam one that gets utterly stuck in the keyhole. I fear I'll be forced to leave it lodged and flee but, with perseverance, it loosens and pulls free. I comb the room for something that might help.

Nothing.

Thwarted.

I stand, looking about, thinking. Do I plan a return and come armed with appropriate tools? Or should I ditch the idea and get out before I'm discovered? While I'm debating my next move, my eyes settle on the hinges of the door, which are on my side of the wall. One of my smallest keys has a rounded shank that protrudes a short way beyond the teeth. I try it and see it will fit snuggly into the hinge pin barrel. Pressing it upwards, hard against the bottom of the lower hinge pin, I force the first pin up a short way before using the key to catch the head and draw it clear of the barrel. The upper hinge follows suit and, with a little coaxing, the door comes free to rest on the floor, still held by the lock on the other side. I drag it open enough to squeeze through into the room beyond. This one is smaller but feels familiar. There are files on a desk and maps and Tobias imographs pinned to the wall. Clearly someone has used this as a Draker case room. A fine layer of dust has settled over everything.

One of the pinned images draws my gaze: another decaying corpse, this one looking remarkably like Tillie Ingham, more so than the one Lizzy and I fixed upon. Is this her, then? The room is dim, the only light coming from the gap made by the unhinged door. I strike a Sulphur to examine the image more closely. The corpse is naked so there's no dress to consider. I look at the other imographs in turn, all women and, judging by the bruising around their necks, they were all strangled to death.

There's also a chalkboard bearing a list of scribbled names. I wonder, are they suspects? All but one name is crossed out: Nathanuel Dover.

The rest of the files scattered around seem to have no bearing on my case, so I disregard them and return to the wall where pins in a map are linked to imographs by lengths of twine. Wishing I'd brought my camera, for there are too many details to note, the best I can do is to draft a quick copy in my pocketbook and note down the locations of the map pins. I can then consult the map later and know where these throttled girls were found. When I've completed my map I carefully replace the door, pushing the hinge pins down into their hinge barrels. I leave with a mounting hunch that the king's brother, Nathanuel Dover, is a killer of women.

I check my pocket watch frequently as the day wears on, not allowing myself to believe that Silver is gone for good, but as hours pass without his appearance, I begin to relax. Willow has left for Rochington with Mardon. Josiah paces the floor of the case room, and Penney and Lizzy are working in reception.

Josiah is unhappy, of course, and barely speaking to me, but he's here. While he's quiet I reassess the progress of our case. I have a long list of loose ends, aspects in need of further investigation that I have simply not had the time for. On my desk my pocketbook lies open.

> The gold ring
> Hinkley Air
> Oliver Ingham
> Zacchaeus Mandon
> Foster Keen
> Martha Judd
> Willard Steeler (frog?)

There is the Hinkley Air building, where Oliver Ingham met his end. Was he thrown from an airship? This idea was never raised by the Drakers and so was never investigated, not even by my father, as far as I know.

There are the three supposed victims named by the first of the green ink letters. At best, I've managed only cursory investigations into these deaths, though they all seem to point to Dover Palace, which in turn could point to Nathanuel Dover.

Viewing my list of initials I see that if Eadward Trent was indeed ET, there are only two others who remain unnamed: YO and ML. Who are these people? And, indeed, who is Assanie Strictor-Booth? Just one more name on the list... We've also been far too distracted to keep up any kind of surveillance on the members of the Order of Lithobates that we *do* know about: Cullins and Gouldstone. What are they up to, I wonder?

I review the map I copied in the Draker case room, that chamber locked and abandoned by the investigators, whoever they were. There is a clear pattern made by the marked locations, for they cluster about the Tower Bridge district with an ever-increasing density around Dover Palace itself. Are these murdered women all victims of Nathanuel Dover, I wonder? And were the investigating Drakers called off the job by an official further up the line? Surely someone closed and locked the door with an instruction to forget the enquiry.

And finally, thanks to Ebadiah's fine detective work, there is the suggestion that Tillie Ingham may have been pregnant at the time of her disappearance. Tillie worked at Dover Palace as a seamstress, a detail that's absent from my father's notes, but it's the kind of detail that might have been too obvious for him to have recorded. It's not something he would have been likely to forget. In any case, I decide to revisit the palace and question the servant girl who spoke with Ebadiah. Who knows what else we might glean?

Ebadiah tells me the girl's name is Poesy Clarence and Josiah mopes the whole way there. We're not allowed into the palace but, after exaggerating my association with Lord Bretling

Draker, I persuade a doorman at one of the servants' entrances to fetch Poesy out and she steps nervously into the sunlight of the palace gardens.

'Good afternoon, Miss Clarence.' I introduce Josiah and myself, adding, 'We're private detectives investigating the disappearance of Miss Tillie Ingham. An associate informs me you knew the girl.'

'I knew Tillie,' Poesy confirms.

'We were hoping you might answer a few questions.'

'Questions?'

'Did you know Tillie well?'

'Well enough. We were friends.'

'And you thought she was with child when she disappeared. What made you think that?'

'She was showing. A few of us noticed, though we didn't say anything. She missed work now and then, complained of nausea. The usual signs.'

'I see, but she never spoke of it?'

'Never. I don't think she wanted people to know.'

'Can you tell us anything else about her? Anything at all that may be useful?'

'I don't know. She was a simple girl, gentle.'

'Is this her?' I present the imograph taken from my father's casefile.

She studies the image. 'Yes, that's Tillie.'

'Did she seem troubled in the days leading up to her disappearance?'

'Not greatly, not other than the sickness. She was quieter than usual, I suppose, withdrawn. She spent some time reading when normally we would sit and talk. We're allowed breaks throughout the day. We would sit together, drink tea.'

'Reading, you say. Reading what?' asks Josiah.

'She liked books. She had a few. She left some here, in fact. I still have them.'

Josiah and I exchange looks. 'May we see them?'

Poesy nods. 'Wait here.' She enters the palace, returning to us a minute or two later laden with books. 'Here.' She offloads them into Josiah's arms. 'Take them. I don't want them.'

'Thank you.'

Poesy hesitates, glancing back towards the doorway before lowering her voice. 'Masters, perhaps it's not my place to say, but it seemed to me Nathanuel Dover, the earl, took an interest in Tillie.' She bows briefly and scurries back to the palace.

Tillie Ingham's reading list is enlightening. There are two romantic novels, one women's fashion catalogue from Finchley & Sons, and three publications, scientific in nature: *Native Birds of Londaland*, *Flora and Fauna of Amorphia*, and an obscure hardback with a peculiar title.

'*Mors Zonam: A Study*,' I say as we ride past the exquisite silker mansions of Tower Bridge at an easy pace. I think back to the books I took from the shelves in the palace, the ones I never got to read. 'Do you think she stole it from Dover's library? I've never heard of this book.'

'Is that unusual?' scoffs Josiah. 'Do you know *every* book that's published?'

'I like to think I know a great many of them.'

He views me sideways, mocking me. 'Must be nice to be educated.'

I ignore the jibe. 'It's a strange topic for a seamstress, don't you think?'

'Aye, but not if you're in trouble and looking for somewhere to escape. I mean, if people were trying to kill you... There's life in Mors Zonam. We've seen it. Perhaps she thought she could survive there, hide there. Perhaps that's where she went.'

'Surely it would be easier to lose yourself in another city or board a ship, go to Amorphia even, or Urthia, Zenzib or Acutane, anywhere. Why Mors Zonam, a place infamously inhospitable?'

He looks at me as though I'm an idiot. 'Because it's the one place no sane person would go looking for you.'

## 22

# The Raven and the Sorrow

*In which Banyard and Mingle attend a masked ball*

We leave the immaculate streets of Tower Bridge and ride into Old Camdon's twisting lanes, where a familiar voice beckons us.

'Mr Banyard, Mr Mingle? Is that you?'

There on the pavement stands Clara Avard, waving. We slow the horses.

'Miss Avard, good day to you.' I doff my hat. Josiah does likewise and we stop.

'Oh, you poor souls! Whatever happened?'

Momentarily baffled, I quickly realise that with our skin burned red and my nose and eyes badly bruised, we must look like we've been in a terrible accident. 'Ah, we're quite fine, Miss Avard. A minor mishap, nothing more.'

She steps closer and runs a gloved hand down Blink's cheek. 'I did wonder what had become of you when you weren't at the ball. Such a pity.'

'The ball. Yes! Of course!' I realise we were in Mors Zonam when the ball took place and had forgotten all about it.

Josiah removes his hat to bow and nudges me to do the same. I follow suit. 'Please accept our deepest apologies, ma'am. We suffered a small accident and were unable to attend.'

I'm impressed. We'll make a silker out of you yet, Joe!

'Apology accepted.' She smiles brightly. 'But I have terms. Tonight, I'm holding another masked ball. The last one was a hoot! You simply must come.'

'We'd be delighted,' I say, and Clara takes a card from her clutch bag and reaches up to hand it to me.

'Eight o'clock sharp. Until later, then.'

We bow briefly, tip our hats and nudge our mounts to walk on and I think, *Josiah must have it bad*: even the charming Miss Avard has not turned his head today.

He continues to sulk, brooding over Willow and my insistence at her relocation. I try to shift his focus. 'A masked ball! This should be fun. Some light relief after all that's happened.'

'What does one do at a masked ball?' he asks, showing little enthusiasm.

'Why, it's a party. You dress up in your finery and wear a mask. The high silkers will be in their ridiculous wigs, of course, and there'll be fine food and drink. You'll enjoy it, I'm sure.'

He throws me that look again, the one that says I'm stupid.

I give up but, arriving home, have him try on his finest silks and we shop for masks in Crowlands, finding two that are suitably ostentatious. Mine is black, adorned with feathers and a long, curving raven's beak. As though to drive the point home, Josiah chooses a Sorrow – a theatrical mask with an exaggerated expression of woe, downturned mouth and blue-glass tears. After dusk, when it's time to leave, we hail a carriage and have the driver take us to the address on the card.

'This might be a good opportunity, Joe.'

'How's that?' he mutters.

'We will be mixing with the high end of society. Nathanuel Dover might even be there. I'm sure Mrs Farringsgate will attend.'

'Can't wait.'

'I mean it may be good for the investigation. Clara knows Gouldstone. He may be at the ball, Cullins too. Who knows?

Other members of the Order might attend.'

'Hmmm.' He stares out of the carriage window at the moonlight on the Tynne's darkly sliding waters as we cross Rook's Bridge to enter Old Camdon. Clara's address is impressive: Steadholm House, Highbridge, not far from the Farringsgate place. It's a residential suburb favoured by politicians, rich investors and businessmen.

'Keep your ears open, Josiah. See what you can learn, and pay particular attention to any names you hear. We have two sets of initials from Tillie's letters to account for: YO and ML. And a name to which we can put no face. I would like to know who this Assanie Strictor-Booth is.'

Josiah continues his study of the night beyond the window, his reply monotone. 'I'll be sure to tell you if I find out.'

The driveway is imposing and we are caught up in a queue of private carriages as other guests, all of them looking far wealthier than us, compete for places to park and disembark. All these grand houses have stone steps leading up to their doors. I can only imagine that at the time of their construction it was categorically the fashion. The more steps and the broader their sweep, the better. It is certainly an impressive house, tall with turrets at the corners and wings either side, adjoining the main building. There are arched windows beneath its gables, gothic columns, battlements and sloping roofs. In short, Steadholm House is a small palace.

'Mask on, Joe. It's time to go in.'

We don our masks, leave the carriage and climb the steps. It's a long way to the top so we have plenty of time to admire the costumes of other guests. There are animal guises, theatrical faces – like the Sorrow but with all manner of other ghastly expressions – obscurities, stylised skulls and strange dreamlike creatures. Some masks glitter and gleam. Others seem to be cast of gold, of silver, or carved from exquisite dark woods. There is lace and silk, feather and sequin aplenty.

We cross a terrace to huge entrance doors that enter onto a balcony with stairways descending either side into a grand hall below, where guests mingle, drink and cavort around a long central table laden with fine foods. It would be a splendid sight if it wasn't so grotesquely opulent.

At the head of one stairway, a servant in cloth of gold receives cards and announces newcomers of note. For those of a humbler approach, which includes us, there is the other stairway. We take it and join the revelling throng. Other servants in cloth of gold meander, offering wine in crystal glasses from golden trays.

We're quick to accept a glass each and stand sipping and feeling thoroughly inept. It is, however, a remarkably good place to eavesdrop on conversations. Concealed behind my mask of feathers, I feel wonderfully anonymous. There is no need to force a conversation when no one can see your face and so we stand and drink, exchanging an occasional glance and grabbing our second drinks when the opportunity arises.

At length, Clara Avard, resplendent in a silver gown and a matching shimmering mask, finds us. 'And who do we have here, I wonder?' She peers at my eyes through the holes of my mask, her identity apparent by the striking curves of her lips. 'A wiry physique, strong and well formed. Raven-haired and keen of eye. He's debonair – a handsome face beneath darkling wings.' She moves on to Josiah, seductively tracing a finger around his nearest shoulder and down the curve of his upper arm. 'Hmmm… Tall, a remarkable musculature. Powerful. A man of *great* physical stature… Is it perhaps the private detectives, Mr Banyard and Mr Mingle?' She laughs and sips crimson wine from her crystal glass.

I force a laugh. 'Ah, you have us, Miss Avard. What fun this is!' It's not fun at all, but she seems to be enjoying it. The conversation is stilted and, each time I blink, other images flash before my eyes: the gawdy masks and smiles are replaced by the decaying faces of the dead.

Blink: I see the poor girl we found overdosed in Harris' room.

Blink: Oliver Ingham is suddenly before me, draped across a

shattered barrel.

Blink: The dead women on the wall of the Draker case room loom, closing on me.

'I wish you could see what I see,' I mutter.

She frowns. The party clamour is loud around us. 'Pardon?'

'I said, I bet you can see the sea. I mean, from the upper windows.'

'Oh, yes. There's a wonderful view. On a clear day you can see right out to the Eyes of Myrh and beyond.'

'Wonderful. Tell me, is this your home or your father's?'

'It is mine, recently acquired, and so you'll understand my desire to show it off.'

'Indeed, I would surely do the same, were it mine. A splendorous mansion to behold.'

'I'm so glad you approve, Michael. May I call you Michael?'

'Please do.'

'Is your acquaintance Mr Gouldstone with us?' I ask awkwardly.

'He may be here somewhere. I believe I extended an invitation.'

'I'm sure all the finest citizens of Camdon City must be attending.'

'I do hope so.'

'Who among them would you say were the most well connected? I did wonder if Nathanuel Dover might be here. Do you know him, the Earl of Lockingshire?'

'Unfortunately, my circle does not extend quite so high. No, you won't find him here, but there are a few high flyers. Let me see.' She scans around for a suitable example and points across the room to a tall gentleman in a wolfish mask who is loading his plate with dressed hallard eggs from the table. 'That's the Earl of Daggonshire, and the lady with him is Baroness Longarton. But if you're looking for businessmen, I must introduce you to Sir Yohn Omediah. He's here somewhere and, of course, there's Morris Lakefield. His father designed Rook's Bridge, the first iron bridge in Londaland. Did you know? I'm sure you'll find him fascinating. One moment.' She disappears into the crowd.

'We should try some of the food,' I suggest to Josiah. 'We might never have an opportunity to eat so well.'

'I'm not hungry,' he mumbles. Instead, he dumps his empty glass on a passing tray and takes a full one. 'I think I'll go out for some air.' He leaves me, drowning in a sea of masked strangers with whom I have little in common.

*Thanks, Joe.*

Across the room a curvaceous figure catches my eye. She is familiar and a few moments' study brings her name to mind. Mrs Farringsgate notices me, too, and waves, her eyes flashing from a golden lace mask in the Morracibian style. I dip my mask to offer a smile. Noticing my glass is empty, she heads over to me, swiping a full glass along the way. I accept it, bowing gratefully.

'Mrs Farringsgate, how wonderful to see you. I do hope you are enjoying the ball.'

'Oh, yes! Isn't it wonderful? Such a beautiful house, don't you think?'

'Indeed, it is!'

'And how do you know our hostess, Miss Avard?'

'I'm not entirely sure that I do. We had a chance encounter in a teashop.'

'Oh, that does sound terribly romantic.'

I try to play down the notion. 'I'm sure it's nothing like that.'

'One can never be too sure, can one? Who knows where such encounters might lead?'

'Very true.'

'Ah, I see an old friend. I really must catch him. Will you excuse me?' She leaves me to cross the room and I stand holding two glasses until a servant passes and I manage to offload the empty.

Clara returns soon after, with a gentleman on her arm. He's wearing a badger mask, which has a distinguished quality in keeping with the rest of his attire. 'Mr Lakefield, this is Mr

Banyard. Mr Banyard, Mr Lakefield.' She deposits him in my care and speeds away.

We shake hands.

'Pleased to meet you, sir,' I say, and he responds accordingly. 'Miss Avard tells me your father is responsible for the first iron bridge in Londaland. That's quite a claim.'

'Indeed, and many other bridges across the land. I do believe I've lived in his shadow ever since.' He chortles, making his bushy grey sideburns shake.

I smile. Mr Lakefield seems affable. 'I'm sure it's a common experience among sons.' I think of my own father, a man who on so many levels I doubt I shall ever match.

'Yes, it is the way of things, I suppose. What is it you do, Mr Banyard?'

'Michael, please. I'm a private detective, like my father before me.'

He studies me. 'How interesting. You must have some stories to tell, I don't wonder.'

'I do. And what business are you in?'

'Iron. I own three yards, all of them smelting iron for bridges, steam ships and the like.'

'Ironworks! Have you perhaps heard of the industrialist Willard Steeler?'

'Heard of him! Why, I married his daughter!'

I stop, feeling I've walked into some kind of trap.

Morris Lakefield. ML. Son-in-law to Willard Steeler! In my pocket my fingers caress Steeler's gold ring. I'm suddenly aware that I'm in conversation with another member of the Order of Lithobates. A quick glance at the gold ring on the middle finger of his left hand confirms it. And what were the other names Clara mentioned? The Earl of Daggonshire and Baroness Longarton... Sir Yohn Omediah: YO.

'Do you by any chance know anyone from Hinkley?' I ask, wondering if I've pushed too far.

'Hinkley Air? Of course. I imagine most people in this room know Albert Silkerton. He's a director. Would you like an introduction? He's just over there.' Lakefield waves at a man in a grimacing golden mask and across the room the man, presumably Albert Silkerton, waves back, though I can see no ring on his hand.

Albert Silkerton: perhaps he is the AS from my list, another member and a direct link to Hinkley Air, where Oliver Ingham's body was found mutilated. Are these the people that Tillie's letters warned of? Should I take him up on his offer of an introduction? My inclination is to flee!

'No,' I say. 'But thank you. Will you excuse me?' Making a short bow, I leave him and look for Josiah, who's nowhere to be found. I search instead for Clara, convinced that she should be warned of the Order, amid whom she has become unwittingly surrounded.

I must find her!

An extensive search of the party leaves me convinced that both Clara and Josiah have left, but where? Have they absconded together? A terrible feeling builds in my gut as I leave the hall to investigate the rest of the house. The servants at the entrance inform me they haven't seen Miss Avard for some time. The wine is definitely going to my head and I drowsily wonder if someone has slipped something into my glass.

They are not in the entrance hall, nor the reception chamber beyond. Room after decadent room. They are not here.

Breaking into a sweat, I retrace my steps and stumble back to the entrance, burst out through the doors onto the upper terrace of the outer steps and stop, swaying gently and staring. Below me on the steps, Josiah and Clara Avard sit in deep conversation, their masks set aside. My head feels strangely light. I swoon and hit the ground.

I feel a sharp blow to my face, followed by another, and open my eyes to Josiah. He slaps me again for good measure.

'Are you awake now, Mr Banyard?'

'I am. You seem to be striking me in the face a lot these days, Josiah,' I mutter blearily. 'It's a worrying trend.'

'Though never without purpose, Mr Banyard. What happened?'

'I think I've been drugged,' I whisper.

He offers a hand and helps me to my feet. 'Let's get you home, then.'

'Are you sure he's all right?' asks Clara, standing a short way behind Josiah.

I brush myself down. 'I'm perfectly fine, Miss Avard. Thank you. Just a little giddy. It's been a demanding few days.'

'I'll have my driver take you home.'

'That would be kind. Thank you.'

Hanging on Josiah's shoulder, I make it to a seat in the carriage and the driver sets the horses into motion with a flick of the reins.

Josiah leans towards me. 'There's a meeting tomorrow. I think it's important.'

'A meeting of the Order?' I ask.

'It could be. There are certainly some big movers going. You know the type, people of influence. People with serious money. I heard Fletcher Gouldstone talking about it with another man.'

'Did they see you?'

'Even if they did, they wouldn't have recognised me.' He holds his mask in place and I see what he means. The Sorrow mask covers almost his entire face. 'Want to know where they're meeting?'


The Hinkley Air skyraker towers over us. At the double doors, people come and go unchecked. Dressed as businessmen with silk toppers, Josiah and I enter and soon find our way into a packed steam lift that chugs us upwards. The lift stops at each floor and some people leave while others enter and off we go again, ever ascending towards the roof of the building. By the time we arrive, we're the only occupants. A bell jingles, telling us it's safe to leave. I open the folding latticework doors and we step out onto the roof and marvel at the huge dirigible before us. Was it from this craft that Oliver Ingham was thrown, his throat cut? My father knew that – for some reason he failed to record – Oliver was not thrown from the roof, but he did not rule out the possibility of it being an airship.

Tethered by a dozen ropes to iron rings set in the expansive flat roof, the aircraft floats like a giant fat cigar above our heads. Its varnished cotton skin is a creamy white, bearing the Hinkley Air logo in red along its side. Beneath and towards the front, a ladder reaches from the roof to the gondola, where the backs of seated figures inside are visible through windows. At the foot of the ladder stands a pair of muscular guards – real bruisers – with pistols on their belts.

I fish around in my waistcoat pocket for the frog ring and slip it on to my finger. The guard on the right steps in front of the ladder to block our path.

'No admittance beyond this point,' he mutters, glaring at us.

'Ah! Well done, my fine fellow. We appreciate your ardour.' I show them the ring on my finger and he moves aside, waving us on.

'Mind your step, sirs.'

Not knowing what to expect, we quietly climb. At the top, handrails ease our entry and we creep in to spy on the meeting from the back.

The gondola is smaller than it looks from the outside: a rounded room with windows on all sides and elegantly decked out. The members are gathered on quilted seats of red velvet, and polished wood panels line the walls to surround a central table on crimson carpet. There is a small entrance chamber before the meeting room and it's here that Josiah and I crouch, to listen and watch, hidden behind the fitted seats and partially obscured by a partitioning door that is flanked by more windows. Among the faces, Cullins and Gouldstone are obvious, but I think I recognise Morris Lakefield's bushy sideburns also, and there is a man with coppery skin, Sir Yohn Omediah, perhaps. The name is Urthian and the skin tone suggests an origin in kind.

There is a great deal of talk about money, the apparently

terminal circumstances of Stallwarts Bank and various payments to individuals, little of which I truly follow – being unfamiliar with those mentioned – but my ears prick up after a long and tiresome financial presentation.

Standing before the others, Gouldstone sums up. 'This concludes the Order's fiscal report, other than to say, with this new threat of collapse from Stallwarts Bank, we have of course arranged a full transfer of the Lithobates' funds. Tomorrow morning, our collateral will be loaded onto a postal carriage bound for our banks in Loncaster. Are we agreed upon this action?'

From around the room, the response rumbles. 'Agreed.'

'I should like to offer my services in overseeing the transaction,' says Cullins, standing. 'I suggest Mr Gouldstone and I see it done personally and accompany the carriage. There will be the usual armed escort, of course, but with such a sum I'm sure we would all rest more easily knowing one or two of us were actually there.' The members nod and mutter their agreement. He addresses Gouldstone. 'Would you care to join me, sir?'

'I would, indeed,' says Gouldstone, mopping his brow with a handkerchief. 'Is this acceptable to our members?'

More murmurs of assent follow as Gouldstone and Cullins retake their seats.

'Pray continue, Mr Direson,' says Gouldstone.

I jot the new name down in my pocket book.

A thin, bony man with a tall topper and long white hair stands to speak, tapping a glossy black cane on the floor for attention. He wears black from head to toe. 'Now, I wish to address the matter of the latest threader girl, the one found on the banks of the Tynne, south of Tower Bridge. Mr Lakefield, perhaps you could enlighten us on recent developments.'

'Certainly.' Lakefield stands. 'I believe the matter has been satisfactorily resolved. The Draker who discovered the body has received the usual sum. The girl has been sent directly to Mort and Jarvis for disposal. There shall be no Draker report filed.

No enquiry, Dover's name has been kept out of the matter and the scene has been sanitised.'

'Just as well,' says Cullins. 'We don't want a repeat of last time. Blood and guts everywhere. What a mess!'

'Here, here,' the others agree.

'But there's no need for concern,' says Gouldstone, gesturing with his cane. 'It was only a threader's blood and guts!'

The members laugh keenly and nod to one another.

'Only a threader's blood and guts! Yes!'

'Indeed, no cause for concern. Hah-hah!'

Grimly, I tap Josiah on the shoulder and whisper. 'Come. I've heard enough.'

# 23

# The Plan

*In which Banyard and Mingle conspire*

A time like this calls for plenty of black bean soup and honey cakes. The bitter drink enlivens the mind and the sweetness brings well-needed vigour to our blood. There are four freshly filled copper cups steaming on Josiah's desk and a plate stacked high with the syrupy cakes. I've asked Penney and Lizzy to join us in the case room because I want them to know what we've learned and to discuss a way forward.

'I'm sorry to pull you away from your other work, girls, but with Mardon in Rochington, we need your thoughts. Josiah and I have been busy.'

Between us, we tell the girls everything we've learned about the Order of Lithobates and the murders the Order has either committed or covered up. We share our suspicions but have no physical evidence to show, only our testimonies. They seem convinced by our story, though, and listen intently, sipping black bean soup while we conclude with a blow-by-blow account of the meeting in the gondola of the Hinkley Air ship.

For a few moments we sit in silence as they absorb everything we've said. Penney is the first to respond. 'So, you can't take this to the Drakers.'

'No. I think that would be a mistake,' I say. 'I've a hunch they know all about Dover's killing spree and they're implicit in the cover-up. I fear Nathanuel Dover has developed an unhealthy taste for threader women.'

'Well, yes,' Penney agrees, 'if what you say about the meeting is true and they're paying Drakers hush money. What will you do?'

'I don't know,' I confess. 'That's why we're meeting.'

Penney puts her cup down, looking perplexed. 'It sounds as though they're too big for us. Too powerful. Perhaps you should walk away, Michael.'

'And let the trail of murder and corruption continue?' I ask. Silence.

'Sometimes, one is simply powerless to change a situation,' says Penney. 'There is wisdom in knowing and accepting when that is the case.'

'True, but I won't give up so easily. Not this time. These threaders, they have no one else on their side. There simply has to be a way.'

Josiah gulps down a mouthful of honey cake and clears his throat. I give him a nod. 'There *is* one way,' he says. The girls watch him, waiting. 'It's obvious, really.'

'Is it?' asks Penney.

'We hit them where it hurts. Rob their carriage. Take their money.'

The girls exchange a glance.

'We heard it in the airship,' I add. 'All their money will be on that coach bound for Loncaster. If they lose that, they'll lose everything.'

'No money: no power,' adds Josiah.

'The Order will collapse,' I conclude.

'And you think this is a good idea?' asks Penney, singling me out.

'You can't rob them,' states Lizzy, matter-of-factly. 'You'd be breaking the law.'

She sounds pretty much exactly the way I thought she would.

Word for word.

'I told you they wouldn't like it,' I tell Josiah. He shrugs.

We receive disapproving glares.

Josiah offers the plate around. 'Would anyone else like a honey cake? They're good.'

'Not for me, Josiah Mingle.' Lizzy crosses her legs.

Josiah takes another cake and crams it into his mouth, looking around the room at anything other than the girls.

'Does anyone have any other ideas?' I ask.

'You could take them to court,' says Lizzy. 'Like you did with Cullins.'

'And we all know how well *that* turned out,' says Josiah, with a spray of cake crumbs. 'Sorry.' He wipes his mouth on his sleeve.

'You must have *some* evidence, surely,' says Penney.

'We have the green ink letters, anonymous and so inadmissible. Besides that, we have only our testimonies. It would not be enough. Not even to raise a summons.'

'Then you need to *find* evidence,' says Lizzy.

Josiah and I ask in unison. 'How?'

Silence again.

'You see?' says Josiah. 'It's not that easy.'

'Even if we had evidence, I don't fancy our chances,' I say. 'When the Order faces a problem it just throws money at it. It would do the same with any case against it. Any witnesses, judges or Drakers would be bribed. Any evidence we provided would mysteriously disappear.'

'Yes,' agrees Penney. 'I see the problem. It's a shame the Drakers are bought so easily. If they were to do their jobs properly, Nathanuel Dover would have been tried for his crimes a long time ago and these terrible killings would have been stopped.'

'Indeed. We don't even know the true extent of these murders. If we could set the Drakers against the Order, we might stand a chance.'

'Then there *is* a way forward,' says Lizzy. 'Find evidence and find a way to get the Drakers on board.'

She's right, of course, but that's easier said than done. For once, I'm in agreement with Josiah. And tomorrow, he and I mean to steal every last guinea of the Order's funds.

When the girls have returned to their tasks, Josiah and I remain in the case room to conspire. Our plan is vague at best, which concerns me. We'll face more guards this time. There'll be Cullins and Gouldstone, too, and there is no way I'm going to take them all on without Josiah at my side, so our identities will be more easily guessed, even with our best disguises. To be honest, we could do with a small army, but we have none, so Josiah and I will go unaided.

### The Good News
No one is making us do this.

### The Bad News
We're doomed.

We decide our previous approach is unlikely to work against a heavier guard. Our only hope is to surprise them from both sides of the road and have our pistols on them before they can react. I wish Mardon was in on it, but he's miles away, and in any case this is exactly the kind of venture he loathes. He would most likely refuse to be involved, and I won't have Ebadiah or any of the street boys risk themselves. It's for that reason I've kept Ebadiah out of it.

'We need a leveller,' I say, thinking aloud.

'What do you mean?'

'Something to even the odds.'

'Like more men.'

'Yes. Or failing that, a scheme that will give us another advantage.'

'Hmmm…' He screws up his face.

'This would be a great time for one of your excellent ideas.'

'I'm trying, Mr Banyard, I'm trying.'

But no excellent ideas transpire so we sit in silence, thinking.

We are about to head home when Lizzy raps on the case room door and enters to deliver a letter. 'This just came for you. A street boy pushed it beneath the door before fleeing.' She hands me the letter and leaves.

'Thank you.' I stare at my name drafted in flowing green ink upon a creamy envelope, slide a letter opener along the fold, open and read out the letter.

> *Dearest Michael,*
> *I write with urgency. Fate has forced my hand for I can see no other course remaining. It may be the last thing I ever do. Meet me on Haylarton Heath tomorrow morning at ten o'clock. I shall await you and your associate by the old mine stack. Bring arms and we shall rid the world of the Order of Lithobates, once and for all! My friend, I pray you do not disappoint me in this, our hour of need. I know I can count on you.*
> *Yours truly,*
> *Demitri Valerio*

I hurry to find a map. Haylarton Heath is around three hours ride north of Camdon. It's too distant to feature on the Camdon City map but I have another that includes Loncaster and shows the heath well enough. I take the map down from a shelf and unfold it to study it more closely, following the road to Loncaster out from the southernmost point where it passes through a few hamlets and patches of woodland like the one where we took Willow from Silver. I flatten the map on Josiah's desk so we can both view it, and trace the line of the road north with a finger.

'The road crosses the heath here.' On the map there's a drawing that looks like the ruin of a mine with a tall chimney stack. 'This must be the place. It's the wheelhouse of an abandoned copper mine.'

'What's that?' Josiah points to a place just south of the mine where the road becomes a pair of dashed lines for a quarter of an inch.

'It's a tunnel.' I recall the place where the north road burrows through the lower slope of a hillside as it bends north-west towards Loncaster. 'By thunder! This is it, Joe. We'll use the tunnel!'

'How?'

'Do you remember? The road narrows to enter the tunnel. The ceiling is low and barely broader than a cart. To pass through, the guards riding on the coach would have to dismount and rejoin it at the other end, unless they're on the driver's bench, of course. Even if half of the guards were to walk ahead of the coach, we could surprise them as they exit. We could stall the horses before the coach leaves the tunnel, and have them trapped in our power. There'd be no way they could retreat. They'd be utterly stuck. I doubt they'd even be able to open the doors. It's brilliant! Precisely the advantage we need.'

Josiah flattens his lips, nodding his approval. 'He's clever, our green ink friend.'

'He is. And tomorrow we'll finally learn his identity.'

We leave the map and the letter on the desk. We will not need them for what we are about to do.

Around seven in the morning we ride north as the low sun streaks the sky with tones of fire that cast the horizon into silhouette, heat rising on the dusty road. Almost three hours later we hit Haylarton Heath and the landscape opens up into a vast stretch of moor scattered with granite outcrops, fells and peatbogs. There are occasional flocks of sheep and glimpses of wild ponies along the way, but the mine wheelhouse and its tall, narrow smokestack are unmistakable, protruding high, solid and stark against the pale sky. It nestles at the foot of the hill beyond the tunnel and we quicken our pace, keen to reach our goal. We thread the tunnel, our mounts' hooves bounding loud echoes about the walls, and hit the light on the far side, slowing on an incline towards the mine. It's a ruin, its stone walls weathered and broken, grey and green with lichen and moss. Looming over us at one corner, the old stack rises, its only flaw a few fallen stones that have broken away from one side of its peak. The building's roof has collapsed but the walls remain two levels above the ground, and its tall, arched windows and doorways are empty and starkly shadowed in the bright morning light.

We ride in a slow circle around the ruin, seeking our green ink ghost, though the place is deserted.

'Where is he?' growls Josiah.

'Patience. He'll be here.' I check my pocket watch before peering around at the vast open heath. 'We're a few minutes early.'

'How do we know he's going to show? We've no reason to trust a word he says.'

'He was right about Eadward Trent. What choice do we have?'

'Anyway, why ten o'clock? We may have missed the coach already.'

'I've a feeling this ghost knows more than he's saying. Perhaps he knows the time the coach was scheduled to leave.'

'Perhaps. You think it will pass at ten?'

'Or soon after. I imagine it can't be far behind us.'

We dismount and tuck ourselves in against one end of the ruin to watch as a cart, drawn by a pair of mules, rumbles into view beyond the tunnel. It disappears beneath the hill and reappears as it leaves the tunnel to pass the mine. One driver. No guard. A load of sawn timber bound for Loncaster. It trundles away and the road quietens again.

A new sound rises: the clop of hooves on the baked ground behind us. We turn to see a cloaked rider wearing a crimson dress fringed with black lace, a black bodice and a squat coachman's hat. Her face is partially hidden beneath a black scarf but the eyes watching us are striking and familiar. We rest our hands on our pistols as the newcomer approaches, riding side-saddle on a chestnut gelding and slowing to a stop before us.

'Good morning, gentlemen.' Clara Avard removes her scarf to smile at our bemused faces.

Josiah scans the area, presumably checking for others. There aren't any and we both reach the same conclusion. 'It's you,' he says. 'You're *Demitri Valerio.*'

'Well done, Mr Mingle. You figured it out.' She grins.

'But...' I can't fathom which question to ask first, I have so many. '*You* are the green ink ghost?'

'We can talk later,' says Clara. 'Right now, we have a coach to rob.' Beneath her words begins the rattle of an approaching vehicle and we turn to see it in the distance, on the far side of the tunnel. I use my stereoscope to get some detail: four harnessed horses, four guards, one driver, two men on horses – they must be Cullins and Gouldstone, I realise – a dust trail rising in their wake to shimmer in the heat haze. Clara, too, spies on the coach through a stereoscope. It's likely they haven't seen us yet because we're gathered in the deep shadow to one side of the wheelhouse and its tall chimney.

Clara repositions her scarf to cover her nose and mouth. We adjust our scarfs to hide our faces.

'To the tunnel!' She heels her mount forwards and we follow, quickly putting the hill spur between us and those approaching.

'Your plan?' I ask, catching up to ride alongside her.

'It's simple,' she says. 'There's a tunnel. I have a bag full of pyronitronite...'

'But that's – '

'Dangerously unstable? Yes, though worth the risk. Any problems, we bring the tunnel down on them.'

'Are you insane? You're just as likely to kill us all!'

She flashes that grin again. 'I suppose that's a possibility. Just follow my lead and have your pistols at the ready. Do as I say and all will be well.'

We pull our hats down low over our eyes, leave the mine behind and ride into the crook of the hill long before the coach nears the tunnel and there we hide, Josiah on one side of the entrance, Clara and I on the other. We listen. It's clear when the coach enters the tunnel. The din is raucous: the clatter of sixteen iron-shod hooves and four iron rimmed wheels echoing around.

Cullins and Gouldstone are no doubt also following behind on their mounts.

I always find it's hard to argue with an unhinged woman carrying a bag of pyronitronite. You tend to let them get on with whatever they're trying to do. And that's exactly what I do, waiting with trepidation, wondering what her next move will be as the horses thunder towards us.

A pistol in one hand and a fist full of explosive cylinders in the other, Clara coaxes her horse down onto the track and tosses the explosives into the mouth of the tunnel ahead of the oncoming horses. There's an almighty eruption that shakes the tunnel and must surely deafen those inside. There's no sign of the guards or Cullins or Gouldstone, so I reason they must be caught up beyond our view, behind the coach, unable to pass.

The coach horses whinny, rear and stamp, panicked to madness, though too fearful to flee through the black mass of smoke that plumes and wafts around the tunnel opening. It clears to reveal Clara astride her horse, levelling pistols at the driver. The tunnel remains intact. There are shouts and curses and the sounds of the panicked horses, but the trapped coach stops. Only the guards are *not* trapped, because one of them squeezes between the coach and the tunnel wall, his gun aimed at Clara. He fires a poor shot that zips past her head.

She shoots back. Boom. He drops, a hole in his forehead.

I blink, see Trent's pale face flash before me, a similar hole between his eyes. I'm unsettled. Clara Avard is a crack shot.

Another guard appears crawling over the roof of the carriage, the barrel of his musket thrusting ahead. Clara discharges her second pistol. The guard on the roof sighs and collapses to move no more.

'Clara, stop!' I shout. This was not my plan. Not my plan at all!

'Quiet!' she hisses. 'Any more chancers?' She raises her voice to those in the tunnel. 'Shoot me and you'll all die. I have a dozen pounds of pyronitronite that will fall with me. In case you didn't know, it's rather volatile. Throw out your weapons or I'll

235

blow you to Amorphia.'

If I'm right about the numbers, there are two guards remaining, the unarmed driver, who has his hands in the air, and Cullins and Gouldstone, too. I catch Josiah's eye. He looks as flummoxed as I feel. I ride down from the verge to join Clara on the road and level a pistol at the coach as though I'm part of this madness.

'Weapons, now!' she urges, gesturing to those in the tunnel with her pistol.

Someone has to take out this crazed woman before she kills again. And that someone is me. While her attention is on them, I reverse my pistol and swing it like a club, aiming for the back of her head. She sees the blow coming and ducks away, twisting in her saddle to train her guns on me, though I'm not worried because she's used both her shots. She knows this, too, and quickly makes a grab for the explosives in her bag. Leaning from my saddle, I lurch at her and while we tussle on horseback, Cullins slips out of the tunnel, his gun fixed upon Josiah. Josiah sees him, but too late. Cullins fires and the shot glances Josiah's shoulder. He falls backwards, toppling from his saddle. As Clara and I struggle, our scarves slip from our faces. Cullins appears before us with surprising speed, his second pistol levelled at my head. A guard joins him as recognition blooms on Cullins' face. He seems suddenly pleased.

'Well, now, I've been waiting a long time for an opportunity like this, Banyard.'

Two guns follow me. There's nothing I can do but release Clara and retreat, my hands raised. Josiah is down, injured and unmoving. I fear he may have broken his neck in the fall.

'Wait!' I say, thinking desperately. 'This is not. I'm not...'

'Shut it, Banyard,' says Cullins. 'You're through. Finished. I'm taking you back to Camdon where you'll hang for highway robbery.' He takes my guns, tosses them a good distance into the heath and turns to Clara. 'And you! What do you think you're doing? Robbing from your own?'

'We're all thieves, Mr Cullins. Didn't you know?' Clara

snatches another cylinder from her bag and raises it threateningly. As she does so, the collar of her dress parts a little, and that's when all becomes clear. At her throat, gold flashes briefly in the light. There's a ring on a chain around her neck: a gold ring set with onyx. I don't need to see the frog motif to know it's there.

Clara addresses Cullins and Gouldstone as Gouldstone leaves the shadows of the tunnel. 'Consider this my resignation from the Order. Do as I say and you will walk away with a third of the bounty. Obstruct me and you will die with the others.'

Cullins considers this. 'You have a deal, Miss Avard.'

Gouldstone nods his approval. 'Indeed, you do.'

'You're one of them!' I say to Clara, still in disbelief. 'One of the Order.' The truth reels my mind. 'But the letters…'

'You still don't get it, do you? I was *using* you. Not that you proved to be of any use. You couldn't remove a single obstacle from my path. You see, the thing is: I'm simply not content with my place in the line. I was hoping you might eradicate some of the competition but, oh no, I was wasting my time with you. It was fun, but I'm afraid you've proved a terrible investment. And now, well, frankly, you're *dead* to me.'

I'm flabbergasted. 'You had us exhume Steeler just to put us on to the Order. You were toying with us…'

'Good,' she says, smiling. 'Now at least we're all up to speed.'

# 24

# Destination Pyronitronite

*In which much happens in a very short space of time*

Clara commands Cullins and Gouldstone while gesturing towards Josiah and me. 'Bind these simpletons and take them to the mine. There are shafts in there a mile deep. Their bodies will never be found.'

Cullins orders me to dismount and, under duress, I oblige. For a moment I fear he will kill Blink – but he doesn't. It's not until he is tying my hands behind my back and I'm forced away from the tunnel that I get a better glimpse of the dead guards. They're dressed in black uniforms with gleaming brass buttons. The Order must have arranged a Draker escort for its money. The other two appear, nervously edging their way out from the tunnel, guns poised.

'Just exactly what is going on here?' shouts the first, clearly bewildered by the fact that Cullins and Gouldstone have apparently teamed up with a highwaywoman.

'Shoot them,' Clara mutters to Cullins.

Cullins obeys before the guards can take aim. His shots streak the air. The Drakers fall to the ground. Gouldstone keeps his pistols on me, giving Clara and Cullins time to reload.

Clara points a newly primed pistol at the driver. 'You there, get these bodies on the coach and bring them to the mine, or you're next!'

The driver coaxes the four horses to move on, drawing the coach out of the tunnel. He climbs down from the driver's bench to load the corpses with Gouldstone's help.

With a gun at my back, I walk the track ahead of Cullins and Clara while Gouldstone and the driver struggle to heft Josiah up and onto his horse. They leave him belly down so that his arms dangle one side and his legs the other, and lead the horse by the reins. Josiah appears to be unconscious, or dead. I can't tell which.

I spit. 'You people revolt me.'

'The feeling's mutual,' replies Cullins, gesturing with a pistol for me to walk on. 'Keep your mouth shut or I'll gag you.' They glance up and down the road, checking, but it seems no one else is coming to bear witness to their crimes, and our disjointed party moves up the track, nearer to the wheelhouse.

I have an extremely bad feeling about the mine. I'm sure Clara spoke the truth: there are shafts that delve a mile deep. It's the perfect place to dispose of a few inconvenient bodies – I should have thought of it earlier – and I imagine Cullins is only keeping me alive so he can enjoy the expression of terror on my face as he shoves me off the edge into the abyss. Perhaps beforehand he'll cut my throat or shoot me in the knees for good measure. For now, he lets me walk.

I glance behind at Josiah. His head lolls with the gait of the horse.

*He is dead*, I think. Something happens in my core, a reaction to that thought, over which I have no control. My gut knots and I double over to retch on the road.

Cullins sniggers. 'My, you've a weak stomach, Banyard. Never mind. You won't need it where you're going. Move on.' He prods me with the muzzle of his gun.

Behind us the driver brings the coach loaded with the money and four dead Drakers. If this is a dream, I'd like to awaken, to open my eyes and sit up, to realise everything is all right. But even if I could, everything would *not* be all right. Not while silkers like Cullins, Gouldstone and Clara Avard are in power. In any case, this is no dream. It is simply my unfortunate reality.

We reach the wheelhouse entrance and I stagger as Cullins pushes me through an arched doorway into the ruined shell of the mine head. I make a fight for it, pull back hoping to unbalance him but he's larger and heavier than me. Perhaps three times my age, his frame is stocky and my efforts reap little reward. In anger he clubs me around the head with the butt of his pistol. The pain is unbearable, my rebellion curbed.

Inside, there are several moss-grown chambers. The upper floor is long gone, the structure open to the sky, but there are two open shafts remaining in the ground, each with its own chamber. Clara directs her accomplices to the nearest shaft, which has a rusting cage suspended over the drop on an equally rusting chain. The chain runs up and over the huge wheel of a steam-powered winch. The cage is large enough for around four people standing with a little room to spare and has a gap around it for clearance in the shaft.

At its open door Clara stops and waves a pistol. 'In there.'

Cullins drags me over to the cage and shoves me inside.

'Down, Mr Banyard,' commands Clara. 'On your face.'

I refuse. She sends a pistol shot over my shoulder and levels her second gun. I comply, dropping to my knees and wriggling uncomfortably on to my belly. With my hands still tied at my back it's an awkward procedure but I start work on my bindings, trying to loosen them from my wrists while Clara reloads.

Gouldstone calls from outside. 'I'll need some assistance with this one. He's a heavy brute.'

Cullins leaves to help drag in Josiah, and gripping him under the arms, they heave his limp frame across the flagstone floor to the cage. They dump him alongside me before revisiting the coach to press the driver into helping them haul in the four dead Drakers. The chain creaks under the strain of the new load and I wonder how long it will hold as the driver, Cullins and Gouldstone pile the Draker corpses on top of Josiah and me.

The weight squeezes the breath from my lungs and I forget any thoughts of freeing my hands. They are squashed at my back and I can barely move. Through the floor bars I see the shaft below: chiselled stone walls diving away beneath us into darkness. My journey's end.

There's an immense pressure on my ribs as I'm crushed against the iron floor bars. It feels as though at some point my bones might all snap catastrophically and my chest will collapse. I wonder if Josiah is breathing but can't see much of him beneath the bodies. Part of me hopes he is already dead. At least then he'll be spared the horror of our final descent when it comes. Voices beyond the cage rouse my attention and I strain to catch glimpses of what follows.

'Take the bag,' says Clara.

Cullins dutifully receives her bag of explosives.

'Now place it up there beneath the winch.'

Cullins moves out of view, presumably to position the bag.

'There's a fuse line in there ending with a powder charge. Uncoil the line and run it down here. Bring the matches.'

Moments later Cullins reappears in my line of vision, a pale cord trailing in one hand. In the other he holds a packet of Sulphurs.

Clara gestures with a pistol to the driver. 'You, get over there by the cage.'

The terrified man crosses the room to stand in front of me. I hear a shot, smell burning gunpowder and he falls to the floor, groaning.

'Mr Gouldstone, I'd be obliged if you would help him on his way,' says Clara.

Gouldstone uses a foot to shunt the bleeding driver over the edge and into the shaft. There's not much space between the cage and the shaft's edge so the driver nudges the cage, setting it swinging as he falls, dying. He screams on the way down, though a breath later there is only the faint creaking of the cage and its fragile chain.

'Good. Light the fuse, Mr Cullins. It's time for us to leave.'

Clara reloads. Cullins sets the fuse alight. It crackles and sparks, throwing out a thin line of smoke as the smouldering fire begins its journey to the bag. 'And now, there's one more thing I must do before we go.' Clara points a pistol at Gouldstone and shoots him in the chest. Gouldstone grasps at the cage for support but slips to the floor at the edge of the shaft.

Cullins looks on, stunned. 'What are you doing? You fool! He is one of us!'

'Not any more.' She turns her loaded pistol on Cullins. 'Put him down the mine.'

Cullins gawps at her. For the first time, there is a glint of fear in his expression. 'A two-way split, then?' he nervously suggests.

'Of course. Why split it three ways when two is better?' says Clara, but presumably I'm not the only one thinking, *In which case, why split it at all?*

'You're a witch.' These are the last words Fletcher Gouldstone will ever speak.

Clara smiles. 'Mr Cullins, if you would oblige…'

Cullins walks regrettably to Gouldstone and, shaking his head, shoves him over the edge with his boot.

'Now, surrender your pistols,' commands Clara.

Heaving a sigh, Cullins takes his pistols from their holsters and cautiously places them on the floor at his feet.

'Kick them to me.'

He boots them across the floor but as Clara stoops to collect them, he makes a dash for the doorway. She rises to shoot, her aim rushed. Cullins takes the shot in his left thigh but keeps running and he's gone before she can shoot again. She curses under her breath as the fuse smoulders closer to the winch.

On her way out she pauses, framed briefly in the arch. 'Farewell, *dearest Michael*.' She blows a kiss.

The fuse has burned down and there are now bodies blocking my view of it. I can hear it, though, a soft crackling that's working its way further around the side of the cage, ever closer to destination pyronitronite. I wriggle and kick, desperate to break free from the pile, but I'm going nowhere. The bodies and the bars of the cage floor are slick with blood, and blood glistens on the flagstones opposite the cage door. Some time passes; I'm not sure how long but it seems an age. It's probably only a few seconds.

Cullins returns. I'm baffled, left wondering what has become of Clara. Is she lying unconscious out on the heath? I also wonder *why* he's back, risking the imminent explosion that will send my cage of bodies plummeting into the shaft and bring down the chimney to cover everything. My question is soon answered. He hurries, limping to the cage, opens the door and leans in, groping among the bloody bodies for a pistol. From the wound in his thigh a stream of blood soaks his britches. He finds a gun and checks it's loaded before stooping over me to club my head with the butt. I throw my head to the side, managing to only receive a glancing blow.

'This is your doing, Banyard! This is all *your* doing!' In a fury, he aims a kick at my head through the door, but with his weakened leg he slips on the bloodied stones of the floor and topples into the gap between the cage and the shaft's edge, grappling for a hold that doesn't manifest. The buckskin of his riding gloves are oiled with blood. For a moment his eyes bulge at me as his body is pinned briefly between the cage and the shaft wall.

'Help me!' he cries, gloves slipping and sliding lower down the bars. His feet kick for a foothold on the side of the mineshaft but this only presses his body harder against the cage, which swings further away from the edge to broaden the gap. Lower he sinks.

His head reaches my level so that the whites of his terrified eyes are a few inches from mine.

'Help me!' he whines through gritted teeth.

'I'm sorry,' I mutter, struggling for breath. 'My hands are tied.'

Flailing for a hold, he slides through the gap to hang from the cage, his grip straining on the bottom of the bars. He's heavier than he is strong, and he struggles to hold his own weight. I watch his fingers lose their hold and he plummets, screaming into the darkness below.

I feel a wave of nausea and the onset of a faint. *Good*, I think. I will not be conscious when the end comes.

It brings a mild sense of relief.

I close my eyes and abandon myself to it.

It is over.

Footsteps tell of a newcomer. I open my eyes and wonder if I'm hallucinating.

'Penney?'

Penney walks towards me, closely followed by Lizzy. Both look concerned and puzzled.

'Michael, is that you?' asks Penney, stooping to peer. They each have snub-nosed pistols poised in their hands.

'There's a bomb on the winch!' I nod my head upwards as best I can as a trickle of blood runs into my eye. 'Pull the fuse before it detonates! Hurry!'

Lizzy runs beyond view while Penney rushes to the open cage door and begins tugging at the bodies that are piled on top of me.

'I have it!' announces Lizzy.

I throw my head to the side. 'Quickly! Josiah is under there! He's been shot.'

'Whatever has happened?' asks Penney. Lizzy joins her and together they manage to drag a body free of the cage, carefully avoiding the gap. The cage swings perilously.

'It was Clara Avard. Cullins and Gouldstone, too, though the men are down the shaft now. Dead,' I say. 'She shot them. What are you doing here?'

'We found the letter and the map,' says Penney. 'We figured you'd try something stupid.'

'Someone has to look after you boys,' says Lizzy.

They heave another body from the cage. I feel the load lighten, though there's an unhealthy groan from the chain, and I stretch my neck to glimpse up at a link that is gradually easing apart.

'Hurry! Before it gives way!'

A Draker enters the wheelhouse, looking bemused, peering behind at the road outside and then at the scene before him. 'What on Earthoria…'

'You brought a Draker?' I ask, astonished and at the same time irritated.

'Help us!' Lizzy shouts. The Draker responds. The three of them drag the remaining bodies onto the floor and finally lift Josiah and me out. The empty cage swings mockingly.

'Now,' says the Draker. 'Will someone please tell me what's going on?'

Penney works my ropes loose while Lizzy tends to Josiah.

'Is he alive?' I ask.

'He is, though he's bleeding. She rests his head on her lap and, taking a silver flask from a pocket, unstoppers it to pour some of the contents into his mouth. The liquor seems to help. He stirs, opens his eyes, groggy and disorientated. He takes in the scene, looking every bit as confused as the Draker.

'Where's the loot?' asks Josiah. He's not too damaged, then. He sits up and glances down at his wounded shoulder. 'I think I hit my head.'

The Draker stamps in frustration. 'If someone doesn't tell me what's gone on, I'm going to arrest the lot of you!'

'It was the Order of Lithobates,' I explain. He looks blankly back at me. Apparently, he is not on the Order's payroll. My hands are free. Gingerly, I get to my feet. 'A secret order of wealthy nobles, sworn to protect the king, but they're corrupt. They were transferring their funds in a coach when one of them, a woman named Clara Avard, tried to take it for herself. They put a bag of pyronitronite back there on the lift wheel to blow us sky-high.' I walk to the arch and peer out. Along with Cullins' and Gouldstone's horses, our mounts are roaming free, feeding on moor grass a short way from the mine head, and beyond them on the road sits the coach. I had expected to find the coach and horses gone, had presumed Clara would have driven it away with the cash, but only her chestnut gelding is missing.

'The money is still out there.' I sweep blood and hair from my eyes.

'Well, the *coach* is still there,' says Penney. 'And there's blood on it.'

Josiah looks bewildered. 'They were going to blow up the mine?'

'With us in it,' I nod.

'Right,' says the Draker. 'Nobody touches a thing. I'm going to inspect that coach. We'll see if what you say is true.'

'So where is Clara?' I ask nobody in particular, while scanning the heath beyond the arch.

The Draker heads out to the coach and we all follow, even Josiah, though he's unsteady on his feet. I'm surprised to learn that there are eight caskets full of bank notes in the back of the coach. A fortune.

Prising the lid from the last casket, the Draker raises his brows and whistles through his teeth. 'Right. This lot's goin' back to headquarters as evidence. You'd better start from the beginning and tell me everything.'

We gather at the side of the track, the Draker's back to the coach as he interrogates me. In the corner of my eye, I see Josiah turn back to the mine. I tell the Draker what happened, leaving out the part about Josiah's and my intention to rob the coach, of course. I explain about the green ink letters and that we came to learn the identity of the author. It's a long story and before I'm through, Josiah rejoins us with Clara's bag in his arms.

'This is the bag of explosives,' he says. 'I suppose it's evidence, too.'

'Indeed,' says the Draker. 'Put it in the coach with the money.'

'Carefully, Josiah,' I add. 'It's volatile.'

With a nod, he heads for the coach and I notice the end of the fuse protruding from his long coat pocket. In the mid-distance, a caravan of threader carts approaches along the road from the north. Josiah pauses ahead of the money coach to unhitch its horses, leaving them coupled. I wonder what he's up to as he slaps the hindquarter of the closest mare. They start and walk on a short way down the road before coming to rest as Josiah disappears behind the stationary coach.

'I still don't understand,' says the Draker. He's intent upon me and quite red in the face, now. 'How did you end up in that cage?'

I repeat part of my story and, as I'm coming to the end of it, Josiah strides briskly away from the coach. He catches my eye and nods towards the open heath ahead.

I take the hint. 'Come, let me walk you through it.' I put an arm around the Draker's shoulders to steer him quickly away from the coach. We're halfway between the mine and the coach when it blows, sending wood and a multitude of bank notes high into the sky. We cower, sheltering beneath our arms against the flying wreckage as the unhitched coach horses bolt. For several breaths debris rains but, when it stops, I look around and find that none of us is hurt. The notes flutter and spin in the air, dissipating over a wide area, blowing on the breeze. The approaching threaders halt their carts and run to gather the falling notes, rejoicing in their good fortune.

'Here! You can't do that!' shouts the Draker in vain, but his attention shifts when there's a deep rumble from the mine. We turn to watch the chimney fall, a ground-shaking collapse that sends a vast dust cloud up into the air. We're enveloped in the choking haze.

I glance at Josiah. With distrust, the Draker eyes us in turn.

Josiah shrugs and shakes out his coat. 'Volatile.'

# 25

# Dover

*In which Mingle empties his pockets*

It's not until later, when we're back at home and alone, that Josiah empties his long coat pockets of the banded bank notes he hurriedly crammed in before lighting the fuse of Clara's bomb.

'At least the money isn't being returned to the Order,' he says, quietly pleased with himself. 'And this bit can pay for new papers for Willow and a few of the other threaders we relocate. And some other expenses. There's quite a lot here.' He piles the wads of bank notes onto the sitting room table.

'Hmmm.' I'm distracted. 'What do you think happened to Clara Avard?'

'Who knows? She didn't get the money either. That's good, isn't it?'

'I suppose.'

I can only imagine Cullins must have knocked her unconscious or waylaid her somehow before he returned to torture me and that, before the girls brought the Draker first to the coach and then to the mine, she managed to escape, nursing whatever wounds she had suffered. Was she out of ammunition and simply decided to run? Her horse was missing, but it could have wandered off and is perhaps lost on the heath. I test other scenarios but nothing much seems to fit.

We enter the green room and relax into chairs. We don't notice immediately but a beating sound draws our attention across the room to where Baker lounges on the floor, his tail thwacking the rug.

'He's made himself at home,' I mutter, unsurprised. Mother must have let him in here. I think nothing else that might possibly happen today could surprise me now.

'Huh,' says Josiah, acceptingly.

Baker yawns and makes a low whining sound.

We sit in silence for a long time. I suppose we're stuck with the hound because we can't rid ourselves of the creature. I just hope Silver doesn't come calling again.

'Of course, the Draker collected some of the money.' I recall him desperately running in circles, leaping at the falling notes as they swirled and fluttered around.

'And you're worried he's returning that to the Order?' Josiah chuckles.

'He may have.'

He whistles an upward note followed by a downward note and mimes pocketing the cash.

Perhaps he's right. The Draker may have returned nothing to the Order. One thing's for sure, though, he did return a lengthy report to his superiors vividly detailing the callous murder of four Draker watchmen. I made certain of that, explained in full how three members of the Order colluded in the slaughter, put it all in writing. I also visited Bretling to deliver a copy of my statement in person and explain what had happened. With a little bending of the truth, you understand. I showed him the third green ink letter, saying that we were compelled to go to the rendezvous if only to learn the author's identity, and *that* sufficiently explained our presence at the mine, although it won me a suspicious glare and a perfunctory puff of smoke. If I'm right, the Drakers and the Order are no longer bedfellows.

As for Penney and Lizzy, we owe them our lives. They have not given us up to the Drakers, and neither of them has resigned. I wonder if we should trust them with more of our secrets.

Soon after the events at the mine, I make a point of thanking the girls in the office late one afternoon. They make little of it and Penney leaves for home, but Lizzy tarries and seems earnest when she says, 'You're a good man, Mr Banyard. Worth saving.'

I'm flattered and left wondering if I haven't been chasing the wrong girl all this time.

Several days pass and Josiah and I take some time to recover from our wounds and the stress of recent events. Josiah's shoulder stopped bleeding shortly after the surgeon stitched up the wound and is healing nicely. In time it will be yet one more scar upon a vastly scarred body. He has quite a collection, though he's fortunate that most can be covered by a shirt. His back is permanently striped from the many lashings administered during his years as a labouring threader.

We spend time honing his writing skills because he's keen to write to Willow. He's desperate to see her, but that's not going to happen. Not for a long time. Not if I can help it. I will help him draft a letter, though, and he's eager to impress, so the better the letter, the more I'm forgiven. Or so I hope. He does well enough, and three days later posts a reasonably cohesive message to his lover in Rochington, though I only allow him to address her as W for security's sake, and to sign it with a simple J.

There's another, more trivial, matter to address, also. With two Willows in the picture, we should really rename his horse to avoid confusion. I put it to him and he thinks about this long and hard, eventually announcing, 'Willie. We'll call the mare Willie.'

Fair enough, I suppose. 'Willie it is.'

That night, I peruse a copy of the *Camdon Herald*, comfortably installed in the green room with a fine glass of port and my father's hat for company. Stocks in Hinkley Air have plummeted. I'm not sure why but perhaps there's a connection with the Order's lost fortune. The most interesting news is the leading headline. Apparently, at some point during the previous morning, Nathanuel Dover, Earl of Lockingshire, the king's brother no less, was found hanging by the neck from a roof beam of a stable on the Dover Palace estate. One has to wonder if the collapse of the Order's arrangement with the Drakers isn't to blame. Did the Drakers take matters into their own hands? Was it a deranged man committing suicide, or did the Order of Lithobates execute one final act before disbanding? We may never know, but either way, Nathanuel Dover has killed for the last time and the streets of Camdon City are a little safer for threader women.

I wonder what my father would have made of it all. My eyes fall upon the tricorn and I hear his gentle voice in my head.

*You did what you could, lad. You did what you could. And no one can ask more of you than that.*

It seems likely my father *was* killed by the Order when he investigated the murder of Oliver Ingham. My money is on Cullins, though I can't be sure. It may have been Gouldstone or any of them really, and, in a way, it was *all* of them, Clara included. Why did Oliver Ingham have to die? Probably because he was looking into the disappearance of his daughter, Tillie, and, if I'm correct, she was fleeing the Order, carrying Dover's illegitimate child. A child who would have brought shame upon the royal house of Dover.

It's a grim story. A spiral of death and deceit.

Of course, there's a flaw in the theory that the Order has already found and killed Tillie. Every Tobias file or imograph I saw from the Draker case room was that of a body thought to be a threader, and Tillie was not a threader. She was, or is, a silker.

I spend some time reading Tillie's book on Mors Zonam, intrigued by a writer who might take interest in such a subject. The author's name is Evantia Mandicut. Another Urthian name.

From what I read he was, or is – I know not if he is living or dead – a viscount of his homeland and a well-travelled adventurer who enjoyed, or enjoys, a good expedition. Several chapters in, I notice a faint pencil line beneath a few words of the text. I've not spotted this before and the observation causes me to backtrack through the pages in search of other such lines. They are so feeble that they are hard to make out, but with more lamplight and a magnifying glass they become clearer and I find a dozen or so more examples, folding the corners of the relevant pages. With some considerable study I realise that they occur only beneath phrases that speak of survival in Mors Zonam. This, then, seems to lend more weight to Josiah's argument that Tillie may have fled there to escape the Order. Was she studying this book and planning a getaway to the least habitable zone of Londaland? It's a crazy idea, but the more I read, the more believable it becomes. I return to the underlined phrases.

> There is life in Mors Zonam, though it is hard to find. Nevertheless, there is life and life cannot exist without water. This is a scientific fact. Ergo there is water in Mors Zonam.

This we already know because a gawper supplied water to Josiah and me – water that saved our lives – and I'm convinced that the gawper took that water from somewhere close by.

A few pages on there's another underlining.

> Water naturally flows downhill to gather at the lowest non-permeable point in the geological strata. Therefore, there could well exist hidden reserves of water beneath the upper layers of toxic desert.

This, too, Josiah and I suspected as we walked out of that acrid, arid land, though we never found it.

The book details several expeditions into Mors Zonam, most of which ended badly for the explorers. I recall the bones scattered about the valley, the feelings of thirst and doom.

Despite this, a notion settles in my mind. I consider an expedition of my own, one I would embark upon alone for fear of leading others to their deaths.

Later that night, when everyone else has retired, I close the book and climb the stairs to my bedroom where I keep a chest at the foot of the bed. I open the lid and take out one of the hide-stitched waterskins left for us by the gawper in the valley of bones, and turn it in my hands. Is this not proof of civilisation in Mors Zonam? Is that where the gawpers abide?

I examine a mask also, still unsure of the material from which it is made. I decide these basic but effective implements might make the beginnings of my expedition kit. With plenty of water for the journey, enough food that will not rot, a compass, some form of sunshade and a gawper mask that makes the toxic air more bearable, I may be able to venture into the zone for a number of days without fearing a painful death. I would need my pistols, of course, and plenty of gunpowder and shot for protection against the creatures that venture out in the green glow of the night. My rapier, too.

The mask in my hands prompts another thought. Each time I have encountered the gawpers I've been struck by their lack of facial features. They have eyes, yes, most definitely, but other features? I've never seen them. I place the mask over my lower face and study my reflection in the mirror on my dressing table. My lower face is a dark, featureless shape. The material seems to absorb the light. Do the gawpers wear these masks? Perhaps they are partly the cause of their strange appearance. Perhaps the gawpers are not so different from us, after all. The more I dwell on it, the more I desire answers. My father would have been thrilled by these artefacts and the things I have learned.

I pause as my thoughts are disturbed by the sound of smashing glass somewhere lower in the house. It's late in the evening and I know that no one else is up. So, who or what is smashing glass in the dark?

Baker?

I drop the mask, belt up my pistols, grab a storm lamp from

my bedside table and leave the room to investigate as a second smash reaches my ears from one or two rooms away. A third comes from the other side of my bedroom door. I re-enter to see my window shattered across the floor. A lump of rock the size of a fist rolls to a stop at my feet. I dash to the window only to glimpse a shadow disappearing around the side of the house. There are further smashes and then a gunshot, loud and startling. I descend the stairs as Josiah enters the landing corridor.

'Tell the women to lock themselves in their rooms!' I hiss, drawing a pistol. He follows the passage to the other bedrooms as I head down to the ground floor.

At the foot of the stairs I pause, eyes straining in the half-light, my senses heightened by a rising fear in my heart. The small hairs on the back of my neck are standing on end. I hear the creak of a hinge. The back door, perhaps.

The hallway leads on to the green room, among others, so I check in there. It's dark and empty but shards of window glass glisten across the floor in the lamplight. Another stone rests among them. I pause to collect the rock and examine it. It looks familiar. Like one of the stones from the decaying walls of the wheelhouse on the heath. I glance out into the shadowscape through the broken pane, where cool air flows in from the night. There is movement. A bleak wind stirs the murky trees. I shudder.

Footsteps, small and quick, somewhere inside.

I leave the green room to work my way through the house to the back door and find it swinging gently open in the faint breeze. Raising the lantern, I see the lock has been shot through, the blast enough to rupture the inner mechanism. I glance out across the back garden, the stables.

And sensing a presence at my back, I turn.

# 26

# The Valley

*In which Banyard prepares for an expedition*

A figure stands before me, pistol levelled at my head. She is changed, though recognisable from a former rendering. From a time when the finest silken skirts traced her form to shimmer in the crystal light. When the exquisite trappings of a wealthy silker woman prescribed a different aura. In that short moment I blink but once and see this single image. She is beautiful, glorious, resplendent and beguiling, sipping tea in a teashop, a lace-edged parasol at her side, her gloved hands genteel, softly caressing a steaming cup. The sculptural curves of her face please. Her eyes are large and innocent, but there is something about them – even then, it was apparent – something untouchable, unfathomable.

I know, now, in this moment, what it was.

*Darkness!*

Clara Avard has changed. When I open my eyes I see her reborn in shadow. In some ways it is a truer translation. Her silks are sullied and torn. There is a damp, animal smell about her. Her skin is grimy with filth and encrusted with dried blood, her porcelain lustre flawless no more. A festering, bloodied gash streaks downward from her left temple where a rock impacted, out on the heath. Her large eyes are now narrowed, crazed and fixed upon me, driven by hatred.

She pulls the trigger. The powder flashes brightly.

At the same moment a shadow bursts in at her side, a huge shape in the gloom, loping at her, displacing the shot and driving her to the floor. Lead burrows into the doorpost at my side. Baker's weight hits her, driving her down. She is pinned to the floor. His slobber drools in her face as her pistols skitter beyond reach across the tiles. She howls in frustration, thwarted, trapped.

Josiah arrives as I lower my pistol at her.

'Be a good fellow and fetch the Drakers, Joe.'

This seems a fitting time to share what little else we have learned about the Order, so I collate a file and deliver it to Bretling. Drakers arrest those they can, among them Assanie Strictor-Booth and Morris Lakefield, and they even track down and apprehend Fat Rat, Gouldstone's portly associate. Of course, there will no doubt be those who manage to squirm away into the shadows, but for now it feels like a victory.

Over the next few days a Draker investigation into the Order gets fully underway, one that unearths a wealth of information. I suppose that when the Drakers who had taken bribes were told to talk amid the new order of things, they had a lot to say. We learn that Clara Avard was not her real name. That was the name of the woman she murdered some six years ago and from then onwards impersonated. The ghost's real name, the one known to the Order, was Assanie Strictor-Booth.

AS.

Clara Avard – or more accurately, Assanie Strictor-Booth – was swiftly tried for an extensive list of crimes. I read in the papers of her incarceration, though rather than the silker prison one might have expected, she has been confined in chains within a guarded cell of Fossgale, an asylum for the insane. I can't argue its suitability but assume that somewhere a good deal of money was exchanged to keep her from the prison. All the same, I doubt her conditions will be much improved. I've heard dreadful rumours about the treatments that go on there.

So, who sent the warnings to Tillie Ingham in the thinly disguised form of threatening letters? I can only imagine it was the servant girl from Dover Palace, Poesy Clarence, or else someone like her. She seemed to have a good understanding of what happened and was perhaps a better friend to Tillie than Tillie ever knew.

I decide it would be worth the trip back to Dover Palace to speak with Poesy once more and confront her with the threatening letters.

'Am I in trouble?' she asks, her face flushed with concern. 'I didn't mean to threaten anyone.'

I smile. 'My dear, it was an act of kindness. Your secret is safe with me.'

I commit the following week to determined preparation. Josiah, adamant that he should accompany me, is only placated when I agree a supporting role for him. He will travel with me to the very ends of the Borderlands, there to set camp and await my return among the wilderness of that perilous zone. Because the land there is poor and damaged, the shanties of the border folk are scattered far and wide with much unoccupied space between, so he should be safe enough if we choose a secluded spot. There he might camp quietly without fear of disturbance. He may even enjoy a few days of reflective solitude, boiling black bean soup over a campfire and lounging in the summer sun.

We shall take a wagon and horses that far and from there I will go on into the sands.

Our wagon, then, is loaded with camping gear, bottled water, dried fruits, ship's biscuits and cured aurochs meat. Enough for the two of us. There is fodder and water for the horses, though we plan to set Josiah's camp near a water source, if a safe one can be found. Beyond that, I have my equipment: my stereoscope, the gawper masks, a great broad-rimmed journeyman's hat for shade, some ironworker's goggles with darkened glass against the sun's glare, my compass and weapons.

At dawn we leave the house, riding the wagon, Blink and Willie harnessed together before us. They seem to jostle along well enough and we set a fair pace.

We also take a pair of spades and, mid-afternoon, without mention of Loegray's digging machine, set to work with them in our chosen spot, out on the far side of the Borderlands. Avoiding signs of settlement, we dig our own well in the sweltering heat, relieved when we finally see a damp patch materialise deep in the dusty soil.

Beneath a darkening sky we gather dead wood, and from old ashblacks, make a fire and sit either side, stewing a pot of aurochs meat and beans over the flames, talking for a while. Josiah then raises a subject we've both been avoiding.

'I'm sorry,' he begins.

'For what?'

'For everything. For killing Harris. For punching you. All of it.'

'Well, that's not a bad thing. To be sorry, I mean. And to be fair, if you hadn't silenced him, we might now be swinging from the city gallows. And Willow might be dead.'

'All the same, it's not something I want to be, a killer.' He seems to have more to say, so I let him talk. 'I won't kill again. I don't like the way it made me feel – the way it *makes* me feel.'

'It is a good code to live by. You have a physique most men would envy, Josiah, a powerful one, which means that with ease you can do great damage. You need to control your temper.'

'Harris was a... *a scoundrel of the highest order*, but I should have found another way. If you've taught me anything...'

'It's all right, Joe. I can forgive you, but sometimes it's harder to forgive yourself.'

For a few moments we watch the flames and the steaming pot in silence.

His eyes find me across the fire. 'Punch me.'

'What?'

'Punch me. I punched you. You must punch me back. It's only fair.'

'I couldn't.'

'Sure you could. Go on.'

'Even if I did, it wouldn't be like a punch from you.'

'You should take a run-up! Do it.' Enthralled by the idea, he stands, sets his jaw as a target and taps the side of his face. 'Right here.'

I stand, too, though I have no intention of hitting him. I wouldn't want to break my hand. 'I can't. It's ridiculous. Anyway, I don't want to.'

'I need you to.'

I study his eyes. He seems serious. 'Oh, very well, if I must.'

I can't believe I'm doing this. I draw back my fist but he stops me.

'Start from over there.' He points into the deepening shadows.

Begrudgingly I go, take a good run-up and plough my fist into his jaw. There's a shock of pain in my knuckles. I stagger, massaging my bruised hand.

Josiah stretches his jaw and laughs. 'Is that all you've got?'

Through my pain I begin to laugh with him. He laughs harder and now we can't help it. We collapse by the fire, guffawing uncontrollably. It's not *that* funny but I sense a measure of relief, as though a neglected tap has been opened and long-bound pressure released, and I don't want it to stop. When it finally subsides, I feel somehow at peace with the world and Josiah.

'You don't have to stay with Mysteries Solved. You know that, right?' He watches me. 'You can go anywhere. Do whatever. You are a free man.'

He nods. 'I know.'

That night we camp beneath a sky lit with the green glow of Mors Zonam. There are noises in the darkness, distant sounds of creatures unknown. I lie awake, listening, for hours.

The fumes are stifling here, at the beginnings of the zone where desert replaces the dusty soil and dry grasses, where stones lie shimmering in the heat. I leave our camp at sunrise and immediately start to perspire.

*Get used to it,* I tell myself.

My morning is punctuated by the appearance of a small lizard basking in the sun, and later a snake, scything across the sand. At midday I stop by a pile of bones to rest, eat and drink a little water. I'm careful with the rations, unsure of my journey's length.

The stink has increased so I put on the mask. I hoist the pack onto my back and walk on alone.

That night is a blur in my mind. I walk the burning sand as the sun drops, flaring the horizon a fiery red before giving way to a pallid green that descends into a dim iridescence. The sandscape is barren and featureless for a good few miles and then, in the gloom, I recognise the stunted trees and see rocks protruding from the dunes here and there. This is Mors Zonam proper, though still only its outer edge, I'm sure. It will be hotter still, further on. I have many miles before me if I'm to reach the valley of bones.

And I must reach the valley of bones. For that is where we met the gawper, and somewhere close there is water.

On soil, or a good road, one might cover twenty miles by foot on a good day's tramp. That doesn't leave much time for resting up, though, and I'm on sand.

Sand, sand and more sand. As far as I can see.

There's no easy way of charting my progress, but I reckon by midnight I've covered around five miles. My feet are sore and they feel cooked, slow-steamed in my boots. I rest for a while, sitting to remove my boots. I drink water from one of the gawper waterskins hung about my shoulders, depleting my supply, and check my bearings against the compass. I chew a few strips of dry-cured aurochs meat before risking a brief sleep.

At dawn I awake, the sun glaring down on me, though it's only seven in the morning. I don my ironworker's goggles, my journeyman's hat and take a sip of precious water before walking on. I pass bones, both animal and human. Sometimes there are rags still caught among them, fluttering in the Toral wind, the remnants of clothes, though it's hard to picture them as such. Other times the bones are simply chalky shapes poking up from the dunes.

On I walk.

It's another day's hard trudging before, in the green haze of night, I come upon an arrow built of stone that is set in the sand. It points at me and I stare at it. I know this place. Sure enough, after a little hunting, I find a drop to my right and I hasten to peer over a stony slope, hoping to find the valley. It's there, plummeting away before me, and along its course lies scattered the pale white-green of more desert-bleached bones. I slide down the dune edge, keen to explore. This is surely the valley of bones. I sit and look around, in wonder that I've made it this far. If my theories are true, this is gawper territory.

I rest, drink, eat and think about what to do next. Josiah and I explored part of this valley but we were not down here long before we came across the gawper, trapped by the shrieking beast. The thought prompts me to check my pistols. One thing's for sure, my powder's nice and dry.

The valley leads me on. Further south. Always south. Away from home. Away from safety. I feel it in my gut with every step.

My true search begins. Water is here. I know. I just have to find it.

I trace fissures in the rock, search out lines of descent carved by wind or ancient tides. Chasing ever deeper. The chasm drops, twisting, and a wind picks up, blasting sand into the air. It is funnelled here by the valley walls, guided, caressed. It is the force that shapes the rock. It builds and I fear it will flay the skin from my flesh. I must hide, must find shelter and sit this out. I rush to put on the darkened goggles that at least offer some protection for my eyes. Through the darkened swirling haze appears a cleft in the rock, a split where sand has fallen away, and I run for it, half-blinded by the gritted turmoil, breathing hard, hot beneath my mask. Reaching it, I hug myself in, tight against the stone. Sand is liquid at my feet. Fluid in the air. The sky is a swirling dune.

I fall. Like hourglass time, I am poured out, only to spiral and tumble down, further and on, giddy, gasping, groping through a glassy gap.

The sandstorm throbs, billows, subsides.

Rolling to a stop, I lie still, waiting for the world to calm, for breath, for quiet, for...

*Water!*

The distant, unmistakable sound of it taunts me; the enticing song of flowing water.

Dripping with sweat and encrusted with sand, I sit up to gather myself, check my supplies. I don't appear to have lost anything in my fall. Encouraged, I rise to follow the dappling sound. It grows louder as I move, and more real, more believable. I am not dreaming. There is a stream. I see it!

And standing over the stream is a gawper.

# 27

# Deadlock

*In which Banyard learns much*

The gawper watches me, its eyes two cold points of light in the night. The greenish glow dances on the shifting water that babbles as it snakes through the bedrock. Behind the figure, a deeper darkness swallows the night; a low mouth in the stone slope. The stream flows into this cave and vanishes there.

The dampness on my skin is not sweat. It is too thick between my finger and thumb, black in the eerie light. It is blood.

The gawper moves. It drops a waterskin, spilling to the ground, and stretches out a clawed hand to one side, palm down. A long staff rises up from the stony bank, summoned into the claw, which closes around the staff. Now armed, the gawper approaches, drifting nearer.

I back away, only to find I'm wading in sand that grows deeper the further I go. My groping hands soon feel the hardness of a rockface at my back.

Nowhere to run. I consider my rapier but reach for a pistol.

On it comes, eyes burning, piercing, probing.

*Say something*, I think. *Think something!*

I abandon any thoughts about the gun and the sword. Bad

idea.

*Stop!* I think it. *Wait!* What was that word? It returns to me. *Shrivened! I have been shrivened,* I think it loud and clear.

The gawper pauses, peering at the hide waterskins strung over my shoulder and the mask on my face, but all too soon continues its terrible advance. Looming over me, it raises its staff as though to strike me down and I know a single blow would open my skull. I cower, only to glimpse the soft greenish hues of human bones protruding from the sand around me.

Terror contorts my heart.

*Hold, Deadlock!*

I hear the words in my mind, recognise the mind-voice.

The staff halts mid-air. The gawper turns, glancing over its shoulder back towards the cave.

*Why?* It thinks. I hear this also, as clearly as my own thoughts.

I glimpse the dark outline of a second gawper behind the first, see its eyes shimmer.

*I know this one. This one is Michael Banyard. This one and another rescued Magwitch from toll-da-roth.* The second gawper touches a clawed hand to a wound on its shoulder.

Deadlock, if that is his name, lowers his staff.

*This one knows where the Dagomites dwell,* he thinks.

They exchange a glance. It seems I'm causing something of a dilemma.

'I've been seeking you,' I blurt, hoping this will help and not condemn me.

Deadlock turns aggressively towards me. *This one does not speak!*

*Only think, Michael Banyard. No talk,* thinks Magwitch. He draws level with Deadlock. *This one has been shrivened. This one lives.*

Begrudgingly, or so it seems, Deadlock retreats from me. *This one has sought us. This one is danger.*

*No danger,* counters Magwitch. *It is written. A life for a life. This one lives. This one gives life.*

Deadlock leers at me. *Bring him. Skallagrim will decide.*

### The Good News
I don't mind this Magwitch fellow.

### The Bad News
I really don't like Deadlock.

### The Terrifying News
*Skallagrim will decide!*

Ominously, Deadlock points towards the cave with his staff. With his other hand he points to the weapons on my belt.

*We go. Weapons stay.*

I rise, ditch my gun belt along with the rapier and walk as they escort me into the darkness of the void. At first it seems I must stumble blindly to a deeper cavern where, presumably, Skallagrim awaits, but once we're away from the entrance a new and different glow illuminates our path. The cavern walls are bright with a turquoise phosphorescence and parts of the stream's bed also shimmer beneath the waters to cast a soft undulating light around the chamber.

Black plants rise from the water's edge, strange lobed branches that remind me of the bladderwrack on the rocks of Lytche's Cove. I pause, reach out a hand to feel the stuff in my fingers. It is rubbery, like the substance of the mask I wear.

Deadlock glares, nudging me forward with his staff. I walk on.

We pass through a narrow tunnel that appears to have been extended above our heads to accommodate the gawpers' extraordinary height. There are tool marks left in the stone where it has been hacked away. Always we follow a path that edges the twisting stream, eventually coming out into a large chamber with a huge vaulted ceiling, carved by larger waters in the far distant past. A new sight greets me. This cavern is inhabited by gawpers. Many of them. My impression is that of a subterranean village. It is my first sighting of smaller gawpers, for clearly the young number among them. To one side where the rock climbs to a natural plateau a throne has been chiselled in the stone and there sits a huge gawper menacing over all.

Deadlock levels his staff at the throne.

*Skallagrim will decide.*

Magwitch and Deadlock bring me before the mighty Skallagrim and I listen with trepidation to a conversation of thoughts as other gawpers close around with interest.

Skallagrim: *What is this? This one is forbidden to enter here.*

Deadlock: *This one found the Dagomites. This one dies.*

Magwitch: *This one lives. A life for a life. It is written.*

Me: *Long live Magwitch!*

Deadlock glares at me.

Skallagrim: *A life?*

Magwitch: *This one saved Magwitch. Gave Magwitch life.*

Skallagrim appears to consider the argument. At length, and with some reluctance in his mind-voice, he pronounces judgement. *It is written. A life for a life. But this one must swear never to reveal our dwelling.*

*I swear!* I think.

It seems I am to live. I'm so relieved that I almost collapse then and there, but Magwitch quickly beckons me away with a curling claw, keen to get me out of the chamber, and he leads me down one of many passages that continue on.

This shaft declines gently to a terminal cave that I can only imagine is Magwitch's own. There are niches cut into the walls, like shelves, where a variety of objects rest. I notice several gawper-made weed masks in one. In another are a group of those hide waterskins and in another there is more of the gawper-weed that has been sliced into ribbons. One nook contains a skull which, by its size and shape, I reason must surely be of gawper origin.

I sit cross-legged on the stone floor.

I have been in close proximity now with Magwitch for long enough to notice other details. The matted hair or rags that I'd always seen upon each of my previous encounters is neither hair nor rags. It is more of that gawper-weed from the stream. It seems to be useful for many things and I realise each gawper is wearing a long, hooded coat or cloak made from it, one that reaches to the ground. I have yet to see a single gawper foot or leg.

Magwitch takes several strips of the shredded weed from the niche and shoves them up beneath his mask. As he chews he offers me some. I shake my head, show him the open top of my rations bag where there is dried meat, fruit and biscuits. He averts his face as though repulsed.

I'm stunned into silence by the realisation I'm here. Alone. With an actual gawper, with whom I can communicate. It is an opportunity for which any scientist would gladly surrender an arm. My problem is that I don't know what question to ask first. Magwitch, however, seems in a hurry.

*Michael Banyard must not linger. Dagomites may kill.*

*I understand.*

*Magwitch has been watching Michael Banyard. This one has seen much death.*

*Too much*, I think.

*This one brings life to others.*

*When I can.*

*This is good. It is written.*

Magwitch takes the gawper skull from its nook and, with great reverence, lowers it gently into my hands.

*This one must take the skull of forefather. This one can meet Magwitch. In here.* He points a clawed finger to his temple.

I study the skull, marvelling at its lines. There is no jawbone but it is not so different from a man's, only larger, the face and cranium elongated. It is light to hold. Smooth to the touch.

*How do you move?* I blurt. *Appear suddenly in the city? Do you have legs? How do you travel? Do you all live here in one cave system? Are there others? Where is it written? And your names…*

It is the first time I hear the sound of a gawper laugh. Although it is deep and throaty, like gravel and water swirling in a barrel, there is something delightful about it.

*In time, Michael Banyard will learn. We hold sacred the holy art of writing. There are books, ancient texts surviving from the time before. It is from these that every Dagomite will take his name.*

*You know about the Old People?*

His eyes of fire simmer with melancholy. *We know much of the Old People.*

*Are there female Dagomites?* I am like a child with too many questions, eager to explore a new-found world. Unable to focus on any one subject.

Again, the grating laugh chugs and bellows.

*Yes, we have females. Michael Banyard must go. Take the relic. Leave the Green Realm and return to the city of men. Go swiftly.*

I nod and begin to rise. *I came also seeking another of my kind. A woman. She may have come here hoping to escape. Do you know of her? Do any of my kind survive in the Green Realm?*

*You seek the Chasm of Pillars in the west. If woman lives, there you will find her. Three caves, low in the hill.*

He beckons me again to follow and leads me out through another passage that rises to bypass the great chamber. It opens on a broad slab of rock, set over another valley's rock-strewn floor.

*Go now, before Dagomites change their thoughts.*

I bow, unsure of the correct protocol for bidding a Dagomite farewell. Magwitch passes a full pair of waterskins to me and I add them to the others hanging around my neck.

*Goodbye, Michael Banyard.*

Clutching the Dagomite skull, I pause.

*My weapons?*

*You will not need them, Michael Banyard.*

I bow again, though less enthusiastically, and stow the skull away in my pack. I take a bearing from my compass and set off into the night. When I glance back, Magwitch has gone.

I walk through the night, pausing occasionally to check my heading and to drink, and I reach what must be the Chasm of Pillars as the sun crests the dunes at my back. It is a chasm with sheer sides of crumbling rock, a challenge to descend, though I manage it, seeking out a spur where fissured chunks of rock have cleft away from the upper layers to leave a giant stairway of sorts. I half-climb, half-drop my way down from rock to rock and begin my wander through the natural stone pillars that rise sporadically from the valley floor.

An hour of searching brings me to the first signs of civilisation. There are three caves, just as Magwitch said, set low in the valley's rock wall and, outside them, are a scatter of features in the sand: a fireplace of burned sticks, a frame formed of branches holding a stretched animal hide, and several iron pots and pans. There is also a sprinkle of small animal bones discarded around the cave's mouth. I examine them to be sure they are not human and can only guess they are from lizards or snakes, or perhaps some other small creatures that eke out an existence here.

I venture nearer to the central cave, the one with the fireplace, and glimpse in its shadows the tattered, faded remnant of a violet silk dress. Beneath it protrude the legs of a young woman. I walk closer to see the body in full. I drop to my knees, my quest at an end. I am saddened and defeated. To be sure, I take out the imograph I have carried all this time and compare it with the face in the sand before me. I have come too late for Tillie Ingham.

I stay there for a long time, just resting in defeat, until a soft sound emanating from deeper in the cave startles me. There, a shape moves. Alarmed, I stand and reach for pistols that are not there.

From the shade of the cavern a pale creature approaches.

He is naked.

He is grubby and malnourished.

He has his mother's eyes.

A Banyard & Mingle Mystery

## Volume III

# THE SHADOW OF GRAYRTON MIRE

## B J Mears

instant apostle

# Prologue

## Sunday night, 4th Honourmoon

Martha gripped the storm lamp, her knuckles blanching as shadows danced on the stone walls and timbers of the croft. Voices rose from the darkness outside: men approaching along the dry path from the village. A hammering at the door startled her. She spun towards the sound. Bit her lip. Turned on her heel again to sweep her lamp around, searching the kitchen.

She called for the boy with an urgent whisper. 'Billy!'

More hammering, each strike like a jolt to her heart.

They've come for him! Where is he? Find the boy. Run. Hide!

The hammering at the door shook her again, a furious percussion. She glanced from the window out into the night, surveying the dank, leaden expanse of mire broken only by the wavering lamps of the gathering watchmen. She counted half a dozen in the steamy murk that hung over the walkways, the reeds and the water.

'Open up, Martha, or we'll break it down!'

The thumping intensified. A boy with crooked teeth edged nervously into the hallway from deeper in the croft, his eyes wide and stark in the lamplight, his hands cradling an injured bird. Martha ran to him.

She knew the man shouting on the other side of the door: Watchmaster of Grayrton, Jan Morecroft. Knew why he had come. Knew he would not stop until he had what he had come for.

She turned swiftly to the child. 'Run to your room, Billy! Bar the door!'

Billy fled but, slipping in from the back of the croft, a watchman appeared before him. Billy almost ran straight into the man's arms.

The Watchmaster broke open the front door and entered.

Martha screamed. 'Don't take him! Don't take my boy, please! I beg you. No!' She planted herself between the Watchmaster and the boy. 'You can't take him, Jan Morecroft! I won't let you.'

The watchman confronting Billy swept the bird from his hands. The creature hit the floor.

'No!' Billy ran to retrieve the bird.

The Watchmaster shoved Martha aside. 'You're obstructin' the course of justice. We're takin' the boy.' He gestured to the watchman holding Billy. 'Bring him.'

Billy struggled.

'No! He's done nothin' wrong!' Martha tugged at the watchman's arms, trying to pull Billy free.

The Watchmaster backhanded Billy across the face.

'No!' screamed Martha. Blood ran from the boy's broken lip. The Watchmaster grimaced at the cut that the boy's teeth had left on his hand.

Wide-eyed, Billy peered from his mother to the Watchmaster and back again as they dragged him away.

'My boy's innocent!' Martha cried.

'The courts'll decide that.' The Watchmaster threw Martha a backward glance. 'You can see him at trial.'

# 1

# The Legend

*In which Banyard and Mingle hear a woeful tale*

## Monday morning, 5th Honourmoon

Elizabeth Fairweather, exquisite as ever, knocks on the case room door before stepping primly inside. She carries in her arms a hat box, cylindrical in form, which she presents to me.

'You asked for this.'

Without rising from my desk I take the box, open the lid and peer inside. It's empty and seems the perfect size. 'Thank you, Lizzy.'

She nods and glances with interest at an object before me on the desk that's shrouded by an oil cloth. 'You're welcome. Do you mind me asking what you need it for?'

'Not at all.' I smile and wait for her to realise I'm not going to tell her. She rolls her eyes and leaves, closing the door behind her.

In the case room today there are two skulls on my desk. One sits in its usual spot on the corner, a remembrance from a past case that happens to make a useful paperweight and, incidentally, a convenient place to rest my father's old tricornered hat: the hat that has become my firm favourite.

The other skull is the one I'm interested in, though. I unwrap it and lift it from the oil cloth, turning it in my hands. I return it to the desk as it watches everything through empty sockets. It has no lower jaw but is otherwise complete, upper teeth and all. The skull looks like that of a man, only larger and slightly elongated in the face and cranium. Its teeth are longer, too, the canines prominent, though no more so than a man's. It has cheekbones that are higher and broader than any other I've seen.

The skull is not human.

The skull is an enigma.

Lounging in his chair, his ankles crossed and resting on his desk, my musclebound business partner yawns.

I frown at him. 'Josiah Mingle, you do know it's polite to cover your mouth when you yawn?'

'Yeah, why is that?' he asks, without glancing up from the pages of his penny dreadful.

Lizzy calls through the door. 'Mr Banyard, a visitor for you.'

I quickly re-cover the skull with the cloth and rise to open the case room door as Josiah puts his reading matter down and slips his feet from his desk to follow me out.

A pale threader woman stands in our reception room on the far side of Lizzy's desk, silent, like a lost ghost that's drifted in from Bunson Street's cobbles. She has a bedraggled, country air about her, homespun clothes all shades of dun except for the pale cream of the lace fringing her bonnet. She looks poor, around forty years of age and lean faced, her features etched deeply with concern.

Lizzy tilts her head in an attempt to glimpse the object on my desk, so I close the door firmly behind me before gesturing towards the visitor's chair. It's an old Grand Wexford, brown leather, its upholstery studded with brass, and is the most comfortable seat in the Mysteries Solved office.

'Please, sit.' I draw up a simple wooden chair so that we can talk with ease in the corner of the room. 'Would you like black bean soup?' This is a standard line we take with potential clients.

The people who come to us have problems they are unable to solve. They are frequently unhappy, vexed and edgy. Black bean soup can help with all that and it gives them something to focus on other than their worries, albeit briefly.

'If it's not a trouble.' The woman nods, although the notion is clearly distracting. She is here for a purpose. I see it now, in the restless nature of her eyes, the resolute set of her brow. She is neither a ghost nor lost.

'Miss Fairweather, if you would be so kind.'

Lizzy glances up from our case book and slaps her quill down upon her desk in a mildly irritated manner. 'Yes, Mr Banyard.' She leaves to fetch the soup.

Josiah drags another chair across the room to join us. Our other operatives are all out in the field and so, for a time, the three of us are left alone. I imagine we make an interesting trio: Josiah's considerable frame, hulking in his chair, his brutish face intent upon the visitor; the woman, slight and frail by comparison, and full of fear; and me, a wiry, raven-haired young man with a nose a little on the large side.

'My name is Michael Banyard,' I say. 'And this is my associate, Josiah Mingle.'

Josiah nods. 'Pleased to meet you.'

Our visitor glances with deepening apprehension at Josiah. I don't blame her. He has all the physical charm of a thug and, even when seated, towers over her.

'Don't mind Mr Mingle. He's harmless,' I say, though he's not. It wasn't too long ago that I witnessed him strike a man dead with a single blow from a fire iron. Even so, she has no reason to fear him. 'Please tell us who you are and why you are here.'

'Martha Landsdale of Grayrton, the village out by the mire. I heard you were a good man, Master Banyard, someone who might help a soul such as me.' She wears a simple copper band on her wedding finger, the sort threaders commonly use because gold or silver is too expensive for them. The copper leaves a greenish stain on the skin. She turns the ring anxiously, glancing back and forth between Josiah and me.

Her nerves seem to have silenced her, so I attempt to put her at ease with a smile. 'Please take your time, Mrs Landsdale. We are all friends, here. How may we help?'

She sniffs, fighting back tears, and dabs at her reddened eyes with a handkerchief. For some moments she is unable to speak. When words come, they fall from her like sorry rags cast on the wind. 'They've taken my Billy. They've taken him and they're going to hang him for something he didn't do.'

'Of what is Billy accused?' I ask.

'Murder, they say, the murder of a man found butchered out in the mire, though it wasn't my Billy who did it. How could he? He's just a child.'

'How old is Billy?'

'He's fifteen. The Watchmaster took him from me in the night.' Martha Landsdale pauses to look us in the eyes in turn. 'There've been others.'

'What others?' asks Josiah, leaning nearer so that his shadow engulfs her.

'Others found savaged, just the same. All of them out on the mire, but my Billy's no killer, I swear. He barely ever leaves the croft.'

'I believe you, Mrs Landsdale,' I say. 'Where are they holding him?'

'He's in Grayrton gaol but won't be for long. They're taking him to the threader gaol in Camdon later today and soon he's to be tried for murder. You have to help me, masters. I've nowhere else to turn.' She appears desperate, tears beading in her eyes. 'Though I don't have much with which to pay you. I'd sell mysen sooner than see my boy hanged.'

'I promise that won't be necessary. Please calm yourself. Perhaps we might discuss payment at a later point. If your son is innocent, I'm sure the court will find him so.' Even as I say it, I feel the spectre of doubt over us like a gathering storm cloud. The chancel judges are rarely lenient on threaders who find themselves in the dock and, if a case is uncertain, the crueller sentence is more often awarded. 'It seems to me imperative that we set to work. Please tell us everything you know about these killings.'

'You'll help me?'

'Why, of course.' Money is really not an issue right now and I'd sooner work for free than see her or her child harmed. 'We shall do whatever we can.'

Her expression eases, and she nods as Lizzy returns laden with bright copper cups of steaming black bean soup that she's fetched from a street vendor.

'Ah, thank you, Miss Fairweather. Mrs Landsdale was about to enlighten us. Please be so kind as to take notes. I'll fill in the blanks later.'

'One moment.' Lizzy passes the cups around and we sip the hot, bitter brew.

'What, no cake?' jibes Josiah.

Lizzy scowls at him, fetches a ledger from her desk and sits to record details, all business. 'I'm ready.'

Martha continues. 'There've been killin's on the mire going back years. I don't know much but I'll tell what I can. There are rumours, y'see, stories about the mire. There were stories long before my time: tales going back to the Old People, even. Ancient bodies found there, preserved in the bog. Dark is the mire.' The phrase hangs ominously in the air as she sips her soup, gathering her thoughts. 'The first I remember was around eighteen years back, before Billy was even born. A local girl went missing and a week later turned up dead. Far from the village, it was, a place deep into the mire where no one goes, only there was a search made and it was then they found her. There are dry paths, safe enough if you know your way. Her body was off the path, half sunken in the mire. She'd been mauled by a wild beast. Bitten. Her flesh torn. What skin remained was as wan as the moon.' She peers up at us with widening eyes. 'They say she'd been drained of blood.'

'Wolves, perhaps?' Josiah shudders and, resting back against his chair, traces a circle on his forehead before touching a point over his heart. This is the sacred sign, a gesture that threaders commonly use in dire moments. I worry about his struggles to kick old habits. It's been a while now since he was a condemned threader – since I rescued him from the noose and brought him to Camdon, paying for his forged silker papers – though he has made some progress. But back to the now…

'Did the coroner examine the body?' I ask.

'I doubt it. It was probably the Watchmaster because the girl was from Grayrton, a threader girl from a poor family. They wouldn't have bothered the Drakers.' The Drakers are Camdon City's watchmen, named after their founder and chief, Lord Bretling Draker.

'I see. You said others?'

'Some years later there was a boy who used to go out snaring birds in the marshes. He didn't return home one day and they found him the followin' morning: torn up, bloodless, just like the girl. He was a local, too. Then there was a man found dead out there. A stranger. A threader, though, by what was left of his clothes, so I don't suppose there was much of a fuss. The next was a woman who used to cross the mire to visit her kinfolk over near Windstrome Bay. She took a basket of food on her arm. Never made it to the bay. They found her three days later, lily-white, her throat torn out.'

'All of them threaders?' asks Lizzy.

'Aye. Though this latest man they found two days gone, the one they're blaming on my boy, is a silker. He was from Camdon so the Drakers were called. That's why they're bringing my Billy for trial in the city.'

'Quite. Is it known what this silker fellow was doing? Perhaps he was killed elsewhere and his body dumped in the mire.'

'He was an imographer, by all accounts. Made a hobby of it. I heard he was out taking imographs. There are plants out there that don't grow elsewhere, and the marshes attract all kinds of birds, you see. Per'aps he was imographin' those. His name was Winsley Dunn.'

I glance at Lizzy. 'Winsley Dunn. Be sure to make a note, Miss Fairweather.' She rolls her eyes again. I turn back to Martha. 'They must be quite convinced that your son is guilty. Do you have any idea why?'

Martha falls silent. Her troubled eyes roam as though searching for a more appropriate answer than the one in her head, before conceding, 'It's because of the legend.'

Josiah leans in keenly. 'What legend?'

Martha's eyes glaze over. 'The legend of the shadow drinker, the Bibit. You will know of it.'

We exchange blank glances.

'We do not,' says Josiah, his interest piquing. He loves his penny dreadfuls and this sounds like a story straight from those pages.

'The legend tells of a spirit creature who dwells in Grayrton Mire, a beast with horns like a stag and the teeth and claws of a wolf. It's been called all sorts. Sometimes the Soul Stealer. Sometimes the Shadow Drinker. Others name it the Bibit.'

'The Bibit?' asks Lizzy, peering up from her notes.

'It means the drinker,' explains Martha, 'for it drinks the blood and thus the souls of its victims.'

'What nonsense,' says Lizzy, noting it all down. 'A beast that lives on the mire and drinks people's souls? It's quite preposterous.'

'I've heard of tribes in the east who believe the soul resides in the blood,' I confess. 'Though I know nothing of the creature about which you speak.'

'Well you might think it nonsense but there's them who don't. The story begins with a beautiful girl, married off for silver by her uncarin' father. She was forced to wed a cruel man, a wicked man who walked among the evil spirits abroad in the marsh, those that wandered at night as ghost lights. The villagers witnessed him dancin' out on the mire, cavortin' with unnatural creatures: evil beings in the form of shadow dwellers. The girl bore him seven children but, one by one, terrible dooms befell each one.'

Martha pulls her shawl tighter around her shoulders as though suddenly cold.

'When the first was found dead, the mother thought it an accident. They buried the child in the marshes. Soon afterwards another child was taken, and another, and still she knew of no reason to blame her husband. At last, only the seventh child remained, but soon the wife happened upon a ghastly scene. She came upon her husband throttlin' the child. The wife flew into a rage, clawin' and bitin' him, drawin' blood, but the husband was too strong for her. He overpowered her and strangled her, too. In the years she'd been with the man, she'd learned somethin' of his dark art. With her dyin' breath she hurled a curse upon him, beseechin' the wild beasts and the evils of the night to finish what she'd begun: to tear him to pieces and to drink freely of his soul.

'The wicked husband could do nothin' more than bury her body in the mire.

'The villagers then learned of the killin's, for over time they noticed the absence of the mother and the children. They sent out a party to bring the man in to answer for his crimes but found him dead, his chest ripped asunder, his heart laid bare. 'Tis said the murdered wife rose from the waters of the mire, reborn as the drinker of souls, remade as the Bibit, and has haunted the marshes ever since, seekin' souls to drink, forever enraged at the killin' of her young 'uns.'

'And you believe this old wives' tale?' I ask Martha.

She stares into her cup and I fear I've embarrassed her. 'I don't know what to believe, master. That is why I've come to you, that and to help my boy.'

Josiah and I exchange glances. We've seen things in the hot, green glow of Mors Zonam's nights, things as equally terrifying as the Bibit, if not more so.

'You may scoff,' says Martha, 'but somethin' is out there killin' folk, though it ain't my Billy. You must believe me. There is a great evil on the mire.'

I frown. 'I'm sorry, Mrs Landsdale, I still don't understand how any of this implicates your son.'

'You will recall I told you he rarely leaves our croft. Well, there's a reason for that. It's his teeth. They're… unusual. They protrude and he has a few too many. It gives him a look that frightens folk. It's blighted his whole life. The other children in the village spurn him, call him cruel names. The villagers have always been wary, superstitious. Now they're sayin' he is the Bibit, that my Billy is the monster on the mire.'

'She's quite the storyteller. The Bibit? I've never heard of it. Must be a local myth,' says Josiah a few minutes later when we're alone in the case room. He voices questions I've also been considering. 'Do you think it's some unknown beast that's strayed from Mors Zonam? Or perhaps a gawper is responsible.'

'If it's real, then I doubt very much that it strayed from Mors Zonam, not without help, at least. It's feasible that someone captured a creature there and released it on the mire, I suppose, but if so, why? And who in their right mind would risk entering a deadly wasteland to attempt such a thing?'

'A good question, Mr Banyard. A very good question.'

'It doesn't sound like a gawper attack to me. I've never heard of them drinking blood or even using their teeth. Most deaths attributed to gawpers are recorded as heart failures.' I know this because I've taken a keen interest in the cases, as did my father before me. They are compiled among other gawper encounters in a thick file begun by my father, who passed away some years ago.

Again I consider the strange skull on my desk. I can't seem to leave it alone. It was given to me by a gawper named Magwitch in a cave in Mors Zonam, way beyond the Borderlands. Mors Zonam is a toxic desert that begins around fifty miles south of Camdon, the city in which we live and run our private investigations agency. It's a place where condemned threaders are sent to die – a penalty deemed worse than hanging. There, undocumented beasts roam, the air is a sulphurous fume that burns the throat and lungs, and the hot sands are riddled with the bones of the dead. It is also, I have learned, the abode of the gawpers, creatures taller than men, who steal out from the shadows or the night fog to gawp with eyes of white flame. They are more legendary than the Bibit, mystical in their presence, and many do not believe in them, though I have encountered them on several occasions and bear the evidence before me now. It is not something I am prepared to share with the world of modern science. Not yet, anyway.

'He said you could use it to speak to them,' says Josiah, glancing at the skull as he pulls on his long coat.

'Indeed. Magwitch suggested I'd be able to communicate with him through it, but I still don't know how.' My recent gawper encounter left me thinking I'd learned a lot, but truly I hadn't. I know where they dwell, that they have a form of telekinesis and telepathy, and that they are able to think in conversation with others without uttering a word. They have some kind of mind gate that they can open and close. I've tried many things with the skull, have placed a hand upon it and opened my mind gate as best I know how, have used two hands and reached out to Magwitch with my thoughts, silently calling his name. I've placed the skull over my heart. Held it beneath water. Warmed it by a fire. I've stared into its empty eye sockets for hours on end, but nothing. No gawper voice of reply. Not a murmur nor the squeak of a mind gate's hinge. It's as if the way is permanently closed, which leaves me wondering: what was the point of Magwitch giving me the thing?

I wrap it in its oil cloth and stow it away beneath my desk in the hat box. Further analysis will have to wait until later, for now – if Martha Landsdale is to be believed – there is an innocent child speeding towards the gallows and we may be his only hope of salvation.

I grab my long coat and head for the door. 'Come, Joe. We have a case to solve.'